Threads of Gold

J.C. WARREN

This book is a work of fiction. Any references to historical events, real people, or real places are used fictitiously. Other names, characters, places and events are products of the author's imagination, and any resemblances to actual events or places or persons, living or dead, is entirely coincidental.

Threads of Gold (2024)

Copyright © 2024 by J.C. Warren

Edited by Chrissy Wolfe

Cover Design by The Cover Cauldron

All rights reserved. No part of this book may be reproduced in any manner whatsoever without written permission except in the case of brief quotations embodied in critical articles and reviews.

First Printing, 2024

To those who feel different.

Trigger Warnings

Alcoholism
Anxiety
Cancer
Death
Depression
Kidnapping
Mental health hospitalization
Profanity
Self-harm (off page)
Sexual assault
Sexually explicit
Terminal illness

Threads of Gold

Chapter One

Go ahead. Have another drink.

Cinzia Clark smiled at the voice, doing her best to pretend it was directed at the bartender as she raised her hand. The voice had a point. If she was going to get up the courage to talk to that tall drink of water on the other side of the bar tonight, she needed another. She peeked over her shoulder to find the guy staring at her. He must have been a year or two older than her, a light shadow sprinkled across his cheeks. An old scar ran from the right side of his chin to his brown eyes. Brown eyes that were watching her with a mischievous glint. Cin forced herself to turn back to the bartender who was finally standing in front of her. He offered up a tall glass garnished with a lime. Gin and tonic.

"You remembered!" she squealed, before cringing and covering her mouth. She took the drink, already regretting it, as the bartender leaned toward her.

"It's from that guy actually. Asked me to bring you another round." He gave her an exaggerated wink before walking away to tend to another person somewhere down the bar. Cin stared at the drink. She'd never been offered a free drink before.

He's just messing with you.

"You don't know that," she whispered.

Who would buy you a drink?

Cin gave the voice a mental middle finger before turning to give the guy a smile. But when she looked up, the spot was filled by some too-tall blond bimbo with a ponytail almost as tight as her back was straight. Behind the blonde, she thought she saw Mira's red hair bobbing up and down. She squinted, but the head disappeared. She felt herself deflate; Mira, her best friend for the last decade since they turned fifteen, would never come to any of these. She hated the music and drunk men hitting on her. This wasn't worth it to her.

See? All alone again.

"Shut up."

"What was that?" a gravelly voice asked from behind her. Cin spun around so fast her head whirled, and she had to catch herself against the rough, worn wood of the bar. It was like a pole on the subway holding her steady as her body swayed with the alcohol. When she stilled, she came face-to-face with the man from across the bar. Up close, she could see she was wrong about his eyes. They weren't brown but a greenish hazel with gold flecks. Surrounded by thick brown lashes, they reminded her of a wetland full of golden lilies she could swim in.

"Hi." Hi? That's all she could manage. Great.

Off to a great start.

"Hey. I'm Ian." He took a step back and offered her a hand. She rubbed her palm against the fabric of her dark-wash jeans before shaking his.

CHAPTER ONE

"Cin. Thanks for the drink." She lifted the beverage to her lips and took a long sip. She hoped it made her look coy and alluring as she tilted her head up at him. Instead, she thought she looked like an alcoholic. She was pretty sure being an alcoholic wasn't alluring.

"You looked thirsty. I thought I could remedy that." He winked.

Take him home.

Cin tried to ignore the voice and focused on the man in front of her. It probably would have been easier if she hadn't drunk so much. "Do you want to dance?"

Ian offered a hand, but she brushed it off. Her palms were sweating again, and she didn't want to ruin her chances already. She brushed past him, carefully letting her ass lightly touch him as she went.

If you're going to act like that, you might as well just take him home.

"Shut up."

"What did you say?" Ian asked, his voice at the nape of her neck.

"I asked if this was a good spot." She did her best to ignore the face he gave her and let the music take over. It was pop-punk night, her favorite, and they were blaring the soundtrack to her high school experience. She threw her free hand up and bounced to the music. After a brief pause where Cin regretted every choice she'd made and she rubbed the perspiration off her hands, Ian started to dance next to her. Why was this guy making her so nervous?

"I used to blast this song when I didn't want my parents to come into my room." His voice was barely audible above the bass. "I know all the words."

"I know every word to every song they've played

tonight." Why did she always feel the need to one-up people when she drank?

Starting off with lies. Good choice.

"So do I." Ian cocked an eyebrow at her. She took a shaky breath as her cheeks warmed.

"Let's make it a bet." She took a sip of her drink and let the alcohol in her stomach swish around, giving her liquid confidence. She spun on her heel so she was facing him and leaned into him. "Whoever knows all the words to the next song gets to decide whether we kick tonight up a step."

Cin winked. He stared at her, his eyes tracing the lines of her body, before nodding slowly. She grabbed his arm and dragged him off the floor to an empty booth at the edge of the bar. In her foggy state, she barely noticed the heat his skin gave off or the mirrored sensation on her wrist where he was holding back. She dropped his arm and squeezed into a seat. She placed her elbows on the tabletop and smiled. "First person to stop singing loses."

Ian laughed, and the sound gave her chills. She hadn't felt so attracted to anyone since Mira, who made it very clear *that* wasn't an option.

"Absolutely not. This will never happen," Mira said—the first time she misread the signs—before pushing Cin to the other side of the couch. Cin had been shocked, mouth open, as Mira narrowed her eyes. "You can't just kiss people, Cin."

She couldn't respond, didn't have the words, but she could have sworn Mira had given her the signs. The subtle brushing of her hair away from her face. The lingering fingers on her arm. The locking of their eyes and breathing. It had been there. She could have sworn it.

You're going to fuck this up.

CHAPTER ONE

The voice brought Cin back to the present as she tried to hide her sudden nerves. They were washed away when the song switched. She threw her hands in the air and whooped. She knew this one like the back of her hand. When the lyrics started, she sang at the top of her lungs. Carried away with the music, she barely registered that Ian wasn't singing with her. Instead, he was watching her with that same mischievous glint in his eyes and a small smirk on his face.

"You didn't play fair." She pouted.

"Even if I won, it'd still be lady's choice. Besides, you look adorable singing." Cin's face flushed again. "Well, what's your choice?"

She tapped her chin thoughtfully. What was her choice?

Take him home before you ruin it.

Cin couldn't argue with it. Not with the amount of alcohol sloshing in her stomach or Ian's gorgeous smile blinding her. Or the fact that he thought she was cute singing when she sounded like a hoarse crow. "Let's get out of here."

"Where to?"

"I could really go for a slice." Once the words were out, she wanted to smack herself in the head. A slice? Who says that?

And there you go.

But Ian was laughing as he stood up from the table and held out a hand for her. "Pizza it is. I know a place down the street with the best pizza."

Cin took his hand and stepped out of the booth. "There are two places down the street. If we're turning left, there will be no more turning left in this little game of ours. There is only one acceptable answer." She tried to look stern but ended up giggling as he looked at her with mock horror.

"Left? Do I look like I'm from Chicago?" She breathed out a sigh of relief.

"Oh good. For a second, I thought I picked up a crazy. No good New Jerseyan eats deep dish."

The only crazy here is you, Cin.

Ian shook his head, laughter still bubbling up, as he guided her out of the crowded bar and down the block to the Italian pizzeria she ended up at every Thursday night. They stumbled through the door, and he had to stop Cin from falling over herself.

"Cin!" a man behind the counter called. She jumped onto the counter and kicked her legs out dramatically at the old man. His familiar salt-and-pepper hair was a wonderful sight.

"Antonio. My favorite pizza maker. Two slices please." She couldn't be sure, but without the music, it sounded like she was slurring. She wasn't that drunk, right?

"Usual?" He didn't wait for her to answer. Turning to the case, he shoved two spicy sausage and cheese slices into the oven before grabbing a water bottle from the fridge and handing it to her.

"How'd you know?"

"Two years, Cin. I better know my favorite customer. Who's the new fellow?"

Ian stepped up to the counter, his shoulders pulled back, and held out a hand. "Ian Santos. Nice to meet you. I'll take a cheese slice." A small bell rang in Cin's head when she heard his name, but she ignored it as Antonio gave her an exaggerated wink and pulled the requested cheese pizza out of the case. He threw it into the oven and pulled hers out.

"It's hot. Not that that has ever stopped you." Antonio laughed, and she leaned over to kiss his cheek. He rolled his eyes before putting the slices on the closest table. She slid off the counter and collapsed into the chair Antonio had pulled out for her.

"If it's not hot, it's not worth it." She took a big bite, letting the cheese burn the roof of her mouth, and moaned. The smell of gooey cheese and tomato sauce filled her with joy.

"Does she have taste buds left?" Ian chuckled, taking the seat across from her.

"Doubt it. Good thing she learned I was the best joint in this part of town, or I'd be out one loyal customer." Antonio slid Ian's slice onto the table before heading to the back of the store. Cin looked around the empty joint, sad to find they were the only ones there, before forcing her attention back to Ian.

She studied his short crew cut, eyebrow piercing, and crooked grin. His face was angular, with high cheekbones that made him look almost as severe as his smile made him look happy. His warm, tan skin was unmarred and reminded her of a scoop of coffee ice cream. And there was nothing Cin liked more in the world than coffee, especially in ice cream form.

"What do you think?"

"About what?" Ian tilted his head before his eyes lit up. "The pizza? Just as good as the last time I ordered it. I live around the block but grew up around here. Never been inside, though."

"Well, you've been missing out. Antonio doesn't just have the best pizza, he's the sweetest man I've ever met."

"Seems great. Really something . . ." Ian trailed off, watching her lips. She flipped her eyes between his eyes and his burgundy lips. But he didn't kiss her; instead, he lifted his hand to wipe a bit of sauce off her lip.

See? He's not into you.

Cin awkwardly grabbed a napkin and wiped her face. "Sorry."

"Don't apologize. It's cute." She smiled at him before diving back into her pizza. By the time she finished her slice, her phone rang with her nightly alarm. She grumbled as she snoozed it. If she didn't have it, she'd never make it home in time. Despite her original intentions, she needed to get home. If she took her sleeping meds after eleven, she wouldn't make it to her early morning lab at the university. She already made that mistake this semester.

You're going to mess up your job too. Just like you messed up tonight.

She stood up abruptly, overwhelmed with her walk home, the sound of the worst part of her yelling in her head, and the ticking of the clock in the background.

She mumbled, "I need to get going. I have to get up early."

She pulled a ten out of her purse and called goodbye to Antonio before skirting around a few tables. Ian stood up and followed her. She turned to give him a weak smile. "I'm sorry. I can't miss my lecture tomorrow. I have to teach at nine."

"Can I see you again? Tomorrow night—meet me here?"

She peered out the window at the rain pelting the ground, soaking it to a smoldering gray color. She frowned at the weather; she should have checked it before she left. "I have dinner with my mom. I'm sorry." She stepped outside, rain destroying the curls she had meticu-

CHAPTER ONE

lously done a few hours before, and pulled off her heels. Her phone rang again—reminding her that she had to go or else.

She waved goodbye before starting to run through the rain. It washed away her thoughts as her clothing started to soak up the rain and weigh her down. She didn't stop, her lungs heaving with the effort. Her legs started to burn and cramp, but she pushed past it. It wasn't until, a few minutes later, she had rounded the corner of her block and could see the lights of the entrance that she slowed to a jog. She eyed the homeless man hiding under the awning of her building before swiping her key card and getting out of the rain.

She paused, thinking over whether or not to let the man out of the rain, when the elevator's bell rang.

Might as well just go upstairs. You're useless to everyone anyway.

She sighed, the high of the night wearing off, and headed upstairs. Her studio was on the second floor and two doors from the elevator—an easy walk for when she was drunk. Opening the door, she smiled at the small space filled with soft rugs and blankets. Her own personal oasis.

She walked into the kitchen, intending to get a glass of water, when a magnet from Antonio's clicked something in her head. She'd forgotten to ask for his number. Or give him hers. Antonio couldn't give it to him—she only ever popped in. Cin refused to order delivery from Antonio on the grounds that it didn't give her a chance to say hi. Did she even have the restaurant's number?

"Shit. He's probably gone now." She heaved a sigh before pouring herself a shot or two of gin from the bottle on the counter. She took a sip of it before dropping it on the nightstand as she snuggled into bed. She ran her fingers through the silky fake-fur-lined blanket. Sliding her legs against the white satin sheets, she closed her eyes in joy. It was like sliding into a cloud. A soft, loving cocoon where she could ignore the voice.

At least, most of the time.

He's better off without you.

"You don't know that."

Look at you. You can't even manage to give a guy your number.

"Shut up." She rolled over to press the button on her noise machine, letting the sound of waves crashing wash out the sound of her own self-loathing. Maybe she didn't give him her number, but at least she had a good night. That counted for something, right?

But it didn't. Even with her pills, all the ones she was supposed to take at night, her mind was reeling with every bad moment—every mistake. She leaned over to pull two pills and took them dry before turning her head to stare up at the ceiling, watching the lights of cars explode across the popcorn before forcing her eyes shut. She could at least pretend to sleep.

Chapter Two

Stay in bed.

Cin did her best to ignore the voice. She had lived with the constant hum of negativity for as long as she could remember. But this morning… this morning the voice didn't sound like hers. Cin's eyes were wide open and had been for hours. She had maybe gotten a few hours after the meds had all kicked in and the voice had stopped reminding her she had screwed up with Ian.

She couldn't remember the last time she had gone to sleep for more than a few hours. Maybe last Tuesday? She counted the days in her head. She was bound to come down soon.

Something about this morning, about this time, didn't feel right. The voice didn't tell her to drive around the block or paint the most beautiful flower before giving up halfway out of frustration. It didn't tell her to write a sonnet or sing at the top of her lungs in the middle of the work bathroom. It wasn't reminding her that she was alone instead of with whoever that guy was last night.

Instead, the voice wanted her to do the opposite of what her hypomanic state normally wanted, and she was definitely hypomanic last time she checked.

Avoid today. Spend the day in bed.

Cin had been what people called "crazy" for as long as she could remember. She knew there was a before—before the first doctor's appointment and orange pill bottle—but it was fuzzy. Almost like everything before this fully formed adult was out of focus—like a camera that couldn't capture the image. It was a part of her just like her boring brown hair, the bright-blue dye she used to cover it, and the scars that littered her arms from years of self-harm.

When she was younger, they were something covered under long-sleeved shirts in the middle of August or the constant cardigan she kept in her backpack. Now they were badges of honor. Constant reminders that she had survived through the worst of it. That she could survive anything the world threw her way.

She knew what was and was not supposed to happen, what was and was not supposed to be. She wasn't supposed to stay in bed. And yet the voice sounded so convincing. More convincing than the one she had ignored for years, despite the constant jabbing at her psyche, that she felt the need to listen.

Maybe it was time to listen. Or maybe there's no reason to focus on the new voice since it was just another figment of her imagination.

Everything good in your life has always been a lie.

Cin turned her head, pulling her thoughts away from the voice, to glare at the small stack of orange pill bottles on her nightstand. The same pill bottles filled with the same pills she'd taken for the last ten years. They were supposed to make the voices go away, help her sleep, make her blend in with everyone else.

Maybe she didn't want to blend in. What if she chose to stand out and be the inspired person she used to be?

Take the pills.

Don't take the pills. Live free.

That. That sounded like her. Cin reached for the bottle and rolled it between her hands. She let the cool plastic soothe her. If she was being honest with herself, the only change she'd experienced over the last ten years was a complete disinterest in the world around her when she wasn't swinging. She was still an outcast, only managed to make one friend who didn't flake the minute she wasn't "normal," and even that wasn't guaranteed. Antonio only tolerated her, and she hadn't spoken with her brother in three years. Not to mention her mom, who felt more like a child than a mother nowadays, who lost her grip on the world. She didn't want to lose her grip, not completely. But she was always going to be *that girl*, even medicated.

"Not today, Satan," Cin mumbled, before slipping two little white pills out of one of the bottles, her morning medication, and taking a quick gulp from the glass on her nightstand. She coughed, covering her mouth so she didn't lose her meds. Gin. Why did she always leave gin next to the bed? After all this time, wouldn't she remember to put a water bottle there instead? Did she always need to be so irresponsible?

It's in your nature to screw everything up.

Cin slammed the glass down, the gin splashing up the sides and sending droplets across the stack of graded reports, and finally rolled out of bed with an exaggerated grunt. She sniffed the reports—definitely smelled like gin—and put them on a stack of other reports that needed to air out before she could hand them back.

Thank goodness she didn't live with anyone. Her studio apartment was her little sanctuary. A place where she didn't need to pretend to be someone she wasn't. That's all she needed. She slid across the shag rug that ran between her bed and the living room area and reveled as the soft fuzz tickled her toes. What a good purchase.

You should buy more rugs like this. Put one in the kitchen.

Lay down on the rug and go back to bed.

Cin ran a hand over her face as she walked into the bathroom and got into the shower. It didn't take her long to shower and then braid her frizzy hair. She ran her fingers over the braid, recognizing it for what it was. Hypomanic Cin always did her hair in elaborate styles—like the curls that had died the night before in the rain; Depressive Cin never did more than a braid or a simple bun. She was surprised she had managed to shower without dragging herself kicking and screaming.

Maybe that second voice was just her depressive state dragging her down. If it was, things would get bad again. Bad like they had last September.

∼

The way the sun had shone, at its highest, when she opened her eyes to a slit. Just enough to see the missed calls from Dean Williamson. They escalated every day she missed without getting coverage until finally twenty-nine.

Twenty-five, the number of years she lived, was the number she needed. She didn't know how many days it had been. How long since her last shower? When she had last taken her medication. She had pulled herself out of bed, clad in long flannel pajamas and a ratty-bat T-shirt, and pulled on sneakers before slipping out the front door and taking the bus to campus.

Dean Williamson had hurried her into his office, asked all the right questions, and promised to smooth over the board in exchange for her making an appointment to see her doctor. She agreed, grateful for the favor, and let him call the cab to take her home.

"Take care of yourself, Cin. I'll do my best to cover for you, but the board will only tolerate so much." It had been solemn and serious. But the reality of how bad she had gotten, how tenuous her position was, hit her like a ton of bricks.

She had lifted the bricks, used them to build herself back up as the depression receded, and stepped into her lab for the first time in two weeks the following Monday with blue hair and a wicked smile.

Cin took a moment to acknowledge how hard the next couple of weeks were going to be—how tough they always were. She would get back up like she always did.

It wasn't until she looked in the mirror, stared down the ever-present black bags under her eyes, that her days without sleep and the night before started to weigh on her as well. The image of a pendulum swinging back and forth filled her head—it was how all her doctors had described her mood—but she wasn't swinging. She was like one of those carnival games where you drop a puck down the pegs to win a prize. Except most of the boxes held "hypomanic" or "depressive" with one, smack dab in the middle, that said "apathetic."

She brushed away the brutal image and focused back on the bags under her eyes. Cin was used to them, but today they looked worse than usual. She pressed two fingers into the puffiness before reaching for something to make her look like she got a few hours of sleep. She thought back to the night before, and Ian's face flooded her mind so clearly it was like a picture. Hazel eyes bored into her. Eyes that were lucky she left when she did. She focused back on her own brown eyes and dabbed concealer methodically.

Satisfied with the end product, she headed to the kitchen area to whip up something to help settle her stomach.

Skip breakfast. Have ice cream.

"I don't need to add a sugar coma to my list of problems today." Bipolar was enough for one person. Let alone anxiety and insomnia.

Finish off your glass of gin.

Have a drink and get into bed.

"I can't teach undergraduates basic chemistry drunk. Dr. Williamson won't be able to cover another episode, and I need this job." Cin grabbed a muffin out of the tin she'd left open on the counter. Stale. Oh well. Better than nothing. She ripped off a piece and shoved it into her mouth. Blueberry? Why did she buy blueberry? She hated blueberry.

Wash it down with the gin.

Cin contemplated her options. It wasn't the worst way to start her morning. Especially when she had dinner with her mother and an afternoon meeting with the dean of the college about the new adjunct she had to deal with. "Chalk one up for Satan," she thought as she walked over to finish off the glass on her nightstand. It went down like fire and warmed her gut. At least she couldn't taste the blueberry anymore as she chucked the muffin and made her way outside of the apartment building.

Go back to bed; you'll regret this.

She lowered her head as she walked past the beefy guy two floors above her who loved to run before the sun was out and the elderly lady who lived next door and walked her cat every morning. When they said hi, she grunted and sped up. She had tried when she first moved in to be friendly to the neighbors she passed. The old woman with graying hair had the most annoying Southern accent she had ever heard that spewed constant, unrequested opinions. Meanwhile, Mr. Beefy was overtly creepy about his intentions toward Cin. Just thinking about it made her shiver. She patted the mace in her purse pocket—she bought it right after her first conversation with him.

I bet you can't mess up getting him into bed.

No, Cin didn't need any friends, especially not friends with benefits. She was happy enough with her half-assed relationship with her brother—where she sent unrequited letters—and Mira. Mira who was probably waiting for her already, iced coffee in hand. She was her best friend, her only friend really, and the other half of her crazy coin. She couldn't imagine anyone else to share her musings and misgivings with. A small part of her wondered if that was because she never tried, but she pushed that away.

"Better speed up, Cin, or people might think you're a zombie," Mira called from her spot leaning against her beat-up sedan. Her short red hair was sticking out in all directions, and with the sun rising behind her, she looked like a firecracker. The irony wasn't lost on Cin.

"Maybe if I was a zombie, I would get fewer looks when I talk to myself."

"You'd also have to eat brains. Do brains sound appetizing to you?" Mira put a dramatic hand to her head as she handed over the coffee and hopped into the driver's seat.

"I don't know, Mira. I'm not sure crazy redheads are a zombie's thing." Cin got into the car, and Mira peeled out, tires squealing. "You know, this is what I mean about not being zombie bait. Did you even look?"

"One day I'm going to replace this brick on wheels with a real ride. Then I'll be crazy. Right now, I'm just the partner in crime to a chick who talks to herself."

"And smells like a distillery on a good day."

"Speaking of, did you start your day with gin again?" Mira gave her a sidelong glance as she pulled off the main road and onto a side road that led to the parking garage. It was sandwiched between the main science building and Mira's office in the psychology department.

"I thought it was water."

Liar.

"You know I can tell when you're lying, right? What happened?"

Mira was right, she knew when she was lying, and it didn't seem worth it to start a fight this morning. A lot of things started fights lately. Cin mulled over whether or not to admit about the second voice or the guy from last night.

Don't tell anyone.

She closed her eyes and grabbed her head. "The voices are worse than usual today."

You should have stayed home.

"I'll take it," Mira conceded.

"Kind of you."

"I'm a great friend, and you know it."

Cin took a long sip of her black coffee and swished it around in her mouth. It was bitter, devoid of sweetness, and just how she liked it. Just how Mira brought it to her every morning. It was their ritual since she started undergrad with Mira and, most days, the only reason she got out of bed. "I'd be lost without you, Mira. You don't need me to remind you."

"Just as I suspected, you're sick." Mira sighed dramatically.

"Sick of you maybe." Cin laughed.

Mira wishes you were sick so you would leave her alone.

Their laughter died down as Cin flipped on the radio. The sound of morning chatter filled the car, suffocating the voices in her head. She leaned back in the seat and let out a long sigh. She closed her eyes and did her best to ignore Mira's constant finger tapping. She knew what it meant, and she didn't want to open the door to Mira's building concern.

"Are you ready for dinner with dear old Mom?" Mira's voice was loud over the radio.

Cin squeezed the bridge of her nose. "Do we have to?"

"Do you plan to go in unprepared?"

"It doesn't matter how many times we do this. I'll

never be prepared for my mother's madness. You think I'm the one who needs medication. All these years and she's still convinced we're witches. We're not magical—we're crazy." Cin did her best to sound unaffected, but the weight of losing her mom to the same disorder that was slowly ripping her brain to shreds this morning hung heavy in the air around her.

"You're not crazy, Cin."

You're definitely crazy.

See why you should have stayed home?

"I hear voices. I'm diagnosed bipolar. What more is there?"

"Having a mental disability doesn't make you crazy."

"Try telling that to the devil in my head." Cin opened her eyes to give Mira a wry smile before turning her attention to the white security booth for the parking garage. It beeped at Mira's parking card before the orange bar swung up. Mira pulled the car into the first spot and placed it in park.

"I'm serious, Cin. There's nothing wrong with you. Don't let your mother get in your head with her shenanigans again. There are no witches, but there are certainly mental disabilities that plague you both. You need to be there for her, but only as much as you can handle. Promise me you'll leave if she tries to convince you that you have magical powers before it damages your psyche."

"I can't promise that."

"I know."

"I'll call you after dinner." It was a lie she always told. She never called, and Mira never tried. It was how things worked—Mira hated her mother's belief that they were witches, and she hated having the same fight over and over.

Mira didn't respond, leaning over to give Cin a strong hug. She wanted to stay there, Mira's comforting embrace wrapped around her, but she couldn't. It wasn't fair to Mira that she was so attached in all the ways she promised her she wouldn't be.

Yes, you can.

Cin felt her hand twitch as the voice invaded again, an even better reason to get out of the car. She pulled herself from Mira, grabbed her bag, and got out of the car with a quick goodbye to Mira. She couldn't believe it, but she might actually be getting crazier.

Chapter Three

Cin was packing up her laptop when a shadow passed over her desk. She wasn't sure which student was standing over her, but without a doubt, she knew they were hoping to get the answer to one of the final lab questions before submitting their report. She stifled her eye roll. All these students just wanted to pass so they could go back to their biology classes. No one actually wanted to study chemistry. "Do you have a question about the lab?"

"Professor Cin, do you have a moment to talk?" She looked up, her mouth slightly agape with surprise, to see one of her favorite students, Adam, standing in front of her. When she thought of students trying to get her to help finish their reports, Adam was never on her mind. His shoulders were slumped under the weight of his backpack, and he was frowning at his clasped hands. When she didn't respond, he looked up through his long black bangs. "It'll only take a minute."

You wouldn't be stressed out if you had stayed home.

Cin looked around the room; the rest of the lab students had left. "Huh, I guess everyone understood the lab this week. That's a first," she thought. She looked down at her watch. She had five minutes before her meeting with the dean, and she hadn't even checked to make sure all the chemicals were put away. She tried not to think of the consequences that would come if she was late before sitting back down in her chair. "What's going on, Adam? Are you struggling?"

He shuffled his feet. "I don't think I'm going to be able to pass this semester, Ms. Cin. My dad is sick, like really sick. I don't think I'll be able to get in my last few assignments in time while trying to take care of him."

Tell him to shove it.

"Did you hand in today's assignment?" He shook his head and bit his lip. Cin couldn't be sure, but he looked like he was about to cry. She had known him for two years—taught him for three different chemistry labs—and she had never seen him anything other than happy. Seeing him so broken up tugged on her heartstrings. Her eyes darted around the room, checking to see if anyone left out beakers before bringing her full attention to Adam.

No one gave you a break.

"I tried. I was most of the way done when I had to bring him to the hospital last night. It's just the two of us, and he was throwing up so much." His voice was ragged with unshed tears.

Her phone vibrated in her pocket. Probably Dean Williamson asking where she was. Meeting be damned, she couldn't leave him here like this. She knew it would be added to the growing list of grievances the board had, but she had agreed to teach so that she could help students who struggled as she had. Not to please a board of stuffy old guys.

Cin awkwardly placed a soft hand on his shoulder. It was the best she could do as his teacher, and it still felt wrong. "Don't worry about the assignment, Adam. How about this? Come by during my office hours Friday and we can work through the rest of it together. From now on, you need to let me know if you can't finish the assignment. We can get together to work through everything. Hopefully, that will speed up the process so you have more time with your dad."

"Really?" He let out a rough breath and hugged her tightly. She tensed, uncomfortable with his sudden closeness. "Thank you so much, Ms. Cin. I'm so grateful you decided to move from general to organic. I'd be lost without you teaching me."

Decided was not the word she would use. She patted him on the back before extracting herself. "Meet me tomorrow morning and we'll get this finished up. If you can't make it, just give me a text." She leaned down and wrote her number on a Post-it Note. "I need to get to a meeting now. Are you going to be okay?"

He nodded, his face still pale and disorienting. "I'll be okay. I need to get home soon anyway. Dad has chemo in an hour."

She guided them to the door before peeking over her shoulder to make one last check around the room. No chemicals in sight. Check. Everything put away. Check. She nodded at the room before looking back to the red-eyed boy. "Adam?"

"Yes, Ms. Cin?"

"If you need help or to talk. Well, my line's always open. Okay?"

He followed her in silence down the hall to the offices on the other side of the building until they passed the elevator. He stopped there, staring at the buttons, while she continued down the walkway. It wasn't until the door dinged that she heard his quiet "Thank you."

Skip the meeting. You're already late.

She nibbled on her lip. She had watched a parent get sick when she was trying to get her bachelor's too. She knew how hard it could be. She only wished she had someone to help her when she needed it. But she only had herself; she had always only had herself. Her brother never came home anymore, and Mira, sweet innocent Mira, just didn't do well with understanding her darker side. Mira would always be her person, but even she could admit that when things got really dark, she tended to freak out way before she stood strong for Cin. For someone who worked in the psychology department, she really struggled with any kind of mental illness.

Mira doesn't even like you.

"You don't know that," she mumbled, before turning to the portly assistant, an older woman named Jennifer whom she generally didn't speak to, who pulled her out of her own misery by motioning for her to go inside as she neared the door to the dean's office. She gave her a curt nod, ran a hair over her braid, and stepped into the room with a fake smile.

She didn't make it far, stopping short halfway into the room by the image of the guy from the night before sitting calmly in the chair across from Dr. Williamson. His brown hair was pushed back, and his eyes were locked on the dean's stoic face. A stoic face that held the fire of a thousand suns firing directly to where she stood with her mouth hanging slightly open. Great. She really screwed up this time.

You always screw up.

"I'm sorry. A student kept me after lab." It came out barely intelligible and all at once. She wasn't sure anyone understood what she was saying, but it was enough to propel her feet forward and land in the chair next to the guy. She tried to peek at him without moving her head, but it was useless. She focused on Dean Williamson's round, disapproving face, his deep-brown eyes burning holes into her.

"Ms. Clark, thank you for finally joining us. I'd like you to meet Ian Santos; he'll be teaching our new environmental chemistry class." Dr. Williamson leaned back in his chair and clasped his hands on the desk. "He's requested our best laboratory instructor to support his laboratory portion."

Ian leaned over, finally putting his eyes on her, and stared at her wide-eyed.

See? Today was a bad idea.

He caught himself much faster than she could've by putting on a neutral expression and offering his hand. She shook it awkwardly. At least her hands weren't sweaty this time, just clammy from stress. She wasn't sure if that was any better.

It's worse.

"Ms. Clark here, despite her inability to be on time, is one of the best chemists this university has produced. I will have her reassigned to your lecture and lab sections next semester. That should give you about two months to get prepared. Is that enough time for you, Dr. Santos?" Dr. Williamson smiled at the two of them, completely oblivious to the tension building in the room. Cin could see his annoyance with her swirling in his brown eyes, but to the untrained eye, he looked every bit the unaffected college dean. She tried to plead with her eyes, but Dr. Williamson wasn't having it.

"Thank you for your kind offer, but I'd like to make sure Cin is comfortable with this new arrangement." He focused his hazel eyes on hers, his hand hanging inches from her leg, and she tried not to freak out. His smoldering eyes and crooked grin made her heart beat like drums in a rock song.

You're just going to fuck this up too.

"Cin, don't you want to help Dr. Santos with his new class?" Dr. Williamson pinned her in her seat with a pointed look. This wasn't a choice—it was her last chance to stay with the college. After her depressive streak at the beginning of this semester, she was lucky they let her finish it out. She knew it was "Say yes," or she'd be searching for a new job next semester.

Cin knew this was how Dean Williamson was watching out for her. Just like he had for all the years she struggled through her master's here. He probably would have been the same way for her bachelor's, but she had gotten her first degree at a small liberal arts college to save money. Despite his frustrations with her, she knew he was hoping this would give her an opportunity to start fresh in the department. To keep her away from the board in charge of the college of science who wanted her gone. She nodded, almost imperceptibly. She wouldn't give up this chance.

Always believing you're above your own nature.

"You're right, Dean Williamson. I think this will be a great opportunity." She focused her attention on the smile that spread across his face. She couldn't look at Ian, didn't dare to pull herself away from the relief that was spread across the dean's face to whatever emotions were playing across his. Out of the corner of her eye, she saw Ian's hand twitch.

"Wonderful. Why don't you give Dr. Santos a tour of his new classroom and lab? I've placed him up on the fifth floor in the empty adjoining orgo room. Dr. Schaffer's old room." He gestured to the door with a bittersweet smile as Ian stood up to walk out. But Cin stayed rooted in her place.

"Dr. Williamson, can we have a quick word in private about one of my students?" He nodded as Ian walked out. When the door clicked shut, she leaned forward with knitted brows. "Adam. The junior who I've been teaching for the last two years? His dad is sick. I'm worried about him. His grades had been slipping a little, but today he told me he couldn't finish his assignment."

"Adam?" Dr. Williamson's voice was raised uncomfortably. She couldn't tell what he meant with his tone, so she gave him a wry smile.

"Yes. Adam Wright? He's a junior?" Dean Williamson shrugged awkwardly but ushered her on. "Is there any way . . . well . . . do you think we could give him a pass on the take-home assignments? Maybe offer him a few extra lab quizzes?"

He rubbed his chin in thought. "We don't normally do special treatment, Cin." She cocked an eyebrow at him. He knew very well he had favored her through her college years and into her role now. "Very well. Come back at the end of the week and provide me your post-laboratory quizzes for review. We can discuss how feasible this plan is then."

"Thank you." She gave him a genuine smile as she stood up and headed to the door.

Look at you. Trying to save someone else when you can barely take care of yourself.

"Cin?"

"Yes?" She peeked over her shoulder.

"Please do your best to take advantage of this new opportunity. I'm not ready to give up on you, but the powers that be . . ." He made a face at her as the weight of everything started to settle on Cin's shoulders. Her shoulders tensed, and she quirked her mouth into something like a smile.

"I know. I can do this."

No, you can't.

"Good luck, Cin." She let go of the tension in her shoulders and walked out to deal with her next problem. Cin walked stiffly past Ian's relaxed lean against the wall outside the dean's offices. She did her best to ignore the smug smile on his face and headed to the elevator. She hit the button and pulled out her phone. She didn't have any messages, but she was hoping that by scrolling through her email and avoiding eye contact that it would get her through this new nightmare.

"So, organic chemistry. Why did you agree to teach environmental chemistry with me?" Ian's voice was much closer to her than she expected, and she fought the urge to take a step away as his arm brushed against her. The chills it gave her made her shiver deliciously.

"Suffice to say, it's not really a choice."

The elevator dinged, and she walked in. Ian shuffled in beside her. "You don't have to teach with me if you don't want to. It's your choice. I thought I made that clear."

You could kiss him. Right now. Do it.

"Like I said, it's not exactly a choice for me."

"And why is that?" The elevator doors opened to the musty air of the unused fifth floor. Looking around, she made note of the cobwebs and dust balls scattered about the hallway. She'd need to request the maintenance crew to come through with a good clean and maybe check on the fume hoods. No doubt they needed service.

"No one uses this floor. Not after . . ." She drew her mouth in a straight line. "Our last fifth-floor professor didn't leave on good terms." The image of Dr. Schaffer's sickly body filled her vision, and her eyes pricked. He had been the second person in the department who took a chance on her.

"Oh. Did he get kicked out?"

"He died."

Good choice—scare him away with your morbid attitude.

She still felt the chest-tightening sadness over the loss. Brain cancer was something no one expected. A silent killer until it's too far along. Barney Schaffer had been a bright light on a cloudy day—had pulled her out of bed to weird overnight experiments and coffee runs that involved beverages she was almost embarrassed to request.

She had been shocked the day he met her here—the last day he ever showed up to the fifth floor. He looked at her with a seriousness she had never seen before. Steady eyes from his place perched on the edge of his desk. "We need to talk."

She placed his iced coffee on the desk next to him before sitting on top of a nearby desk. "Everything okay, Bossman?"

He shook his head slowly, deliberately. "I have cancer—brain cancer."

She felt the tears well up, burning her eyes. She straightened her shoulders, and in her most clinical voice asked, "What are the next steps?"

"It's inoperable. I have a few weeks left." Her stomach dropped. He gave her a weak smile. "I have no one else—no wife or kids. Do you think you'd like my apartment?"

She had been living with roommates she hated—having moved out of her mom's place a few years prior. The first few nights had been weird—the feeling of Barney still lingering—but the more time she spent in the hospital, the more time she made his place hers, the more she felt at home. She still lived there, in Barney's old apartment.

Maybe he'll die too.

The voice snapped through her head angrily. Cin walked away from Ian's shocked face and opened the door to the classroom. She flipped on the lights and watched the fluorescent bulbs flicker a few times before steadying out. She made a note to add new bulbs to the list as she counted the ones that stayed off. Most of the tables were covered in dust. For almost a year without use, it was a surprise the room wasn't worse. She walked over to the whiteboard where Dr. Schaffer's name was imprinted on the dirty surface.

Cin sighed, memories of Dr. Schaffer's antics trying to bubble up to the surface. The wacky, crazy scientist wig he wore on the first day of lecture. The banana oil experiment he demanded they do every year despite the smell that penetrated three floors down. But the one that made her smile despite the circumstances was the way he doodled on every surface. The doodles, in purple marker, were scrolled across the bottom of the whiteboard. She traced them lovingly.

It's your fault he died. Remember?
You'll kill Ian too.

She wanted to argue, but she never did. Brain cancer wasn't her fault, but they were a team and spent so much time together. If she had just paid attention more, maybe he'd still be there.

"I used to work under Dr. Schaffer before he passed." Cin grabbed the whiteboard eraser and scrubbed uselessly at the board in hopes to erase the memories of his demise etched in her mind. The image of his limp body rotting away in a hospice bed. She had only left for a few minutes. Went to pick herself up a coffee and bring in his dinner. He should have been fine when she got back. He was fine. The sound of Ian's Converse shuffling across the room pulled her back to the present, and she tapped the board. She added to her mental list. "I'll ask them to replace this with a new one—a fresh start."

Fresh start doesn't mean you'll get a new outcome.
Well. No turning back now. Guess you'll just screw this up too.

"You don't control everything," she hissed under her breath at the voices.

"I'm sorry, did you say something?" Ian's breath was hot on her neck, and she shivered, the memories of the night before flashing before her eyes. She turned around to find herself nose to nose with a smiling Ian. "You know you tend to talk to yourself, right? Are you okay?"

"I hear voices," she blurted out, before taking a step back right into the whiteboard. Ian narrowed his eyes and took an awkward step away. "Shit. Well. I guess if we're going to be working together, I might as well tell you now.

I'm bipolar. Have been for as long as I can remember. I'm stable now, but the medication only does so much."

"Oh." Ian bit his lip as he walked over to the nearest chair and sat down. He patted the seat next to him. "Come here."

Cin leaned against the whiteboard and crossed her arms. "Is that a problem? Should I explain to the dean that our newest employee is discriminatory?"

Ian laughed.

Tell him to fuck off.

Walk away. Go home.

"What? What's so fucking funny?"

"You didn't even give me a chance." Ian shook his head. "It's fine. I only wanted to ask you what you needed from me as a co-worker to make this easier on you?"

"Oh." Cin's face burned. She really dug herself a new hole this time. Always jumping to conclusions. One day she was going to jump right over the cliff into a crazy town just like Mom. "I'm sorry. I just . . ."

"Assumed the worst? Not terribly shocking. I doubt anything has been easy on you."

Cin knitted her brow as she studied the curious man in front of her. She'd been crazy for more than half her life and never, not even when she'd told Mira, had someone just told her they would accommodate her. Mira, her brother, even her insane mother who had the same issue had asked her all these questions. Wanted to know if some scenario they had been through was because of the issues with her own psyche. No one had ever just asked how they could *help.*

He doesn't actually care. No one does.

"It's been fine."

"Oh—lying. What a great way to start this partnership." Ian rolled his eyes at her. Cin tried to shove her indignation aside, but it only worked so well.

"Listen. You don't know anything about me." Cin walked to the door, placing a hand on the metal handle. She used the cool surface to rein in some of her annoyance. Ian opened his mouth to speak, but she cut him off as anger filled its place. "Tell me when you want to meet to work on lesson plans and I'll be there. Other than that, leave me alone. I don't need your pity."

"Pity?" Ian barked another laugh out. It grated on her. "Is that what you thought last night was? Pity?" Cin froze. Her body stiffly holding the doorframe.

Pity. He pities you.

"You think I would spend the night with a girl because I pity them? That's ridiculous. You don't know anything about me!"

Tell him to fuck off.

It was the second voice—the loud, intense hatred of the man in front of her—that snapped her back into the world. She pivoted to glare at him with burning eyes and her most vicious grin. She dredged up her coldest voice, the one reserved for people like her deadbeat father who showed up when he needed money. "You're right. I don't know anything about you, and honestly, I don't want to. I'll meet you here on Monday at three p.m. to discuss our plans for the next semester and deal out tasks. Goodbye, Dr. Santos."

She gave him a once over, making sure the venom she let drip was making him squirm, before walking out the door. When she heard the click of the door behind her, she ripped off the heels she was wearing and ran down to the stairway. As she started down the steps, two at a time, she heard his barely audible call after her.

Can't do anything right, can you?

Cin pushed herself faster, her breathing coming in rough, jagged breaths and her legs burning, until she could feel the fresh evening air on her skin. She pressed herself against the cool brick exterior of the science building, letting the bite of the rough brick rip at her bare arms. A few seconds later, the chill of December in New Jersey made her shiver violently.

"Well, Cin, look at the mess you've gotten yourself into this time."

Chapter Four

Leaning against her building an hour later in a fleece-lined leather coat, Cin checked her phone only to admit she was already running late for dinner and was just avoiding it. She hailed a cab to drop her off at the psych ward. The doors to the facility loomed in front of her like the gates of hell. The more she stared at them, the more they felt like the doors to her future. She eyed the small, plain white sign—RIVERHEAD HOME FOR ADULTS—before she pushed open the creaking doors that felt like she was willingly giving up on herself, like she had given up on her mother all those years ago. As she crossed the thick, black line in the floor and her heels hit the almost opalescent white tile, her skin started to crawl. Everything about this place gave her the creeps. She already regretted coming here, but regret wouldn't stop her from seeing her mom.

"Ah, Ms. Cin, Lucy is in the games room waiting for you." Cin barely turned to nod at whoever was talking as she marched through the main lobby and into one of the larger gathering rooms. It was sparse, filled with a few tables and one other person besides her mother. A small stack of board games sat on the table in front of her. She looked up at Cin when the sound of her heels echoed in the room.

"Darling." Cin sighed. Her mother's brown hair was hanging in loose threads, matted in places, and framing her face. A face that held the same dark bags and washed-out complexion as her own. It was this, the moment she saw her future self, that made coming here so hard.

"Are you taking care of yourself, Mom? It looks like you haven't eaten or showered in days. Do you want to go over to the dining room? Are they taking care of you?"

Always taking care of others. Never yourself—no wonder you're a mess.

"Cin-Cin. Never mind the food. I see it now. I see you." Her mother reached a hand out to touch her arm gently. Her papery skin gave Cin chills, but she fought to ignore it and leave the hand where it was.

"What do you see, Mama?" Her heart twinged to see her like this, no matter how many times she had. She reached up and placed her hand on her mom's.

"I see you've been tied together with strings."

Cin wanted to roll her eyes but stopped herself when she saw Lucy's hopeful face. "Mom, I'm not made of string. Come now, let's eat. Please, for me?"

"No. Cin. You must listen."

"Mom, I listen to you all the time. I can listen while you eat." Her mother tilted her head, her brown hair falling into her face. Cin reached out to brush it away. But as she touched her mother's cool skin, Lucy grabbed her hand with force.

"Cin." Her mother's brown eyes searched hers frantically.

"Mom, calm down. Please."

This is how you're going to turn out.

"Cin. You need to understand. Now. Before others see. I need you to know." Cin pushed aside her feelings of unease, giving Lucy a placating smile. It was easier when she got like this to call her Lucy instead of Mom. A degree of separation.

"Need me to know what?"

"You're tied to death. Just like your brother."

Cin forced herself not to roll her eyes. This was going nowhere. "Come on, Mom. Let's get some food." She put her elbow under her mother's armpit and lifted her out of the chair. She didn't fight as Cin pulled her out and into the room next door before getting her situated in a similar chair and table surrounded by a few other patients. She walked over to the cart full of dinner trays and grabbed the top one. Roasted turkey and green beans. It looked gray and unappetizing—no wonder her mom didn't eat.

"Cin-Cin. Come here, Cin." Cin forced her feet to carry her back to the table where her mom's eyebrows were knitted and dropped the tray there. She gave her mother a wan smile.

This is your future.

"Mama, please. I'll listen to you if you eat something. Please."

She's crazy. Just like you.

"Cin." Lucy touched her hand gently. "You must understand that you have always been a witch. We have always been witches. We come from a long line of them."

You come from a long line of crazies.

"Yes, Mom. You've told me this. I know. Like I said, if you eat, I'll listen to everything you have to say."

"You don't know, Cin. You've never believed, and now . . . now you're tied to death." Cin fought the urge to tell her mother to shut up. Why was she always harping on this? It's not like anything magical had ever happened to them. Before her mom got placed in this facility, she had tried to show her some of this so-called magic, but she was so drunk Cin wasn't sure what was supposed to happen.

That was her mom. Stumbling through the condo, an empty bottle of wine clutched in one hand, and laughing at jokes no one told. It wasn't far off from how she acted alone in her apartment, but that was different.

"Mom, I promise I'll listen if you just . . ." Her mother scowled but took a bite of the turkey Cin was holding out for her. She watched her with a full heart. She might be stubborn and talk all kinds of crazy, but she was still her wacky mother. No matter what, she would always help her.

"There. Now will you listen to me?"

"I'll listen, but I can't promise I'll follow through."

Does staring at your future scare you? It scares me.

"Cin." Her mother gripped her forearm and pulled herself across the table so they were inches apart. "I have never once lied to you. If you don't . . . you must understand who you are. Who we are. You can't end up like me—like my mother. I should never have put myself in here."

Cin took a shaky breath as she pushed her chair back. "Mom. You're in here because you walked into a grocery store naked and threw produce at people. Why do you think you had a choice?"

"That's what you think. Your brother pushed me into here at my first doubt. Said it would be safer this way."

"That's what the police told me, Mom. Are you telling me the police are lying? James was there, is he a liar too?"

"That's exactly what I'm telling you. You're in danger, Cin. You need to believe in yourself and your power. You must be able to use what you've been gifted, or you'll end up like me. Or worse, you'll end up dead. Be wary of the people you surround yourself with. Mira isn't who you think she is."

Cin stood up, throwing her chair back, and glared at her mother. "I can't with your antics. I really just can't. You can't just go around accusing people of things and claiming miracles, Mama. How are you ever going to get out of here if you act like this?" She clenched her fist, pulling in all her frustrations. "I'm sorry. Please just eat your dinner without me tonight."

"Please, don't leave."

Cin blew out a long breath, gripping the chair, and eyed her mother. "Mama, you can't keep doing this. It's hard enough seeing you in here."

"I'm trying to protect you sweetie. I know you don't believe me, but one day soon, you won't have an option. I'll be waiting when it does. I'll always be here. That's what moms are for."

Cin walked around the table and wrapped her mom into a hug.

"I'll always love you, Mama, but I just can't do this tonight. It's been a long day. Please eat your dinner. I'll see you next week. Same time as usual." She kissed the top of her head before turning on her heel and walking out of the room.

In the distance, she could hear her mom calling, but

she ignored it. She couldn't let her mother drag her into the craziness that she lived in. Not today, not after that last twenty-four hours. She needed to get out of there. It wasn't until the cool evening air hit her face that Cin couldn't control herself. She stumbled back against the hard brick wall of the facility and fell to the ground.

It's already starting.

"Get out of my head," Cin hissed, before pulling herself up. She was stronger than this, better than what she'd just witnessed. She could control the demons inside her. Right?

∼

She didn't remember the walk from the facility to the bar around the corner, but suddenly she was sitting on a tattered barstool with a gin and tonic in front of her. She took a sip, the alcohol burning on its way down, and eyed the crowd around her. The bar wasn't super busy, but there was the usual mess of college kids who wanted to feel edgy and the regulars who liked to hang out at bars all night long. Every seat at the bar was filled, though, and each person seemed to live in their own bubble.

The blonde at the end of the bar, her eyes flashing between the door and her phone, caught her attention, but Cin couldn't place her. She felt familiar, but maybe she had just seen her before at the bar. She could be a regular like Cin. Their eyes connected, and Cin turned to look at the rest of the crowd.

The crowd seemed to stare back at her, watching her, almost waiting for her to lose control of the demons inside of her. She wanted to stare back and scream that she was stronger than the demons. But that wasn't right.

CHAPTER FOUR

She wasn't stronger than anything. If she was, she wouldn't end up at the bar every time something didn't go her way. She wouldn't end up at the bar every time she had dinner with her mom.

Cin pulled out her phone and checked for texts, hoping for a comforting message from Mira. She stared at the message thread with Mira and sighed. Of course, she hadn't texted, she never did. Cin wouldn't know how to respond if she did text.

You don't deserve Mira.

Cin took another sip of her drink, the burn easing the more she drank, and flipped her phone over in frustration. She was tired of doing this all alone. She wanted a support system, people to help her. She missed the mom she grew up with; she missed having someone in her corner who supported her.

Chapter Five

When the phone rang two days later, Cin didn't answer it. At least not the first time. She was cooking ramen, her go-to meal on lazy nights, and it was time to start pulling it off the burner or the poached egg would be destroyed. She was pouring it into a large, wide bowl when the phone rang again. Once she placed the empty pot on one of the cool burners, she fished her cell out of her pocket and answered it the minute she saw the caller ID.

She's calling to tell you not to come back.

"Mom? Is everything okay?" She tried to mask her concern. Her mom never called. She was always too out of it for anything more than their weekly dinner with her crazy ramblings. The guilt of her being too overwhelmed to listen to her last Wednesday started to slither around in her stomach like a snake. She clutched her belly with her free hand.

"Ms. Clark? Cin Clark?" the voice of a male

attending asked. She vaguely recognized the voice, but she only visited once a week—she couldn't name anyone.

Or you should give up now because you can't do anything right.

"Yes. Has something happened? Is my mother okay?" The words rushed out and smashed into her chest like a sucker punch. The sound of her gasping for breath made it impossible to catch everything the attending was saying, but she caught enough.

This . . .

"Signed out."

Is . . .

"Emergency contact."

Your . . .

"Nothing to worry about."

Fault.

Cin dropped to her knees as they hung up. The words swirled in her head—weird and uncomfortable. Her phone dropped to the floor as she leaned her head back against the oven. Her mother—her insane, loving, unstable mother out in the world all alone. The thought of her trying to make her way without her pressed down on her chest uncomfortably. Her head was reeling. But the image of her poor mother out there forced her to push past it, reach for her phone, and press her emergency contact.

The sound of the ringing echoed across the kitchen, bouncing against the tile, ricocheting like the sudden tears that were flowing down her face. Guilt burned through her. Why had she walked out on her mother like that? She knew she wasn't stable. She should never have treated her that way. Lucy had done nothing but treat her with love and kindness. Why couldn't she take a page out of her book?

Because you're a screw-up.

When Mira picked up, Cin couldn't speak. She opened her mouth, but all that came out was a gurgle and a sniffle.

"I'll be right over." Mira's voice spilled out of her phone like a lifeline. It was enough to pull herself off the floor and grab the bottle of gin as she stumbled on weak legs to the couch. She took a swig of the bottle before collapsing on the couch. Cin pulled a blanket over herself before having another long swig of gin. It burned in the way that cleared her mind of everything bad.

She had barely moved when Mira let herself in with her key. Her face was smashed into a fur pillow, the soft fuzz tickling her nose, as she listened to the sound of Mira's sneakers on her laminate flooring. The squeaking brought Mira close enough that she could smell her lavender and vanilla perfume, and her heart ached. Sweet perfume for the sweetest person she'd ever met.

You're not good enough for her.

Kiss her.

"Cin." Mira's presence on the arm of the couch, her hand resting lightly on her shoulder, warmed her. It was a sensation she never expected to feel at a time like this, but it was surprisingly comforting. But as it started to settle and mix with the guilt and concern, her stomach started to roll with nausea.

"She's gone, Mira. Signed right out and disappeared. I didn't even know she could sign herself out!" Her voice was husky from crying. It felt like something was stuck in her throat, but she couldn't clear it out.

"You don't know that. How long ago did they say she left?" Mira rubbed circles on her back. She sighed before rolling over. She looked up at her best friend and locked eyes as Mira watched her with kind, concerned eyes. She leaned up, putting herself on her elbows as Mira leaned away to give them some space. The extra space made her heart twinge.

"I don't know. It was hard to focus. Couldn't have been long. I was there two days ago."

"Exactly. It could be fine. We can check out her place tomorrow morning. Once you've sobered up." She lifted the mostly empty gin bottle with a wrinkled nose.

"I didn't even get to apologize to her. I was so horrible to her the last time I saw her. I walked out. I stood up and left her all alone. There's no one else to even visit her. James doesn't even live near here anymore!" Cin collapsed back onto the couch. "I was all she had."

You're a horrendous daughter.

Maybe this is for the best. You don't need her; you need Mira.

Mira ran a comforting hand through Cin's hair, and she did her best to ignore the fluttering it caused in her chest as her mind battered her for being a good-for-nothing child. "Your mom knows how much you love her. I'm sure you'll be able to tell her how you feel soon enough when we find her at her condo."

Maybe she's dead—just like Schaffer.

"You don't know that."

"And you don't know otherwise. Move over." Mira slid onto the cushion, forcing Cin to the next cushion, and wrapped an arm around her shoulder. Cin rearranged herself into a ball and dropped into Mira's lap. Mira rubbed Cin's shoulder soothingly, and her skin rippled with goose bumps. A small part of her, past the alcohol and tornado of emotions, recognized that they were approaching dangerous territory. Territory they had approached once, and that caused a three-year split that tore Cin to pieces in the process.

Kiss her.

Do it.

༄

Mira had pushed her so hard her head slammed into the beige concrete block wall of her dorm room. It wasn't decorated yet; she had moved in only a few days prior, but without a dorm room for herself, Mira wanted to share her space—show her what it was like. Her mom could never afford that—especially with James being in college too.

Cin had stared back, eyes wide. "I thought . . ." She left her voice to hang there—like a heavy mist of regret. She thought she was doing what Mira wanted. She had pulled her onto the bed, ran fingers through her hair with a trickling laugh.

"You thought wrong." Mira glared before pointing to the door with her middle finger. It was obvious that she was directing it at her. "Get out. How dare you!"

She had rushed to pack her bag up, shoving syllabi into it haphazardly. When she reached to open the door, she looked back to see pure hatred flowing off Mira in waves. She wanted to say something, anything, to make it better, but she just left. The door closed with a solid click. No turning back.

༄

Cin brushed the thoughts aside the best she could. She couldn't let that happen again. Besides, they were just *her* demons talking, right? "Mira. I really messed up this time. I should have never let it get so bad."

"You couldn't have known this would happen."

You knew it was a bad idea to leave her like that.

Cin rolled over so she could look at Mira's caring face and frowned. "She said something to me. I don't know. She's so concerned about me not believing her."

"Believing her about what?"

"Witches. Magic. Everything she's been preaching about since I was first diagnosed."

"None of that sounds new . . ." Mira trailed off, her voice approaching annoyed. She stared down at Cin with burning eyes and a wrinkled brow. "Are you starting to believe that stuff?"

"I . . . well . . . I don't know." Cin didn't know what to say. She wasn't willing to give up on her sudden and confusing pull to the new chemistry professor or the comments her mother had made about strings connecting her to death. But she also didn't know what any of it meant. She barely even knew Ian, despite her reactions to him implying otherwise, and her mom had been unstable for years. Not to mention her MIA brother. "No. No. I'm not falling for her *bullshit*. But maybe if I had at least pretended, she'd still be here. Maybe if I believed our family history, James would still be around."

Liar, liar.

The words felt wrong on her lips, she couldn't even argue with the voice in her head, but Mira gave her a reassuring smile. When she spoke, it registered how her smile didn't reach her eyes. "Your mother had lost control over the disease that plagued her. You won't end up like

CHAPTER FIVE

that. You've got this under control. Look how strong you've been."

"Strong? I'm an alcoholic with the ability to blow things up with household chemicals. At best, I'm a ticking time bomb. At worst, the bomb will go off without any warning and destroy everyone close to me." *Look at everyone I've cared about,* she added silently before taking a deep breath. "And well, there's another voice in my head lately."

Mira leaned down to kiss Cin on the forehead, causing disorienting shivers over her body. She tried to push past it, reminding herself that her longtime affection for her best friend was not a path she wanted to travel again, but it was hard with the alcohol fog. She had made that decision when they took that leap after high school graduation, and she didn't plan on going through that pain again. She was stronger than her urges and the voices battering her.

"Oh? Really?" Mira replied, her voice high-pitched and slightly screechy. She pursed her lips at her best friend, trying to understand her reaction.

"I'm worried I'm getting worse." Cin sucked her lips before taking another sip from the almost-empty gin bottle.

Of course, you're getting worse.

"If you're so worried, you should talk to someone. Can you book an appointment with Dr. Cohen?" Mira stood up, walking into the kitchen area and shutting off the burner that Cin had left on.

"I can try."

"Call him in the morning. Promise me."

"I'll call him before you pick me up."

"I'll hold you to that." She surveyed the now-cold

bowl of ramen with a sigh before dumping it into the trash can and pulling out the Chinese menu. "If you're going to sober up to check on your mom and book that appointment, you'll need to stop drinking that and eat something. I'll get your usual, yeah?"

She mumbled her agreement as she pulled herself off the couch and carried the bottle of gin into the kitchen. She placed it on top of the fridge in hopes that that would deter her for the night before pulling Mira into a hug. "I'd be lost without you."

You're lucky she puts up with you.

Mira chuckled. "No, you wouldn't. But it would definitely take you longer to get anything done. Go shower while we wait for the food. You reek of chemicals and gin. Yuck."

Cin nodded into her shoulder before stumbling off into the bathroom and getting under the warm water of her shower. As it pounded into her back, she took a deep breath and made herself a promise.

No matter what happened, she would figure out the truth about her mom.

From how much of what she said was true to where she had disappeared to.

She would never discount her again—if she showed up safe.

Chapter Six

When Mira showed up the next morning to bring them to her mother's apartment, Cin felt as if her feet were waterlogged, trudging through a never-ending stream of water that was trying to pull her under. It wasn't an unusual feeling, the weight of depression dragging her down, but it was a burden that made getting into the car almost impossible.

When she finally slid into the fabric seat and turned her head to Mira, she found her friend smiling. "Good morning, sleepyhead."

"I wouldn't call this a good morning."

Mira pulled her car onto the road before grabbing a cup out of the center console and handing it to her. "Here, drink this. It'll make you feel better."

"There's nothing that will make this better," she whined. She gingerly sipped the coffee, letting the bitter liquid clear her mind.

"You know what would really help?" Mira shot her a sideways glance.

"Don't say calling Dr. Cohen. It's already on my list."

"It should be crossed off by now, Cin."

"I don't need you to replace my mother," she snapped. She leaned her head against the cold window and stared out at the buildings. Mira never responded.

They spent the rest of the car ride in silence, and Mira had dropped her off in front of the building with a muttered comment about finding parking. Cin had wanted to apologize, to stand up for herself, to do anything to stop the silence, but she couldn't do it. She just let Mira drive away like she always did when Cin was difficult.

Who wants to deal with you anyway?

Cin stared at the chipped black paint that covered the door. Her eyes scanned the area for signs of life before landing on the forty-seven made out of spray-painted white metal, that was nailed at eye level. Her mother's condo, which she had owned since James had left for college, felt like a barrier she wasn't ready to cross. Situated at the end of a long hallway on the second floor of a building in a decent part of town, the condo had always felt like it was safely tucked away from the bad of the world. Now it felt like a portal into a world she wasn't ready for. A world without her mom. If she crossed that threshold and her mother wasn't there, Cin didn't think she would be able to pull herself out of that depression alone.

She leaned against the parallel wall, waiting for Mira to park her car, when the dinging of the elevator made her jump. She turned her head just enough to see the silver door slide over and reveal Mira. She looked

CHAPTER SIX

content, happy even, with a wide smile and a bounce in her step. Her perfectly curled bob swayed as she made her way down the empty hallway. If Cin didn't know any better, she would almost believe that Mira was happy her mom was missing.

She'll be even happier when you're gone too.

"Are you ready?" Mira asked, grabbing Cin's hand and giving it a squeeze.

"What am I supposed to do if she's not there?"

"I don't know. I wish I did, but no matter what, I'll be here for you." Mira kissed her forehead before giving her a light shove toward the door. She took a deep breath as she rooted through her pocket for the key. It felt heavy in her hand as she turned the lock, and then the door creaked open. The sound vibrated in her chest.

"Are you sure this is a good idea?" Cin asked as she peered into the empty room. It was exactly how she had left it last time. The sound of Cin's heels clicking against the beautiful wood floors of the two-bedroom apartment echoed uncomfortably around her. It forced the hair on her neck to stick up, and Cin rubbed at it. When she hit the center of the room, she turned in a slow circle to take the room in.

She doesn't want you to find her.

The kitchen, untouched since her mother had been committed, looked like a picture frozen in time. The few wine glasses that hung from the bar area were covered in a layer of dust. The living room, her mother's usual spot, still had the blue knit blanket folded and laid over the back of the couch; not even a mark from a water glass marred the spotless table. All she could see, walking slowly around the living room, was thin layers of dust over the belongings she had meticulously cleaned when it was clear her mother wasn't coming back anytime soon. There were no signs of life, no movement, nothing to indicate her mom had stepped foot in here.

She left you behind.

As the dread started to settle in her belly, Cin began frantically searching the bedrooms. Starting with her old room, still covered in posters of bands she grew up listening to, she peered into its closet and under the bed. But everything was untouched, unloved in the way her mother loved her home—the way her mother taught her to love her home. Dust covered the desk and dresser—nothing was out of place. By the time she reached her mom's bedroom, Cin's hand had pulled at her braid so many times it was sprayed around her in knotted tresses, the hair tie barely holding on to the end. She collapsed, face-first, onto the yellow quilted bedspread and breathed in the faint smell of dust and cinnamon—her mom's favorite household fragrance.

She didn't notice that she was crying until Mira's body forced her to roll to the side. When the air hit her wet face, the cool feeling helped soothe her—almost as much as Mira's hand, which was rubbing circles into her back. "Are you okay?"

"Do I look okay, Mira?" she snapped. When she looked up, she saw the hurt brimming in Mira's eyes, but she didn't apologize. She was tired of apologizing every time Mira pretended to care but didn't.

And there you go. Ruining everything again.

"I'm sorry. We'll just have to keep searching."

"Where else is she going to go?" she whined, before rolling back over so her face was covered in the blanket.

Far away from you?

"Cin, we've only searched one place so far. I promise

CHAPTER SIX

we'll keep looking until we find her." Mira pushed herself off the bed, the spring groaning, and started to pace. Cin listened to her sneakers squeak for a few minutes, contemplating new locations to check, before rolling over and looking to Mira's uncomfortably neutral face.

"You don't look upset." She studied her with a pinched expression. She stopped pacing, turning on her heel from the other side of the room, and frowned at Cin. It was a practice frown that she knew well—it told her more than Mira probably intended.

She doesn't care about you or your problems.

"Of course, I'm upset. But we can't both be emotionally distraught, or we'll never find her."

Always distrustful. No wonder no one likes you.

Cin grabbed her head, closing her eyes, as she pushed away the voices. When she opened them, Mira was looking at her with a tilted head. "I'm sorry. The voices . . ." Cin twisted her mouth before correcting herself. "The voice is just getting really harsh lately."

"I know it's hard, Cin. But you need to push past it." Mira gave her a stern look.

"Push past it? Mira, you've been with me since my first diagnosis. You and I both know it's not that simple. How could you say that?" Cin asked. Mira averted her eyes. She couldn't be sure, but the ashamed attitude looked forced—faked even. It stung worse than the practiced frown.

"You're right. I guess I'm stressed too." She looked down at her phone. "We should get going. There's nothing here."

The bar had just opened, and the sun was shining through the glass windows of the front doors. She had never been to the bar this early in the day before. She had never stooped so low that she could see the grime of the bar floor in the golden rays. Cin was so early that the rest of the place was empty. Not empty because it was a Monday and only regulars were there. The bar was empty except for her and the bartender who was watching her with pity.

This is all you're good for . . . nothing.

"One gin and tonic," she said, finally sitting down on a worn-down wooden stool. She never noticed they were a nice mahogany color. They always looked black at night. The bartender nodded at her, and she watched his profile as he pulled glasses out. He was classically handsome with a strong chin and piercing blue eyes. His brown hair was cut short and spiked up at the front. It was an older style, but it looked good on him.

He handed her the drink and walked away. She studied it before looking down at the bar top and studying the scratches across it. She didn't really want this drink. She didn't know why she was even at the bar. She was supposed to be looking for her mom. She was supposed to make sure her mom was safe.

She took a sip of her drink and grimaced. It was stronger than she had been prepared for. She put the drink back on the bar and sighed. She was going to be useless if she started drinking tonight, and she had no idea how that would help find her mom. Cin pulled out her card and dropped it onto the counter before calling the bartender over to close out her tab. She wouldn't stay. She would do something productive, something to find her mom. She would find her mom.

CHAPTER SIX

The next morning, Cin was awake when her alarm went off. Normally, when she was depressed, getting up was one of the more difficult things she needed to manage. But Cin hadn't slept. She spent the night tossing and turning, trying to remember the exact words the facility had said to her. All she could remember was that her mom had signed herself out.

The words bounced through her mind. Her mom had signed herself out. She still couldn't figure it out. Why would her mom have done that?

She wanted to get away from you.

Cin rolled out of bed, doing her best to ignore the voice, and moved to open the fridge in hopes of finding something to eat with her meds. She needed to have the clearest head possible for the day ahead if she was going to make any headway in finding her mom, or at least getting someone to search for her. Her fridge was empty except for a pitcher of iced coffee she had made a few days before.

Pouring herself a glass, she surveyed the rest of her kitchen. It was mostly empty as well. She couldn't remember the last time she had bought groceries. She would have to stop at the store on the way back from the police station. Cin turned to her nightstand, grabbed her medication, and swallowed her pills with a gulp of coffee. She was off to a better start than she had managed all week, and she wanted to be proud, but everything going on overshadowed the small victory.

The police station on the far side of the city by the facility was bustling despite it being ten in the morning on a Sunday. Cin sipped from her travel mug of coffee as she waited to be called back and tried to ignore the woman crying a few seats away. The woman, a thin older lady, kept blowing her nose and mumbling about how unfair the world was. She had a bruise forming around her eye. She must have been mugged. Cin looked around for a purse, but there was none in sight.

You're a bad person.

"Cinzia Clark?" a voice said. Cin turned to see a young cop waiting at the front desk for her. He reminded her of the guy who lived in her building, with the same build and sneer directed in her direction. She cursed under her breath. There was no way this man was going to believe her. He already looked at her like she was the scum of the earth, and he hadn't even spoken to her.

The cop cleared his throat. "Are you coming?"

Cin jumped up, grabbed her bag, and followed the cop to a desk. The desk was orderly, everything placed just so, with no photos or knickknacks. It was the opposite of everything she was, and her stomach did a little flop. She wanted to just leave, to run away from this man that would most definitely not believe her, but she rooted herself in the seat and plastered on her most serious face.

"All right, Ms. Clark. I'm Detective Williams. I understand your mother is missing. Why don't you tell me about that?" He smiled reassuringly at her, but it didn't reach his eyes.

She nipped at her lip before spilling out all the details she knew about the situation. She explained how long Lucy had been at the facility, the phone call she received, and everything she could about her mother. It had been three days since she had signed herself out, and Cin hadn't heard from her. Her mother was a lot of things, but she had always cared for Cin. She had never left her behind, and she wouldn't leave her behind now.

Who wouldn't want to leave you behind?

Cin smashed her lips together to keep from talking back to the voice and focused on the detective who was saying something to her. "I'm sorry, can you repeat that?"

He sighed. "I was saying that because she signed herself out, there's nothing we can do right now. We can go to her apartment and mark her as a missing person, but there's not really much to go on here."

Cin wanted to scream. "She's endangered."

"She was sane enough for them to let her out of the facility. I'm not sure I agree that she is endangered," he said coolly.

He thinks you're crazy too.

"I'm worried about her," she replied. Cin took a deep breath and stared the detective down. "I'd like someone to look into her disappearance."

Detective Williams frowned at her but nodded. "We'll do what we can, but just know that we don't have a lot to go on. If you are really worried, you should put up some missing person posters."

Cin nodded before getting up. "Thank you for your help," she managed to say, before shaking the detective's hand and walking away. Heading out of the building, Cin turned toward the closest bus stop to make her way to the university. She didn't have the heart to call Mira and tell her how poorly the whole thing went. But she could make the posters, and she could ask Mira to help her hang them up once she had them all printed out.

Once all the posters had been designed and printed at the main office for the chemistry department, Cin headed back to the computer to do some research. She didn't think she would find anything, but it was worth a try to see if anything showed up about her mom. She spent an hour looking through the news without much to show for it. She learned that some famous actor was coming to town, but that wasn't anything she cared about. All she wanted was to find her mom.

Chapter Seven

By the time Mira had stopped for a second round of coffees on the way into the university midmorning Monday and parked in the parking deck, Cin was able to rebraid her hair and clean up a majority of the streaks of makeup that had been running down her face. They had spent the morning hanging up all the posters Cin had made. Cin had cried the whole time, but Mira had stayed stoic as she stapled sign after sign into any telephone post she could find. Cin had gotten so frustrated with Mira's disinterest that she had told her they could stop after the first hour. It was disappointing, but she wanted to believe that Mira was just being strong for Cin.

She doesn't care that your mom is missing.

Cin gritted her teeth against the voice and focused on her face in the mirror. With one last look, Cin swiped away the last bits of black smudge and tried to fake a smile. It was a little crooked, but it would do. She didn't need anyone else to know what was going on.

"Are you going to be okay while I go into my meeting?" Mira put a gentle hand on her shoulder and gave it a loving squeeze.

Cin leaned toward her. "I'll be fine. I have a meeting I need to go to."

"Who are you supposed to be meeting with? Dean Williamson again?"

Realization settled into the pit of Cin's stomach. It had been almost a week, and she didn't even tell Mira about Ian. Mira would hopefully understand. She bit her lip as the nerves started to make her body shake. "No. Um. The meeting is with Dr. Santos. He's our new chemistry professor—he took over Schaffer's old lab."

Mira's sudden intake of breath and long pause afterward made Cin shuffle in her seat. "Dr. Santos? Is that who the meeting was about last week?"

Don't forget failed drunken exploit.

Cin swallowed and nodded. She didn't want to admit it, but Mira's voice was harsh—it felt like a blow to her chest. She didn't even ask about how she felt with someone new in Schaffer's room. "He seems nice enough."

He's got ulterior motives.

"I'm sure he does." Mira turned Cin's face toward her. Her eyes burned with an intensity she hadn't seen in a while. "Don't let yourself get wrapped up in this new guy. Something tells me he's bad news. It can't be a coincidence he showed up as your mom disappeared. Bad omens and all that." She wiggled her fingers at Cin. "I say stay away."

He's very bad news.

Cin studied her boots as she tried to blink away the

prickling sensation in her eyes before agreeing and hopping out of the car. She scurried away, trying to get away from the horrible thoughts taunting her. She made it to the concrete archway that marked the entrance to the stairs when she heard the door slam. She called over her shoulder with faux enthusiasm, "See you later."

∼

She was still feeling uneasy when she climbed up the five flights of stairs and walked down the hallway to the door for the lab. She could see the lights on and Ian's figure pacing by the whiteboard. She stood rooted as she listened to the sound of his shoes squeaking on the tile. She knew she should go in there—she looked at her watch—but she was early. She could avoid this conversation just a little longer. She could give herself more time to process her missing mom and the new doubts Mira introduced.

"Cin? Are you coming inside, or do you want to have the meeting in the hallway?" Ian's suddenly close voice made her jump as he popped his head out from behind the door. His teeth flashed in a broad smile. He studied her with twinkling eyes.

"Why do you look so excited?"

"I have a lot planned. Come inside so I can show you the magical world of environmental chemistry."

She snorted out a laugh before pointing a finger at him as she followed him in. "Laughing at your unnatural excitement about chemistry does not mean we're friends."

"Laughter is better than the scowling you were so fond of last time we saw each other, so I'm chalking that one up as an improvement. Chalk one up for Ian." He wiggled his eyebrows at her.

She tried to scowl at him, to pull up some annoyance from his mocking, but she was still laughing too much at his cheesy attitude for it to be effective. "Fine. You win this one."

"Don't you worry. I'm sure I'll win a few more." He winked before pulling over his laptop to one of the larger benches. He motioned for her to join. "So I made a few PowerPoint slides on what I thought we could do for a few of the lectures."

She smirked at his childlike excitement as she sat down on a stool and studied the slide deck. "By a few, do you mean over a hundred?"

"Okay, maybe I went a little overboard." He shrugged awkwardly.

"I don't know if I would call this a little—there are three hundred slides here. Did you plan out the entire first semester without me?"

"No." He paused, tilting the computer toward him and pressing a few buttons she couldn't see. "Maybe."

He flipped it back toward her, and she tapped the screen. "Did you delete a few slides so I could plan something?"

Maybe he's trying to be sweet.

Cin tried not to choke on her own saliva as the words circled her head. She had been ignoring the voice in her head for so long, uncomfortably burdened by the onslaught of negativity, that she didn't even know how to process what might be a positive thought. It jarred her to the point that when the second voice came in, it ripped a hole through whatever positive attitude she was building after her morning with Mira.

He just wants to sleep with you.

She felt her stomach clench, and she hunched over slightly toward the laptop. She hoped it looked like she was trying to read his notes, not like she was about to throw up everywhere.

"Hey, is everything okay?"

She looked over to Ian's concerned face and tried to nod as her stomach bubbled up like a bad reaction. "I'm fine. I'm just . . ." She sighed. "Tired."

"I'm going to let that slide."

Suddenly she wasn't upset, or nervous, but so irritated that her skin was pricking. She rubbed her forearms angrily. She knew this was her bipolar, not her own emotions, but they felt so real and imposing. "You're going to let it slide that I'm tired?"

Ian twisted his mouth and shook his head. "I'm going to let it slide that you are willfully lying to me."

She grabbed the lab bench and clenched it until her fingers hurt as she seethed. "Do I suddenly owe you the truth? I didn't realize that after one night at the bar and a crappy tour we were best friends."

"No—we're colleagues. It's my hope that we can be honest with each other so that we can have a productive partnership." He blinked a few times, studying her calmly.

Cin almost smacked herself in the forehead as she tried to pull her foot out of her mouth. "I'm sorry." She rubbed her face roughly. "It's been a really bad few days. I promise I'm not usually like this."

"Something tells me you are."

She pulled her shoulders back and faced him. "What is that supposed to mean?"

"It means . . . I have a lot of close family members

and friends all over the neurodiverse world. I understand what that means. I understand how people in that world react differently. I don't want you to feel like you can't be yourself. It's okay if you are normally irritable or constantly bouncy or just a giant lump who won't leave your couch." He studied her face and bit his lip. "This is probably coming out all wrong."

Cin wrinkled her nose as heat started to spread in her chest. He was right, it was coming out like a jumbled mess, but the sentiment was there, and she couldn't ignore it. Not once, but twice Ian had proved that he wasn't going to hold her limitations against her. That he was okay with who she was, no matter how ugly it turned out to be. The heat creeped up her neck until her face was pink. Why couldn't Mira understand?

"I shouldn't have said anything," Ian added, his voice hesitant in the sudden silence as she processed his words.

"No . . . no. Well, you probably should have rephrased some of that, but I appreciate it. There aren't a lot of people who can tolerate my swings. It's nice to know that I don't have to try to mask my feelings. It's a constant drain."

Ian patted her wrist, the same place he held on to at the bar, and she gasped at the sudden appearance of golden thread. It was tied around her wrist and led to a knot on Ian's arm. She gulped and blinked a few times before Ian's arm jerked back, and he shoved his fist to his mouth, covering it.

"What was that?" She gasped, her thoughts sliding back to her mom's words. *Tied to death.* Words that kept circling in her head as she waited for Ian to respond.

He blew out a breath. "I don't know if it's a good idea for us to talk about that right now."

"Look who's hiding things now."

"I'm not hiding things," Ian said, his voice indignant. "I just think you'd be better off hearing this after you . . ."

"After I what?"

He ran a hand through his hair. "After you come to terms with your family history."

She balked. "What do you know about my family history?"

"I know that your family history is similar to mine, but you've never accepted the truth your mother tried to share with you."

Maybe he has a point.

"Oh great. So you think I'm a witch too?" she asked in a low, dangerous tone. Cin wanted to scream, but everything was coming out deadly calm. She could feel herself falling into a fight-or-flight response, and it was leaning heavily toward fight. The pain of her mom hissed within her, and she gritted her teeth as she focused her anger on Ian. "Thanks but no thanks," she spat, before turning toward her things.

She grabbed her stuff, shoved it angrily back into the bag, and stormed out of the room. The door slammed behind her, echoing down the empty hallway. A small part of her was proud for not losing her shit on Ian, but the rest of her was grappling with everything. She couldn't get the golden thread out of her mind. She had never seen anything before that made her believe anything out of the ordinary would be possible, but when she looked down at her wrist, the string was still there. It was taut as she walked away from Ian.

So untrustworthy. Where did that get you with your mom?

"You don't know anything," she muttered weakly. Rubbing a rough hand over her face, she leaned against the wall and slid down. Maybe it was time to give this "witch" business a try. Maybe Ian could help her find her mom. That was if she would just tell someone what was going on beside Mira—who, in Cin's opinion, wasn't trying very hard to help.

If she were honest with herself, she was getting close to trying anything to find her mom. Even if it went against everything she fought against for the entirety of her life.

His shadow passed over her before sitting down next to her. "I know you are. I am too. A lot of people in our world are." Ian held out his hands and drew golden threads between them. She stared at them with wide eyes. "We're both capable of so much more. My coven of witches—they are meeting at the end of the week. Would you come along? Give it a chance before I explain what you saw?"

"No. No. What the hell was that?"

Ian shrugged. "Just a little something to prove to you it's real. It's always been real. Please, just come to one meeting."

Cin thought about it before hesitantly agreeing. "If I don't like what I see, I don't want to hear about this again."

Ian nodded enthusiastically. "Absolutely."

"If anything weird goes on, I'm out." She eyed him and waited for a nod. "Fine . . . I'll go."

"Wonderful. Everyone will be so excited to meet you." He gave her a little squeeze. "Now, are you ready to dive into these slides?"

Cin shrugged, doing her best to comment on the slides, but her mind wandered. The potential of having a group of people who knew more about her mom than she believed was possible, people who might be able to help her find her, swirled in her mind in an endless loop of nerves and excitement. It was marred by her morning with Mira, still stabbing at her psyche, but she couldn't stop the balloon of hope building in her chest.

    Maybe she really was capable of finding her mom.

Chapter Eight

Cin had managed to trudge through the two full days of teaching without much to say about it. She showed up on time and dressed relatively appropriately. She taught, with little interest but thoroughly. And then she ended each day roaming her mom's condo. Each time, the only signs of life were her own. She tried not to let disappointment weigh her down too much. It was Wednesday, and she was supposed to be having dinner with her mom. A twinge of sadness hit her as she thought about her mom lost out in the world without medication or a support system.

The hospital, the police, they all said the same things when she called. They didn't have anyone matching her description from the hospitals in the area, and she wasn't missing, she had signed herself out, but they would keep looking from the police. Something just didn't sit right. The coven meeting Ian had invited her to was like a string holding her to reality—tying her together just enough to function.

You're lucky he even wants to see you again.

But as she tried to pull together something that didn't make her stick out, her stomach started to gurgle with nerves. Brushing aside the idea of looking put together, she grabbed her softest band tee and jeans to pair with her leather jacket and matching heeled boots. After a quick look in the mirror where she smoothed her circles, she breathed out a small breath of relief. Cin might not look professional, or witchy, but she definitely looked kick-ass and felt comfortable in her all-black outfit. And that would have to do.

She made the quick walk to campus where she was meeting Ian, a dance number in efforts to keep her moving toward the destination. She put in earbuds, blaring her favorite New Jersey artist, and tried to dance her way past the ebbing ball of discomfort that was blooming in her gut. The music cleared her mind of the voices and worries and fears, filling it with a peace she only got with something playing at top volume.

Ian's face, bright and excited, waited for her at the science building steps. She smiled back, letting his genuinely happy attitude lift some of the weight from her shoulders.

"Are you ready?" he asked when she had pulled out her earbuds.

"Is anyone ever ready to learn that you've been lying to yourself for years and making up excuses not to be who you're supposed to be?"

Ian shook his head ruefully. "You're too hard on yourself. It took me years to accept my family history. Let me guess, you thought your mom was just plain crazy?"

She nodded.

"Me too. I ignored my parents completely for so long. Anyway, it'll be fine. I swear." Ian squeezed her shoulder.

"Your constant positivity may destroy me one day." She jabbed him with an elbow playfully. He chuckled before lapsing into silence for the rest of their walk to the church.

But when the church appeared in front of them. The pit in Cin's stomach started to grow back into a deep, dark cave of regret. The doors to the church, bright red against the dark-gray brick, reminded her of the doors to the facility her mom had been trapped in, and she was most definitely not ready for any of this. But Ian's shuffling next to her, the perpetual smile on his face and uncanny happiness, helped ease some of the worries. She knew why she was uncomfortable but couldn't put her thumb on the worry lines building on her co-worker's face. But co-worker didn't feel right—Ian was more than that already, friend? Support system? Annoyingly positive pain in her butt?

Despite his smile, the hunch of his shoulders and the shuffling made it clear he wasn't excited about this. What was he so nervous about? "Why did I agree to let you drag me here?"

"Because you wanted to get a handle on who you really are." Ian tapped his arm, bringing her attention to the small golden thread that tied them together. It glistened under the flickering streetlights and the amber glow of the lamp illuminating the entranceway. It was a reminder that there was so much she didn't know, but she was going to find out. She pulled her shoulders back and faced the door.

You'll mess this up.

She felt her shoulders droop a little before she gestured for Ian to open the doors.

This is a bad idea.

"Are you ready?" Ian reached for the red doors and pulled them open with a loud creak. "We meet in the basement."

Cin gave him a wan smile before following him down the barely lit, damp stairwell crammed into the corner of the main lobby. With the large fake plant covering the alcove, she was sure she would've missed it without him. As they descended, Cin ran her fingers against the smooth stone walls and let the coolness soothe her frayed nerves. She mumbled her mantra, the one she'd been saying all day, "You'll be fine," until the stairs turned into solid ground and the walkway expanded into a large, open room filled with eight people milling around a table covered with coffeepots and donuts.

She scanned the room, trying to commit the new faces to memory—people she recognized from campus but couldn't name. She probably would forget by the end of the meeting anyway. Those people weren't the reason she stopped in her tracks, her metal heels scraping the concrete floor and drawing everyone's attention to her. Three faces, faces she'd recognize anywhere, had her pinned to her spot in the middle of the room. Faces like her mom's best friend, Ms. Wilkerson.

"Dean Williamson? Adam? Ms. Wilkerson?" She pivoted to Ian, her blood boiling. "Is this some kind of joke? Are you all playing a fucking joke on the crazy chick? This isn't funny."

It was the shock played out on Adam's face that stopped her from going full-out volcanic eruption.

Genuine, raw shock at her reaction. It was Dean Williamson who spoke first.

"You walked her in here without telling her anything?" He pulled his eyes off Cin to level them at Ian's bright-red face.

"I . . . well . . . I . . . I thought she knew." Ian mumbled. "I thought she knew about you guys but just didn't believe her mom. I thought . . ."

The dean pinched the bridge of his nose and sighed. "Cin, I'm sorry. It seems Ian doesn't remember how hard walking into this room is for people without familial knowledge. Please, forgive us for his inability to properly introduce you."

You should probably run now.

I told you this was a bad idea.

The voices, loud and clamoring in her head, were easier to ignore than usual. Maybe it was the softness of Dr. Williamson's voice or the look of concern flitting across Adam's face, but she felt more in control of her own actions for the first time in years. Even with the meds, she had never felt so strong and powerful. She had to know more, had to at least give them a chance to explain.

"Fine, but I'm staying near the door." There—at least she had the advantage.

"You're welcome to do what makes you feel comfortable. As well as calling me Floyd. In here, I'm not your boss, but your equal."

"That goes for me as well. I know you've only known me as your mother's best friend, but you can call me Megan." Mrs. Wilkerson said, giving her a soft smile.

"It's been a long time, Megan. I don't even know the

last time we saw you. I know you haven't visited her in the facility. Can you really call yourself a best friend?"

She sucked in a sharp breath but didn't argue. Couldn't argue.

Ian tapped her shoulder, causing her to jump. She hadn't even noticed him moving. "Please give this a chance. I promise, it'll help."

"Adam, Megan. Can you please bring Cin a cup of black coffee?" Dean Williamson said, waving a hand over to the table surrounded by what she could only assume was the rest of the coven. Adam scurried to the table as Dean Williamson started to pace the length of the room in front of her. "You see, Cin, there's so much in this world that you've pushed out of your life. We've been waiting to be given the opportunity to welcome you to our coven."

Cin barked out a laugh. "You're just as crazy as my mother. Why did I come here?" She turned and took a few steps toward the stairs, the click of her heels echoing in the silent room.

"Your mother and I were very close when we were growing up. We lived around the corner from each other," Megan added. Cin stopped walking but kept her eyes trained on the stairs. "She was my best friend. What happened to her . . . it was terrible. It is terrible. She doesn't deserve to be in that facility, none of us do. She's not crazy; we're not crazy. You're not crazy, Cin."

You're definitely crazy.

Walk out. You don't need these people.

But like before, the voices didn't have the same power here. Something about these people eased the burden. She scanned the crowd, noting all their hopeful expres-

CHAPTER EIGHT

sions, and narrowed her eyes at Ms. Wilkerson. "You don't know anything."

"No, Cin. You don't know anything. All you know is the pain of carrying this burden alone. I watched what that did to your mother. I won't let it happen again." She glided up to Cin and grabbed her shoulders. "We won't lose you too."

"She's right." Adam's voice was clear, stronger than she'd ever heard it. He stood a few feet away with a Styrofoam cup in his hands. Ms. Wilkerson released her shoulders as Adam offered it up. She took it wearily and sniffed it for any weird chemicals. It wouldn't surprise her to find the faint smell of cyanide with this many chemists roaming around.

"It's not poisoned. We're not the bad guys here. We just want to help," Adam said, giving her a look that told her she was acting ridiculous. Cin tried to fight the sudden melting of her resolve at Adam's sweet face, but it was useless. She shrugged her shoulders. She'd had to at least hear them out. Gosh darn Adam and his good-guy attitude. It was impossible to tell him no.

Taking a sip of the lukewarm, bitter coffee, she leaned against the hard wall and nodded to Adam to keep talking. "You come from a long line of witches. We all do. Your mother was one of the more powerful weavers and the leader of this coven before I joined."

"We had hoped that when you joined the college," Dean Williamson started, "you would join us, but when Lucy went into that facility before you gave her a chance to show you who she really is, we didn't know how to bring you into the coven without freaking you out." Floyd grabbed a seat at the circular table on the far side of the room and gestured for everyone to join him. As Cin plodded across the room, the rest of the group sat down, leaving her with a seat between him and Ian. She paused, eyeing the people on the other side of the room who clearly weren't going to get involved in the discussion, before focusing on the group of people in front of her.

"Why did you invite me now?" Cin asked as she took a seat in the remaining chair. It creaked under her weight in the silence. Everyone was looking at each other with a myriad of uncomfortable expressions. "Well?"

"I'll take this one." Ian looked into her eyes with a wry smile. "Most of the time, when witches do not want to continue in family tradition or don't believe their relatives about the power they hold, we just leave them to live their lives. We have a section of the police force specifically trained to keep an eye on these people, who ensure any incidents caused by unmaintained magic are cleaned up properly and the witch is brought in for proper medication and treatment."

"Proper medication and treatment?" Cin almost spit up her coffee. Had she walked into some kind of cult? "Drink this, you'll be just fine," and then everyone dies. No thank you. She put her coffee mug on the table and eyed it cautiously.

"Yes, each one of us are"—Dean Williamson waved at the group around them—"special. To the average human, we are what the world calls 'crazy.' But within our ranks, which are constantly growing, we are something more. The differences in our brain chemistry, what makes people think we're different from them, is what makes our particular skill sets possible. Everyone has their own diagnosis, their own magical power, but our ability to see the world differently is what makes us special."

"What does medication have to do with this?" Cin

couldn't pull her eyes from Dean Williamson's solemn eyes.

"Without the medication, our magic is erratic, dangerous when our emotions are out of control. We don't have power or the understanding we need, and we end up harming people or things around us. Whether it's from the mental illness or the magic itself, we don't know. But we've had to clean up the mess of uncontrolled magic enough to know that proper medication and strong covens are the only way to ensure the safety of our people."

"Are you saying my mother wasn't properly medicated and I am?" Cin asked.

"We don't know. They won't allow us to see her since we aren't family. No one can tell us what actually happened. As for you, if you weren't, we would've had a much bigger problem on our hands. Your connection to Ian is something of concern. These are rare, and the link is why we brought you into the fold despite your disbelief," Floyd said, looking down at her wrist where the golden thread hung between her and Ian.

She wanted to roll her eyes at their dramatics, but she managed to draw her mouth into a thin line and keep it shut.

Ian touched the place on her wrist that she was staring at, and said, "He's right. I knew it the moment you touched my arm. Your magic, it's bubbling to the surface. It was either we showed you what was lurking in the wings, or you would end up like your mother."

"I don't understand."

"Bonds are like lifelines," Ian said. "They connect witches to their counterparts. It's like a highway for the magic. Yours practically hit me like a lightning bolt. I thought I was going to fall over with the intensity of it."

"What Ian is trying to say is that we're worried that you're on the brink of something truly harrowing. All we want to do is help guide you," Adam said, running a hand through his inky hair and twisting his lips. "You've done so much for me over these last two years. I couldn't let you harm yourself unwittingly."

Cin looked at each person in time, watching their concerned faces and listening to the words of her mother play over and over in her head. All these years. She had always thought her mother was crazy, but these people . . . these people aren't her mother. They aren't spewing nonsense or talking to themselves, they are calmly and concisely explaining to her that everything she'd been told from a young age was actually true.

"Let us show you what we are capable of. Ian, can you show her how weavers work?" Ms. Wilkerson asked, smiling from a few seats away.

Ian nodded, pulling away from the table and moving to the middle of the room. "Weavers, like your mother and me, are able to weave things into existence. We can see the strings of magic that hold the world together and, much like weaving together a piece of fabric, use those to build something anew."

Cin watched as he pulled his hands apart from the center of his chest in a bobbing motion. It took a few seconds, but the golden string holding them together, the one she could see clearly and as if the room was suddenly dusted with glitter, was joined by hundreds of others. It looked like a ball of yarn was pulled through the room, and Ian was manipulating it. His eyes were closed, but the shape of a fox started to form. It was small, almost the size of a small dog, and golden in color.

When he finished, the fox materialized from the strings and circled Ian's feet. Cin watched, her mouth agape. "Whoa."

"This is for you," Ian said, giving the fox a little push toward Cin. He trotted over to her, and she ran a shaking hand through his soft golden fur. It sniffed her twice, licked her hand with a rough tongue, and curled up at her feet. "You can name him whatever you want. He'll be your guardian from now on. We all have one—a familiar to keep us on our medications and a proper training regimen. Mine's a husky."

With the fox purring at her feet and Ian's expecting face, it was suddenly too much. She clamored to her feet. "Thanks but no thanks."

She could feel the group's eyes watching her as she ran out of the room and up the stairs, but it didn't stop her. Not Ian's voice calling after her or the uncomfortable sound of the fox padding behind her. She didn't stop until she had made it back to her apartment, a few blocks away, and landed onto the mattress. She lay face up, her vision blurry from the frustrated tears she was crying, and she moaned.

"What the fuck have I gotten myself into this time?"

Chapter Nine

Cin didn't have any classes to attend to the morning after the coven meeting. Thursdays were her day off, but it wasn't going to be a day she spent doing nothing. Instead, she was going to inspect her mother's place with the help of the fox that now wouldn't leave her alone.

When she stepped out of the shower, he was curled on top of the toilet seat and squinted at her. She eyed him wearily before his yipping made her jump. "What am I supposed to do with a pet fox?"

He let out a little bark before prowling over to her and running his soft fur against her bare ankles. If he were a cat, Cin was sure he would be purring. She grabbed her phone off the counter and dialed Ian's number.

"I was wondering when I would hear from you." Ian's casual attitude made her grind her teeth, but she bit back her snotty comment.

"How am I supposed to hide a fucking fox? They're

illegal to have as pets." What would Mira say the next time she was here?

If Mira wants to deal with you again.

"Well, if you hadn't run out so fast, I would have shown you a masking spell. If you want, we can video chat."

The question hung in the area as she stared at the white towel wrapped around her naked body. Her blue hair was closer to royal blue than the vibrant sapphire, and large droplets of water fell off the lank strands hitting the sink. She watched a blush creep over her neck and cheeks before she coughed out, "No . . . uh . . . can you just walk me through it?"

"I could try. Have you named him yet?"

"I'm supposed to name it?"

"It's not an *it*, Cin. He's your protector." As if the fox could hear him, it added a few barking yips.

"Fine. I'll name him."

"Once you've named him, you can perform the spell. This is one of the easiest, which is why it's the first one we have people perform. You'll need to burn some sage—that should be easy enough for you to find, or I can bring you some later—and then just burn it while running your hand through your fox's fur, chanting their name, and imagining them as a more subtle creature."

She eyed the fox. "What am I supposed to imagine?"

"Well, with a fox, I recommend a dog breed. Do you have a favorite?"

"Yes. Well, thank you, Ian. I'll let you know if it doesn't work out." She hung up and turned to the fox. What had she gotten herself into? Magic? Maybe it was all a dream, and if she just shut her eyes, it would disappear.

You're not magical. You're crazy.

But when she opened them, the fox was still curled up next to her. She looked at her protector and gave him a weak smile as she decided on a name. "Well, Link, it looks like I'll be taking a trip to the grocery store. Maybe I'll make a stop at the mental facility and check myself in while I'm at it."

∽

When she returned, a bunch of sage gripped in her hand, Link was waiting patiently in a ball on her fuzziest blanket. "All right, Link. Let's get this over with."

She searched her kitchen drawers until she found a matchbook. She pulled out a match, lit it, and set the bundle of sage on fire. When she blew it out, smoke streamed out from the end, and Link was rubbing himself against her calf. She crouched down to his level and started murmuring his name.

Once she had pictured the blue-gray pit bull in her head, golden threads started to draw themselves where her fingers weaved through the soft, golden fur.

See? Crazy.

The strings disappeared, and Cin grumbled. "Helpful," she muttered to the voice. It had broken her concentration. She took a deep breath, centering herself away from the voices, and focused on chanting Link's name. Then before her eyes, a golden image of a pit bull was drawn over Link. She could still see the fox underneath, but something made her believe that she had done it right.

She leaned back on her heels and took a shaky breath.

Could it really be? Could she really be capable of magic? Was her mom more than just a crazy person?

The thrill of her successfully completing the spell made the corners of her mouth pull up. The magic burned through her like a shot of gin, but without the hefty consequences. She still had a lot of work to complete, but with the help of Link, and maybe even Ian, she might be able to accept her family's history and find her mother.

∽

The coffee shop, one she didn't visit often, was bustling for the late afternoon. Its busyness was one of the reasons Cin didn't come all the way across town despite how good the coffee was. It was one of the best coffees in town, but she hated the crowds, no matter how well deserved they were. Cin eyed the cold brew she ordered. Her nerves didn't need more coffee, but she took a sip of it anyway as she studied the people in the shop.

There was the older couple sitting in the opposite corner from her, each with a book in their hand and a singular mug of coffee between them. She watched the older man place a hand on his wife's shoulder and give it a squeeze. The pair looked at each other with soft smiles before going back to their respective books. Cin sighed, wishing for the uncomplicated world the married couple probably lived in, and then looked down at her coffee and took another sip. It was strong but not bitter like the coffee Mira brought her every morning.

Pulling her phone out, Cin looked at the time. Mrs. Wilkerson was late. Not by much, but she was supposed to be here a few minutes ago. She bounced her leg up and down while she waited. It had been a few years since she had spent time with Megan, and she really wasn't sure what to expect. It felt weird to call her anything other than Ms. Wilkerson. Especially when she had been like a second mother to her growing up. Every time her mother had relapsed, Megan had been there with dinner and a movie. She couldn't imagine her childhood without her.

"Hi, sweetie," Mrs. Wilkerson said, her voice flowing from behind Cin. She turned around and caught Megan's auburn hair floating by. "I'm going to grab myself a cup of decaf before we talk."

Cin studied the woman standing at the counter and tried to place this person who practically raised her with the woman who had abandoned her when her mom went into the facility. The hair was the same, the wrinkles around her eyes new but familiar, even her smile was the same crooked thing with dimples. Nothing and everything had changed.

Everyone will abandon you eventually.

"Shut up," she muttered to herself as Megan walked over with a steaming cup of coffee. She had opted for a mug instead of a paper cup. Clearly, she planned to stick around long enough to finish her coffee, and that gave Cin the courage she needed to talk.

"I'm glad you called," Megan said, sitting down across the table from Cin. "Accepting your heritage was just as hard for your mom as I imagine it will be for you."

Cin cleared her throat. She didn't even want to think about the coven. It was the least of her concerns, though she needed to deal with it eventually. Right now, she needed to focus on something more important, something more pressing. "That's actually not why I called you." The shock on Megan's face was enough to crumple Cin's courage, but she gritted her teeth and continued. "My mom signed herself out of the facility."

"No, she didn't," Megan whispered. "She couldn't have."

"I got the call last week. One of the orderlies called me because I'm her emergency contact." Cin took a sip of her iced coffee, savoring the liquid before she locked eyes with Megan. Taking a deep breath, Cin spilled the story the best she could for what felt like the hundredth time. Megan nodded along, letting her speak without interrupting. When she finished, she frowned, and added, "I haven't been able to find her."

She doesn't want to be found by you.

"What have you done to look for her?" Megan asked, her voice cautious and steady.

Cin let the steadiness soak into her. "I've been to her place a few times, but it's the same as when I cleaned it up after she was committed. I went to the police station, and they are searching, but I don't think they actually care whether she's found. I keep calling the hospitals in the area to see if someone matching her description shows up."

Megan patted her leg, and Cin let out a soft cry. Her eyes started to burn, but she bit her lip and held it back. She didn't need to cry in the middle of a coffee shop, and she definitely didn't need to cry in front of Mrs. Wilkerson.

"We'll help you find her," Megan said finally. "You don't need to do this alone."

Chapter Ten

"Can you come in here for a minute?" Floyd popped his head out of his office as she stood in front of the printer the next day. She smacked it twice, waited thirty seconds for her weekly quiz to print out, and then gave it a final hit before turning around.

She plastered on a smile. "Everything okay?"

"I just wanted to check on how your tour with Dr. Santos went."

The printer whirled to life, shooting out papers into the tray. She turned back to it, reaching for the papers. "I'll be right there."

The leather chair she slid into felt unyielding as Floyd watched her with cautious eyes. His dark skin was pale, washed out in the fluorescent lights of his office. Dark rings hung under his eyes. He clicked his keyboard before focusing back to her. "I'm worried about you. That your mother disappearing will spiral you. You can't have another break like this fall."

She bit her lip, tears pricking her eyes. She rubbed at them angrily. "I just want to find her."

"We all do, Cin. My biggest concern right now is getting you through the end of the semester. I have people looking into this—looking for your mother—but you're on thin rope here." He leveled her with a look.

"It won't happen again. I have control." She squared her shoulders.

"I really want to believe you." He clasped his hands on the desk. "I can only help you so much. I don't have control over the board, and they'll notice if you don't manage to finish the semester out."

She stood up and walked to the door. Looking over her shoulder, she pursed her lips, then said, "I hear what you're saying."

When she made it to her office, the quizzes were crumpled, and she couldn't stop the hiccuping sobs wrecking her chest.

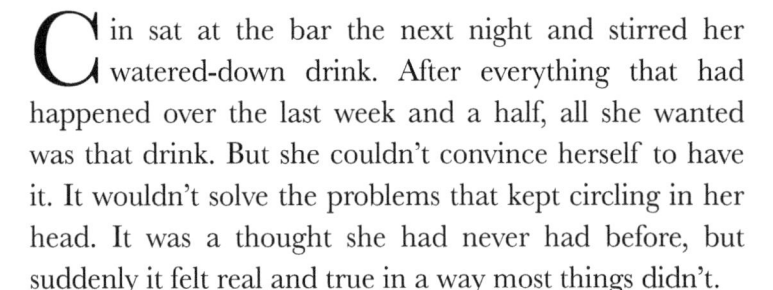

∼

Cin sat at the bar the next night and stirred her watered-down drink. After everything that had happened over the last week and a half, all she wanted was that drink. But she couldn't convince herself to have it. It wouldn't solve the problems that kept circling in her head. It was a thought she had never had before, but suddenly it felt real and true in a way most things didn't.

"Did you want me to remake that?" The bartender, a girl she thought looked familiar but couldn't place, asked while pointing to her drink.

Have another.

"Could you actually get me a Diet Coke?"

"With rum?"

Say yes.

Cin shook her head. "Just Diet Coke." The words felt final, hitting her chest like an arrow—sharp and deafening.

The bartender gave her a look but swiftly replaced her drink before closing out her tab with the credit card she handed over. She sipped the Diet Coke while surveying the patrons scattered around the bar. With her drunk eyes, she had never noticed the creepy guys who leaned against the edges of the bar leering at the girls dancing to the theme-night country music or the way the girls spilled drinks all over each other, covering their shirts and getting their hair stuck together. It made her shiver uncomfortably.

It was the first time she had ever felt this way—felt like she didn't belong at the bar. It was a weird feeling that she wasn't sure what to do with. Much like everything else going on in her life. She dropped a five on the counter under her empty glass and slipped out the front door and down the block. She thought about stopping for pizza, but her stomach was swirling with the overwhelming guilt of the past week and unease from the leering men. She could already feel the soft bedspread, the way Link felt curled up against her belly, and the smell of the fresh, unread pages of her novel.

Cin walked, her heels making the satisfying clicking sound, and made it to her apartment in record time. Maybe sober Cin was more adept at making her way home. Or maybe she was speed-walking. Whatever it was, the brick of her building appearing in the distance, the sound of the elevator ding, and the soft, yellowed lighting of the hallway made it easier to breathe. She stuck her key into the lock, jimmied it, and let it fly open as she took in the man standing in the middle of the studio. Her stomach dropped as she studied him.

"James?" she asked, stunned. It'd been at least three years since she last saw him, but he hadn't aged a day. It was as if he had been preserved in amber, his skin unmarred by early wrinkles and no sight of the gray hairs that plagued their family after they hit that dreaded thirty marker—a number she was, unfortunately, far too close to. She could have sworn he was starting to sprout crow's feet and a salt-and-pepper beard the last time she saw him, but his beard was gone now, so she wasn't sure. "How did you get into my apartment?"

He smiled, one side lifted a little higher than the other. It gave him this off-putting look she couldn't quite name but made her shiver like she had at the bar. "It's only been three years, little sis, and you haven't moved." He pulled a key out of his pocket and held it out for her to see.

She narrowed her eyes at him. Did he just call her little sis? She wrinkled her nose. "What are you doing here, James?"

"Can't a big brother come visit his sister without being interrogated?"

"Like you said . . . it's been three years." Their eyes locked, his familiar chocolate-brown ones searching hers.

"I heard about Mom. I came to help look."

"*Bullshit.* You're the reason she was in that place to begin with—she went off the wagon after you disappeared. Why are you really here?" James's face twisted into a frown, and he tapped the key on the dining room table. She watched it create a small divot in the wood with growing annoyance.

CHAPTER TEN

You're lucky he came back to help you.

"I made a mistake, okay? I shouldn't have left you alone to deal with Mom. Can you please just let me help you find her?" He dropped the key with a thud.

See?

Cin blew out a long breath before walking into her kitchen to grab two glasses. She filled one with gin, the other with water, and carried them both back to James. "I assume you still follow the family's perchance for gin."

James took the glass and swirled the clear liquid a few times before taking a sip. "I could never say no to gin. Sometimes I think part of our blood isn't water but gin."

"Gin and bad genes. That's what we've always been made of." She sipped her water.

James made a face at her glass. "Not drinking anymore, Cin-Cin?"

She cringed at the name; she only ever let the two of them call her that, but he had lost the privilege when he left. "Trying not to."

Cin finished her water slowly, watching James investigate her apartment with practiced disinterest. It was something she'd seen on television so many times that it seemed surreal to see in person. She opened her mouth to speak, but James was watching her suddenly. His eyes squinted as if he were looking at the sun instead of his sister.

"You've grown." Was it just her imagination, or were his eyes trained to the spot on her arm that was tied with a little bow of golden string? The string she was constantly trying to *not* look at. "Do you have any leads about Mom?"

She shook her head. "All I know is that it's been two weeks, and her condo is still empty. I called the police and filed a missing persons report. They said since she signed herself out, she wasn't really missing. She was just missing from us."

I'd run from you too. James already did it.

"That's garbage." James dropped his glass on the counter in front of him, the sound of the glass clanking on the marble surface making her jump. Being near James, smelling his weird lilac smell, made her skin crawl.

"Which is why I've kept searching. I've been by her apartment a few times, but I haven't seen anything change. I'm starting to run out of options." She drew circles on the table with her chewed-up fingers. "I'm worried about her."

"I am too." James plopped into the seat across from her and leaned back in his chair with a melodramatic flap of his arms. "I wouldn't have come back if I wasn't so worried."

Cin nodded solemnly. "Where are you staying? I'd offer my place but . . ." She gestured to the small studio with one bed, before adding, "You could stay at Mom's."

Cin looked around the room for Link but couldn't find him. She didn't want to be too obvious about it in case James could tell he wasn't what she had made him to look like. Where was that stupid fox when she actually needed him?

"I might do that. I have a hotel for the week. Convinced my boss to fly me out here and let me cover a week of meetings with the bigwigs across the river. Anything more than that, I'll have to stay at Mom's. Hopefully, it won't take that long."

"You think you'll be able to find her when I can't?" She scoffed. "You haven't changed at all. I'm not your unstable, erratic little sister anymore, James. I have a handle on myself and Mom. We don't need your pity."

Do you really think you can handle this alone?

"Do you? Because last I checked, Mom was *missing*."

Cin snapped her mouth shut and drew it into a tight line. He was right. If she really was able to handle this, Mom would be at the home getting better. Maybe she wouldn't have been at the facility at all if she had just believed her all those years ago when she said they were special, magical. Instead, she helped keep her in that useless facility when she finally broke the last straw. "I'm sorry. I should have taken better care of her. But you're the one who left, James. You're the one who ditched *us*. You practically threw Mom into that place and just left."

Her eyes burned, and she swiped at her face angrily. She didn't need to be weak, not in front of perfect James. James who didn't inherit their mom's craziness but instead was gifted with Dad's ability to desert when things got hard. She pulled away from the table and walked to refill her glass in the kitchen. Taking a soothing breath, she tried to push out the negative feelings, the hurt, and focus on the man sitting in her studio offering his services.

At least someone is helping you since you can't help yourself.

She rubbed her temples in an effort to shut up the harsh whispers in her head.

"I'm sorry," he mumbled. She turned around to see him staring at the glass he was twirling in his hand. "I shouldn't have left like Dad. I should have stayed. I know you're mad at me—for a long time I wouldn't come home because I was afraid of what you would say."

"I'm not mad at you, James. I'm disappointed. You've disappointed me and Mom." She watched the words slice him straight through the middle, his eyes hooded and mouth twisted in pain. It was a pain he deserved, a pain she had felt for the last three years, but she didn't feel better. She just felt lonely. The loneliness only a sister can feel when your battle buddy leaves you on the battlefield alone while they searched for bluer skies. She sucked her teeth, before blurting out, "You were supposed to be my partner. We were supposed to support each other, James. You promised. The two of us against the world."

You'll always be alone.

He stood up, making his way into the kitchen, and grabbed her hands. "I know. I promised—here in this kitchen—that I would never leave you to do this on your own. I regret every step that took me away from you guys after that. I should have said goodbye."

She averted her eyes, focusing on their linked hands, as she listened to his story. It was a pretty picture, but it wasn't a real picture. James had left with a bang. His voice ringing across their mom's condo as he promised to never return. The look of pure hatred as he dismantled her and their mom with his eyes. His face was as red as his sweater, wrinkles digging into his forehead, as he opened his mouth and drove a knife between them. "You both belong in straightjackets."

"James," she pleaded, holding on to their mother.

"No. This is goodbye." Her heart still ached, watching her mom crumble as the door slammed shut and silence rung in their ears. She pulled herself together faster, picked up her mom, and got her into bed. It wasn't until she was curled up in her bed alone that the tears had fallen, that the insurmountable grief had wrecked her body so badly she couldn't move. Mira had tried to come over, to solve the problem, but she had told her no. Had promised there wasn't a problem. She never spoke of that day, of the pain James had inflicted on their weak family.

She narrowed her eyes at him. "And you left anyway. How could you?"

He didn't speak, just wrapped her in a brotherly bear hug, and let her feel at home for the first time in a while. That's what she wanted to feel, at least, but this James— he wasn't the brother she remembered. Instead, he made her skin itch, made her want to crawl free of it. He was different, and his lies about the last conversation they had told her more than she wanted to know.

Once James had left, Cin rummaged around her apartment for Link. She was searching under her bed when she noticed the whining. She stopped what she was doing, letting the silence fall, until she could pinpoint where the sound was coming from. She raced over to the bathroom, its door shut, and ripped the door open. Link ran out and into the apartment with a growl. He circled the place several times, his fur sticking up, until she assumed he had determined that no one was in there.

Link ran over to her, sniffing her, before he rubbed his head into her calf.

"How did you get stuck in there?" she asked.

Link whined, looking toward the door James had just walked out of. Cin frowned, scratching Link's head. She tucked that weird piece of information away.

Chapter Eleven

"Cin, I'm concerned about you." She looked up from her stack of ungraded reports to study Ian's frame leaning against the doorway. She had skipped their usual Monday scheduled meeting and decided only to show up for her assigned classes that day. When their eyes met, he entered the room and pulled up a stool to her desk. She sucked her teeth before focusing in on the suddenly blurry scrawl. She thought the formula looked right, so she marked it with a red check mark. "There's nothing to be concerned about."

"I know I don't know you that well. But you can't imagine I'm missing the red-rimmed eyes for the last three meetings we've had this week. Do you want to tell me what's going on?" He fidgeted on his seat uncomfortably. She watched his tapping fingers. If he didn't seem so unnerved, she might have spilled her heart out, but no, she didn't need to burden anyone else. She already burdened Mira. Mira whom she hadn't heard from after she told her about Ian.

"Like you said, I barely know you. Unless this is affecting my work, it's my problem." The words ripped through her as she shuffled the papers in front of her uselessly.

Always so stubborn. This is why you're going to die alone.

"It's affecting my ability to work with you. I can't handle looking at this mopey face when we need to talk about whether or not we should teach a few lessons outdoors." His harsh tone forced her head up to study his face. The knitted brows and down-turned mouth didn't match it. Neither did the concern swirling in his eyes that she tried to ignore. "Listen, I understand you might not trust me. But there's something I need to tell you—I think it will make you trust me, even a little."

Screw this guy.

"There's nothing you could say that would make me magically trust you." Cin stood up and walked over to check the lids inside the fume hood. She carefully unscrewed and rescrewed each container as she listened.

"I know about your mom; Dr. Williamson told me you'd been struggling with her sudden disappearance. I know what it's like to worry about my family. My parents were like you . . . well, like me as well. I spent a lot of time trying to shove away their ideals and beliefs until I couldn't anymore. At one point, they disowned me. I was left out on my own for a few years. It wasn't until I accepted who we were that they welcomed me back. I know it's not the same, but I just wanted to be there for you."

"You're right, it's not the same." She paused in her inspection. "You don't know what it's like to be second-generation crazy 'witch.'"

Second-generation certifiable.

"That's the thing. My family, we might not be bipolar, but I come from a long line of witches too." Cin glared at his reflection in the glass as he lifted his hands and golden threads appeared between them. "Do you see the magic we're both capable of?"

And there it is. You're officially crazy.

She laughed wryly. "Do you enjoy making fun of me and my family with your parlor tricks? I know that's not real." The lie stung, but she just couldn't manage it all.

"It is. I'm trying to help, to empathize with your struggles, and offer to support you in your search."

Is this just some cruel joke right now?

Tears pricked her eyes. "Why are you doing this to me?"

"I just want to show you the options. Your mom isn't crazy, she never was, and neither are you. You both just need the support of a coven."

Cin spun around, storming across the empty classroom to shove her tearstained face into Ian's face. "Everyone wants to *help*. They want to *empathize*. But you can't. You can't understand it or figure it out. It's my reality, and I don't even know who's in charge—me or the disease. I'm the one who has to listen to all the voices and try to pick out which one is the real me. I'm the only one who never knows who I am. I don't need you messing with my head too."

Ian opened his mouth to speak, but she glared at him.

"No. Don't. You've just made this so much worse. Do you realize I almost committed myself at one point? I've always prided myself on knowing the voice wasn't real. Now I got two voices and a missing mother. You're just making fun of me. Why would you ever think pretending to go along with my mother's crazy beliefs would help me? You're trying to rip the rug out from under my barely surviving feet. I don't want anything you have to offer. I don't need you to be anything other than my co-worker, you hear me, Dr. Santos?"

Ian pulled back, looking like she had slapped him. She couldn't blame him because the words hurt as much for her to say as they did for him to hear. Her eyes burned with fresh unwanted tears, and she rubbed them away as she made her way to the front of the room. Her emotions were completely out of whack, she was a wreck, and she didn't even know if she was making the right choice. All she could feel was fear—the fear that everything was just one big joke on the crazy chick.

You just love to screw things up.
No one needs him.

Cin ripped open her laptop and started rapidly clicking at the keys. She focused all her attention on pulling up the slides onto the whiteboard behind her and tidying her papers when she got her computer set up. Anything to avoid the disbelief and concern spread across Ian's face. A face that was staring at her from across the room. She didn't need his bullshit disguised as support; she had enough of her own bullshit. That's all she had. Bullshit, guilt, and remorse. There was nothing redeemable about her.

Because you're a screw-up.

She flipped through the graded report in her hand and started to alphabetize them, carefully picking them out by letter and stacking them on the desk. The quiet ruffle of the sheets was all she could hear. It was so silent, her brain shutting up for the first time, she could hear the quiet whirling of the hood fan to her right. So quiet that when Ian finally blew out a long breath.

"I'll be here when you're ready to get the support you truly need," he added, before walking out of the room. She could make out each footstep as it took him away from her. What had she done? All he had offered was the idea that her mom wasn't as crazy as she always thought, had shown her possibilities to make her life more manageable. What if that was true and Ian knew more about her own mother than she did?

Look what you did.

What had she done? How could she let him walk away? She needed to stop this. She wanted to stop this. But her body wouldn't listen. She stood like a statue until the sound of the door shutting clicked so loudly she jumped. Why couldn't she have just unburdened herself? Why was it always so hard for her to trust people? Ian seemed genuinely interested in helping her, had proven to be genuinely interested in helping her. Unlike Mira.

You're better off without him.

The words rang in her head, the echo viciously ripping through her psyche. She wanted to lie down on the floor and just cry, wanted to smash all the glassware sparkling in the afternoon sun. Her thoughts screamed at her to take action, break something, break down, anything but stand like the lifeless zombie she was being. It wasn't until a knock sounded at the door that her body finally cooperated, jumping to life so quickly she smacked her hip into the lab bench in front of her.

"Fuck." She took a sharp inhale of cold lab air and blew it out slowly before peeking over her shoulder. *Crap.* The class was waiting for her.

Cin swiped at her face, trying to clean up the makeup that was no doubt running down her face. Hopefully, she looked more punk goddess than druggie.

You're already an alcoholic, why not add drugs?

"One second!" she yelled hoarsely, before taking a peek in the front camera of her phone. Definitely bordering drug addict but it would have to do.

See?

She let the class in, barely registering whether or not they were dressed properly. She didn't really care. They could be wearing shorts, and Cin would probably let them in. When everyone was standing in their spots, she stood in front of them with her eyes trained on the ceiling. She knew they were staring, wondering, but she didn't need their pity. She pitied herself enough.

"All right, everyone. You know what you are doing today. I'm going to play some music. Get started." No one moved until she turned on some classic rock. Once she heard the sounds rubber squeaking and glassware clanking, she forced herself to look at her students. Most of them looked away from her, avoiding eye contact. She couldn't blame them.

You don't need any of these people.

But one was standing to the right of her desk. She gave him a weak smile. "Can I help you, Adam?"

"Are you okay, Ms. Cin?"

She laughed wryly. "I'll be fine. Thanks, Adam. How are you feeling about the lab? Did you need help with the formulas? Do you need an extension on the report?"

He paused, watching her. It took all her willpower not to look away. She needed to be strong. She didn't know why, but she needed it.

Don't lie to yourself. You'll always be weak.

She wanted to scream, but she bit her tongue as Adam opened his mouth. "Actually"—he pulled open a notebook and pointed down at a formula—"could you help explain the calculation here?"

Cin looked down. It was a simple conversion. Adam could do this on his own—she knew it. He knew it. She narrowed her eyes and looked up to find him giving her a genuinely hopeful smile. "Please?"

"Sure. Pull up a chair and we can work through it together." He practically jumped away from her and grabbed the first seat he could find, bringing it up to her bench. She placed the notebook in front of them and started explaining the problem. He nodded along happily.

When she finished, she pushed the notebook back to him. "You better get to weighing, Adam, or you won't be able to finish the lab with everyone else."

"Thank you, Ms. Cin. I just want you to know that I'm here if you need to talk about anything. I promise I've been there."

She shook her head ruefully as he scampered across the room. Despite herself, she could feel a genuine smile crawl across her face. She wanted to thank him back for giving her an easy, achievable problem to solve. A problem so unlike what her life was slowing turning in to. She was going to have to apologize to Ian at some point, explain that she wasn't being herself. But that was a lie, and she knew it. This was all her; it always would be.

No one wants to deal with an emotional wreck.

Cin clenched her fist and narrowed her eyes at the wall of glassware in front of her. She wasn't an emotional wreck. She was a woman with a demon. Or was it demons now? That didn't make her a mess, it made her . . . well . . . Cin didn't know what it made her, but the words *emotional wreck* felt harsh and wrong. The voice felt stronger than usual and far more vicious.

Emotional tornado? Seems more appropriate after today.

With a sigh, she reached into her purse that she had slung over the hook on the laboratory bench and rooted around for her pills. She popped the top inside the oversized tote and grabbed one tablet before closing the bottle and grabbing water. She took the pill and closed her eyes in hopes the emergency anxiety pill would help calm her turbulent emotions.

That won't change anything. You need the witches.

Cin bit her tongue as she opened her eyes to the shelf in front of her. Anger poured out of her like bubbles out of a boiling pot of water. She couldn't control it, couldn't control herself anymore. She let her nails bite into her fleshy palm, but it didn't help.

That's it. Let go. Give into your demons.

"No," she hissed, before her vision went red. She heard the crackling of glass before she saw the beakers spiderweb. She bit at her palm harder, drawing blood, the familiar smell wafting into the air before the glass shattered. Shards waterfalled down the shelves, puddling on the floor in a glittering heap. For a moment, she just stared as her vision turned normal again. All the students stood still at their stations, their eyes trained on the shelves.

One student—Adam—watched her with a critical eye.

Cin swallowed roughly as images of her mom's panic attacks as a kid—the shattered wine glasses, the cracked plates—came crashing down in front of her. The reality that she had done what her mother had for years. The power that surged through her whispered the word over and over again in her head.

Witch.

But she wasn't a witch. Ian and her mom were wrong, right? But the proof was in front of her. It was a wonder that she couldn't keep it straight in her head with Link's constant presence around her at home. Maybe it was just the years of constant denial she couldn't brush away.

Cin shook away the thoughts and the kids' horrified faces focused in front of her. "It's okay! Everything is okay."

Cin grasped at straws trying to come up with reasons, but she didn't have anything viable.

Look what you did—Witch.

She ignored the uncomfortably truthful voice as she started to sweep up the mess. By the time everything was cleaned up, most of the students had dropped their reports on her desk and left. The only one left was Adam, waiting by the classroom door with a solemn face.

"We're here for you when you're ready." His twang soothed her jagged thoughts. She gave him a slight tilt of her head as he turned to leave. When the door whacked against the wall, she let out a shaky breath before shooing him out the door.

She didn't have a choice anymore. It was time to step up, face this head-on, and learn about who she really was. Or things would just get worse.

Chapter Twelve

The last time she'd spoken to Ian, her irrational outburst, replayed in her head like the soundtrack to her morning as she prepared for their rescheduled weekly meeting the following day. She had barely listened as Mira spoke about what ridiculous thing the girl at the coffee shop said to her. She managed enough affirmations that Mira didn't question her too much, not that Mira cared much when Cin was quiet since it gave her more time to talk. She didn't offer up the news about James, didn't want to talk about the mess her head was, and Mira didn't ask.

She didn't even notice when Cin walked away without saying goodbye, lost in her own anxiety that was building in her chest as she walked to her building and hit the button for the elevator. She threw her earbuds in and tried to let the pumping bass of her '90s dreamboat playlist drown out her worries. Ian said he was understanding; hopefully, he got this too.

He won't.

It wasn't until she made it to the classroom, light off and no note, that her dread started to make her heart beat so fast the whooshing sound overtook the music, and she contemplated running to the bathroom. But as she spun around, Ian was stepping off the elevator with two iced coffees and the biggest smile she had seen all week. She felt her dread slip away as she left out her breath.

"Cin," he mouthed or said. She wasn't sure. But she pulled out her earbuds soon enough to hear him add, "I brought you coffee. Is iced black okay?"

She smiled as she took it, her anxiety pulling back like a dark cloud after a big storm. "How did you know?"

Ian gave her an awkward smile. "I asked Adam. I hope that wasn't overstepping."

She chuckled. "If anyone would know, it would be Adam. He's seen me bring the same coffee for two years. Was lucky enough to be treated with a fresh cup before finals last year." She took a long sip, savoring the bitter drink, before winking as she added, "It didn't round his ninety-one point five up at all."

Always watching out for everyone by yourself.

"I'll remember that when we grade his final next semester."

"He's taking our class?" The excitement swelling in her chest was hard to contain.

"I saw him on the roster. We managed to get a whole twelve students. Can you believe that?" Ian started to lead them into the classroom. "Your students must really like you. Floyd said that every one of them has taken you for lab at least twice."

They just think you're easy.

He handed her a thin sheet of paper with the printed names. She read through it a few times, putting faces to each of the names, before giving Ian a wan smile. "It probably has more to do with all these girls"—she pointed to the eight names on the list—"who want a chance to spend time with the new, young chemistry professor."

She arched a brow at him.

"They're going to be sorely disappointed when they find out I have my eye on someone more my age." Ian looked at her pointedly as she blushed.

She looked away, uncomfortable with his boldness, before pulling out her laptop and opening it to a fresh word document. She tapped the keyboard. "Ready to get started?"

Ian's shoulders slumped, but he nodded and pulled out his own notes. She watched, trying not to smack her forehead. Someone who didn't mind her quirks or antics showing actual interest, and her response was "let's get to work"? She really couldn't get anything right.

That's right. More failure.

He's bad news anyway.

She let his slow and steady discussion of whether or not they should introduce partition coefficients during the first third of the semester ease her mind. It was easy, listening to Ian talk, compared to anything else going on in her life. But when he looked up, his brow knitted and eyes boring into hers, her comfort slipped into dread again.

"I was hoping we could talk about something, but I don't want to upset you."

She slid the laptop shut and pivoted to face him. She bit her lip. "About what?"

"Are you okay? You ran out of our meeting so fast, and then everything with your mom, I didn't have a chance to check in."

She tapped her fingers on the desk.

"It's okay if you need more time. We don't mind waiting until you're ready."

"And if I'm never ready?"

"Then we'll still be here as a support system. No one should manage this alone." He gave her a wan smile.

She opened the laptop again, logging in and flipping to their slides before looking back at him. "I'll think about it. Okay?"

∼

Ian had suggested they spend the rest of the week apart, giving her time to process her feelings about the coven while also allowing her time to focus on getting her final exams prepared. He told her that if she was feeling up to it, the coven had another meeting on Wednesday, and she was welcome to join them. Cin didn't know what to do with that information, but she kept it locked away in her mind. She didn't tell him about James —not because she didn't want to, but because she genuinely didn't know how to explain him. He was still a mystery to her.

James suggested they get dinner every night, taking her out to all these fancy restaurants that she couldn't afford. It wasn't that she was poor, but with rent, teaching supplies, and groceries, her budget was too tapped for five-star restaurants. Each dinner ended with him promising to talk to her tomorrow and her feeling bittersweet about the whole experience. It wasn't that she didn't love her brother, she did, but she didn't know what to do with him and the lies he kept trying to feed her.

It wasn't long until James decided it made more sense

for him to stay at their mom's condo. Cin didn't want to argue about it, so she had mumbled words of agreement as she helped him get packed up and moved. His hotel, one of the nicest in their small suburban city, was packed with people she didn't recognize and weren't accustomed to her bright-blue hair and combat boots.

She was used to the looks, but the mouth-agape staring she was getting screamed, "I've come here to see the big apple," but also "I thought New Jersey was the normal state." Joke's on them. The looks just made her laugh, especially when she stuck her tongue out and made them hiccup in fear. She normally wasn't that malicious, but the last few days with James, and without Mira or Ian, had started to wear her down to . . . to sticking her tongue out at strangers.

By the time she had pushed past all the people, James was walking out of the elevator with a rolling suitcase in one hand and a duffel in the other. She hurried to him, grabbing the suitcase. "Ready?"

He nodded. "Is your cab still waiting?"

"Yep. Better hurry, though. This guy is costing me an arm and a leg. While I don't mind, I also want to eat something other than ramen this week."

"I can pay for the taxi, Cin. It's not a big deal."

She sucked her teeth. It was a point of pride that she could handle this. She didn't even know why she made the comment. "Don't worry about it."

Because you've used up your entire month's budget and will need to eat ramen for the rest of it?

"You should really ask for a raise at the university—you know that, right?"

She narrowed her eyes as she shoved his suitcase into the trunk of the taxi. How did he know about her job?

She hadn't told him—not even in her unanswered letters. The last job he knew about was when she worked at the local coffee chain while doing research with Dr. Schaffer. She added this misstep to the growing list in her head of weird comments James had made. "Maybe next year."

"You're too easy on them."

"You're probably right, but I have enough."

Liar, liar.

She took his duffel and started to push it into place as James got into the passenger seat. She slammed the trunk before sliding into the back seat. James hated sitting up front, hated talking to cab drivers, hated talking to strangers in general. She'd only seen one person sit like that in a taxi—Mira. It was just another line item for her list.

"Surprised you decided to sit up there, James," she commented once they were en route.

He turned to give her a bright smile and winked. "All the better to pay."

She faked a laugh and cheery smile before pulling out her phone. "I'm going to let Mira know she can meet us at Mom's for dinner. I'll make us some grilled cheeses while we brainstorm."

"Mira?" James asked, his voice rising a few octaves.

"My best friend for the last decade? You remember Mira, right?"

"Yes of course. I just—I've never liked Mira. Do you think we could do this just us?" James watched her in the mirror of his visor with calculating eyes. She did her best to make her shrug look casual, but it felt stiff and uncomfortable. James stared for a few extra seconds before muttering a thank you and gluing his eyes to the road ahead of them. Cin tried not to let his weird behavior upset her, tried to rationalize it, but the hair at the nape of her neck was standing up so straight she had to rub at it.

Let him be! You're so judgmental.

She wished she had taken Link with her. She didn't realize how much his presence and constant watchful eye made it easier for her to breathe, easier for her to function sober. What she would give for a drink to get her through this horrible experience. But without the alcohol, and without Link, Cin realized how vulnerable she really was, and there was only one way for her to build up her defenses—no matter how ridiculous it sounded.

Chapter Thirteen

Cin knew she needed to go back. She knew it was a bad idea—the first meeting was a disaster—but she couldn't help feeling drawn to the connection to her mother. Especially after that awkward reunion with James and her ineffective sleuthing. It was clear her mother wasn't going to head back to her old condo and with James's sudden appearance and need for housing, he was more than capable of confirming that she wasn't there.

Which meant Cin needed to start looking for other places her mom might turn up and the coven meeting was her only lead. She contemplated calling the police again, but they had made it clear that she was just missing from Cin—not actually missing. It was on her, and she knew that this was a place she might actually be strong in. There she stood, staring at the creepy red church doors and contemplating whether or not she had other options when Ian's gravelly voice made her jump.

"Whoa. Didn't mean to scare you. I'm just surprised you showed up again. You didn't seem on board last time we spoke." Ian lifted a corner of his mouth in a comfortable smile as he studied her. She tried to hide her shock; with her messy bun, lack of makeup, and haphazardly thrown together jeans with a baggie university sweatshirt. When she had looked at herself in the mirror before running out the door, Cin had taken a moment to question if she really wanted to leave the house looking how she did, but she was growing desperate with the lack of leads and running out of time before the meeting.

"My mom is still missing. As much as this"—she gestured at the building—"isn't what I believed was real . . . doesn't mean that it's not a lead to follow."

Liar. You just want more time with Ian.

"So you finally believe your heritage?" He squeezed her arm, making the golden thread appear between them.

Cin blew out a breath. "Do I believe I'm a witch?" she laughed. "No. But I don't not believe it. And that, my dear Ian, is all you're going to get from me."

"It's an improvement. I will never ignore improvement." He stuck his tongue out at her before looping their arms and pulling her inside. She shook her head ruefully but didn't fight him as they transcended the narrow, dark staircase to the group of her co-workers and select acquaintances that were slowly becoming familiar.

"Ms. Cin! You came!" Adam called, walking across the room with a red plastic cup filled with something red. Ian nodded before plodding across the room to talk with Dr. Williamson and Megan. Adam, drawing her attention away from Ian, handed her the cup. "Megan brought punch tonight. It's really good. Give it a try."

She inspected it. "Is it spiked?"

Adam chuckled. "No, of course not. It's hard, almost

impossible, to practice self-medicated. You haven't been drinking tonight, have you?"

Cin bit her lip. She had a shot before leaving the house. She swallowed it hastily, whispering that it was her last. The only one she had planned for the night, which was why she asked, but all of a sudden she felt self-conscious.

"It's okay if you have," Adam added noting her unease. "Most of us used alcohol to self-medicate before we knew better. You're just starting out. There's so much knowledge to share—you shouldn't feel nervous. Do you remember what you said the first time I visited your office hours?"

Cin couldn't help the smile that spread across her face. Two years ago, Adam walked into her little hole in the wall they called an office with thick black eyeliner and a perpetual frown. She didn't expect, especially after his constant grunting responses in lab, for him to end up being her favorite student. But, without the pressure of the other students, Adam smiled at her, explained how badly he was struggling, and pleaded with her for help. "I told you that you should never feel bad for not knowing something but for being unwilling to learn. I remember."

"Well, the roles have flipped, but the sentiment is true. Don't be so nervous," He jabbed her with his elbow, "everyone just wants to share what they know with you. No one will make you feel bad for not knowing."

A tall, brooding girl with long brown hair and dark, turbulent eyes stormed into the room, boots smacking the ground with loud thuds, and took a seat at the table. She muttered a few curses but otherwise kept to herself unless addressed. Adam lifted his chin toward her. "Except her. Georgia is just a bitch." Adam shrugged. "Sorry to be so blunt but there are no other words for her unnecessary attitude and constant shit-talking."

"Time to get started," Floyd called, forcing everyone's attention up and over to him. Adam gestured to the table.

"Good to know," she whispered into his ear before heading to the table, Adam in tow.

"I would like everyone to give a warm welcome to Cin—Lucy's daughter. She joined us last time but tonight will be her first full meeting." Dr. Williamson gave her a look. "She has a lot to learn about our history and her place here—I expect you all to make sure she feels welcomed." He looked at Georgia pointedly.

The group all chorused a hello.

"Wonderful. Now, since we didn't have a full meeting last week—we don't need to discuss previous minutes—so I'll jump right into new business. Megan, can you start with our new business?"

Megan stood up and leaned against the back of her wooden chair and shuffled the papers in her hands. "There were a few reports from the health center." She knit her brows together as she skimmed her notes. "From what reports we've received, there is a belief that a wraith has infiltrated campus."

A murmur grew around the table, and Cin tried her best not to stare at the bickering pairs, but she couldn't stop looking at Georgia, her sour pucker and furrowed brows. When Georgia's eyes flicked to her face, Cin attempted to pivot her attention but was pinned before she could.

Fuck off, she mouthed, forcing Cin to flush before leaning over to Adam.

"Are you sure she doesn't have anything against me?" Cin whispered.

"I don't think so . . ." Adam trailed off as Dr. Williamson banged on the table in front of him.

"Enough. We need to start assigning roles in the investigation." Dr. Williamson surveyed the table. She followed his eyes, studying all the coven members. She ticked off the people she knew—Adam, Ian, Megan—and focused on the others. Some weren't there last time. Others she recognized by appearance only. There was Georgia—the sour puss—the older couple with graying hair and light wrinkles that she knew worked in the geology department, the three graduate students from the physics department that she was convinced were attached at the hips, and lastly, Dr. Sanjit Ramesh—Mira's boss from the psychology department.

The locked eyes, his crinkling as he smiled warmly.

She wanted to ask him if Mira knew about his extracurricular activities, especially with her opinion on whether or not any of this was real or just a ploy by her mother. At the very least, she wanted to make sure he kept this whole thing a secret from Mira for as long as possible. She didn't need the stress of what she knew would be a huge fight when Mira eventually found out.

When she dragged her mind away from future-Cin problems, she turned back to Floyd just soon enough to hear her name. ". . . so that settles it. Ian, you'll take Adam and let Cin tag along."

"Thank you everyone for coming out tonight," Megan added, standing up next to Dr. Williamson. "Please help yourselves to food and drinks. Sanjit provided butter chicken, naan, and some kind of chip—it smells delicious." She waved to the table in the corner, and everyone jumped up, scrambling to the table.

"Sanjit's wife makes the *best* food," Ian said, offering a

hand to help her up. She squinted at it but with a little pause, took it, and allowed Ian to help her out of her seat.

She pulled her hand away before the tingling feeling shooting up her arm and straight to her uncomfortably fast-beating heart. "Don't get used to that."

"Don't get used to helping you up?" Ian chuckled. "You are something special. You know that?"

"What you mean is especially insane."

"No, I mean something special."

She opened her mouth to add another snide comment when Sanjit handed her a plate filled to the brim with naan and butter chicken. She inhaled the delicious smells and started salivating. Mira had told stories of Rose, Sanjit's wife, and her traditional dinner parties. She took another whiff of the food, her mouth practically dripping, and grabbed it greedily. "Thank you. Mira has raved about Rose. Did she make sesame chips too?"

"Ah. Mira. What a spitfire." He took a bite of naan. "I'm pleasantly surprised you recognized the chips. Most people haven't heard of them before. We call them Tilachi Chikki."

"I had a friend in elementary school who had just moved here from Calcutta. Her mom always made them for us after school." Cin smiled before shoving a chunk of naan into her mouth to avoid explaining that her *friend* had dropped her after she had her first big breakdown and Cin wasn't willing to smoke weed to "chill out." It had been the first friend she had as a kid and her first broken friendship. One of many that dominoed through high school and undergrad. Until she stopped trying.

It was why Mira was so important to her, even if she couldn't always handle her at her worst. Mira still put up with more than anyone else. Anyone but maybe Ian—

who not only handled one screaming, irritable Cin but two. There he stood, willing to put aside her bad days to see her good days. The last episode she had, when her mother had first gone into the mental facility, Mira had walked away for almost a month, claiming she needed "space."

"Ms. Cin, are you okay?" Adam asked, pulling her back to the conversation.

"I'm sorry, I spaced out. Did I miss anything?" She looked around to see it was just the two of them.

"No, Sanjit and Ian went to talk to Floyd about possible solutions to our little wraith problem. I was hoping we could talk, though, if you're up for it." He stared down at his feet while shuffling them before giving her a weak smile.

"Did something happen with the assignments? With your dad?"

"Well, he's going in for some scans and testing. We're supposed to find out something more about whether or not chemo is working."

"So it could be good news," Cin offered with a weak smile.

"Yeah, I guess." Adam fidgeted with the hem of his shirt in the long pause as Cin tried to come up with something to say other than "this sucks." She didn't think Adam would appreciate that. Before she could speak, Ian came stalking back over with a sour face. She'd never seen Ian annoyed before and couldn't help the giggle that spilled from her lips.

That earned her a glare and mumbled, "Shut up."

"Well excuse you. Did something crawl up your ass?"

"I'm really not in the mood for your particular brand of sass right now, Cin."

"Oh, I'm sorry. Let me turn the sass spigot off." Cin mimed her turn a valve by her head which earned her a snort from Adam and another, less severe glare weakened by Ian's smile.

"You're lucky you're cute or . . ." He trailed off.

"You'd what? Kill me with that glare of yours?" She laughed. "So what's got you all riled up."

"Ugh, it's just Georgia. She's being a pain again. Nothing you need to worry about."

"What did she say?" Adam asked, leaning toward them with a curious face. Cin shot Ian a look before chorusing the question. She didn't want him to push Adam away when he was finally perking up.

"Nothing that needs repeating. She's just bad news. If we could kick her out, I would second that. You guys don't need to worry about her. I'm going to teach you"—Ian squeezed her shoulders—"everything you need to know about what we do around here with the help of my favorite coven member."

"What is it, exactly, that you do here?"

Adam leaned a heavy arm on her shoulder and gave her a crooked smile. "We keep the people of this fair city safe from any and all paranormal activity. It covers quite a lot of problems but for the most part, we are prone to wraiths. Other outposts have different issues but ours always, always, always has been and will be wraiths."

"Don't make light of our roles," Ian added. "It's hard work, it's complex and unforgiving. Before I joined, I had heard horror stories of coven members dying at the hands of lower-level wraiths. But don't worry, I'll make sure you know everything you need to."

She paused for a minute, contemplating once again what in the world she had gotten herself into before she nodded. She did her best to follow along as the boys walked her through the ins and outs of wraith hunting, coven life, and everything her mom should have been teaching her, but she couldn't get the nagging idea that she had walked into a world crazier than her own. All she wanted was her mom to ease her into whatever this was, but her mom was still gone, and she didn't even know where to go in her search after her disappointing effort at her condo and James's sudden appearance in her life. She didn't even know what to ask yet.

It wasn't long before people started to disperse from the church, and Cin was forced out into the dark, creepy night. She couldn't stop fretting over her mom, and suddenly all the shadows down the poorly lit street looked like scheming shadowy wraiths. At least what she imagined wraiths looked like. She searched the stairs of the church for anyone, but all the coven members had disappeared. Where had Ian gone to? He hadn't even said goodbye.

"Looking for me?" Ian said. She turned to see him exit the church.

"Even if I was, I wouldn't admit to it."

He widened his eyes comically. "How silly of me to think you might want my company on the walk home. I'll just go now."

Ian started to walk past her down the stairs. She watched him, unwilling to admit that she really wanted him to stick around, and started off in the opposite direction when he didn't stop toward her apartment. It wasn't until she made it halfway down the block before she heard footsteps running up behind her. She spun around just in time to smash into Ian before falling hard on her ass.

"Shit," she muttered.

"Are you made of stone?"

"Maybe. I thought you were leaving me to walk alone . . ." She wanted to cross her arms but decided she didn't want to look like a child. Or did she?

"You were supposed to make me feel wanted."

She stared at him mouth agape before collecting herself enough to ask a question. "You wanted me to what?"

"Whoa. You actually thought I was just going to leave you alone? After all our talk of wraiths? Come on." Ian stood up, helped Cin to her feet, and looped his arm through hers. "Let me take you home and answer any questions you might have. I'm not going to leave you to heft this burden alone."

She nodded, a grin breaking out on her face, before they set out down the street and down her long list of questions that were constantly plaguing her mind.

Chapter Fourteen

She didn't know where to start, choosing to focus on the sound of her heels on the pavement rather than the words she didn't really want to say. Besides, having Ian's comforting presence next to her made all the shadows and dark alleys between the church and her apartment turn to unassuming shades of gray. Ian who kept brushing his hand against hers while rambling on about all the different things the coven does on a weekly basis.

"What do you think?"

Ian's question, probably repeated a few times, jerked her out of her thoughts. "I'm sorry—think about what?"

"A-ha. I knew you weren't listening. I thought you had questions." He poked her side.

"I do. I have a lot of them."

"But you're not asking because . . . ?"

Cin bit her lip as she tried to convince herself to just spit it out. It was harder than she thought, especially sober. Where was a good bottle of gin when she needed one?

Already running back to the bottle? It's been two days since you swore it off. I thought that shot was your last?

The voice was right, and much nicer than she remembered it ever being. She needed to stay strong and learn to say the hard, honest things when she wasn't slurring and falling all over herself. She was never going to okay with who she was if she didn't put in the effort to take care of herself physically and mentally. This was an opportunity for both. "Why me?"

"Why you?"

"Why me what?"

"Why did they bring you here to bring me into the coven? Why didn't Dr. Williamson do it?"

Ian looked at her with a creased forehead and dilated pupils. "You think they dragged me back from the Atlanta outpost just to bring you into the fold?" She nodded, and Ian took her hand, stopping them in the middle of the sidewalk. He lifted her chin to look at his eyes. "Cin, they didn't drag me here for you or to force you into the coven. I requested to transfer home. Us meeting at the bar, the thread that connects us? All of that was pure luck."

Her heart twisted. Somehow that made it worse. That they didn't even care if she ever joined the coven. But the fact that Ian wasn't a pawn in this game eased the churning in her stomach a little. Her mind reeled with more questions, but staring at him while she asked was too much for sober Cin. She let go of her hand and started down the sidewalk again.

When they made it to the next block, she finally spoke. "Why did you move back here?"

He blew out his breath. "I had an ex in the coven

down there. When we broke up, she made it impossible to work together, and we agreed it made sense for me to return."

She didn't want to acknowledge how the idea of Ian caring about anyone made her head spin. It was a foreign concept to her—the possibility of her caring about anyone who wasn't Mira—but she couldn't deny that it was there, looming over her like a storm waiting to pour. Then, before she could stop herself, she blurted out, "What happened?"

Ian took a sharp intake of breath, before letting them walk in silence for another block. That left three more blocks until she had to decide whether she was going to invite him up. The silence just opened her head up to the possibility that he still cared about her—whoever she was—instead of giving her the opportunity to make a choice.

It's not like he would ever be interested in you.

Who needs him anyway?

"Shush," she mumbled as a car sped past them. She wasn't sure if he heard, but if he did, he didn't comment.

The silence and condescending voices in her head were starting to build a migraine at the nape of her neck when he finally sucked his teeth and spoke. "She wanted to have biological kids, and I didn't."

Cin let go of the breath she didn't know she was holding. It was a hurdle she had never planned to cross. That was the beauty of Mira; she never had to cross the hurdle of discussing kids with Mira. She didn't need to justify why she wanted to adopt; just that she did. She added this little piece of information to the list in her head. "That's all?"

"Can you imagine raising a child who struggles with the same things you do? Could you proudly announce that you love who you are? Because up until moving here, I really couldn't."

"No, I can't imagine forcing all these struggles, or this world, on a child. I remember how much I struggled as a kid with what I thought was just my mom making things up. But I always imagined I would adopt. Provide a home for a child who might not otherwise have. Now, I don't know." Once the words were out, they hung heavy and truthful in the air between them.

Ian paused, and when she turned, he was watching her with an expression she couldn't place. "You don't want to adopt anymore?"

She could hear the nerves in his voice but didn't have an answer. They walked, passing a few closed storefronts, before she had churned through her thoughts enough to respond. "I had always thought I would. The only person I had had feelings for was a girl, so adoption was my go-to choice. Now that I know everything my mother told me was real—if I adopt, they won't be a part of this life. I don't know what's worse—knowing you're setting your child up to struggle or that you're setting them up to be left out of what appears to be a huge part of your life."

She waited for him to comment, or run, when she told him about her sexuality, but he just nodded. "I've thought about that a lot. At the end of the day, I think that I'm starting to open up to the idea of having my own kids—biological or adopted—and I have time to figure that out with my partner."

Cin didn't know how to respond. The conversation was turning more intimate than she had anticipated, and her heart was starting to beat so rapidly that she was getting lightheaded. She faked a cough. "Why did you leave in the first place?"

If Ian thought her topic change was abrupt, he didn't comment. "College. I decided I wanted to go somewhere similar to home but not, so I picked the University of Georgia. You'd be amazed how much UGA is like Rutgers. I used to joke that it was the Rutgers of the South. It's not exactly close to Atlanta, but I had joined the Athens coven for the four years I was in undergrad before applying to get my doctorate at Georgia Tech. I had originally planned to stay until . . . well, you know."

"That's a good school. I could never imagine leaving my mom alone—especially after my dad left. So I kept to something close by."

"The City Campus has always been underrated."

Cin smiled. "It has some of the nicest little park areas in the city. I've never felt like I missed out."

"I'm glad I transferred. I always felt a little out of place in the South. It feels good to be home, smelling the city air."

Cin laughed. "No one has ever missed the city air and constant smell of trash and urine."

"You have never left the city long enough, my dear Cin. You know what that means?" Ian stuck a tongue out at her.

"What?"

"We're going to have to get you out of the city. Next weekend, we'll drive up to Bear Mountain. I used to wander those roads when I needed to get away in high school. I promise it'll be fun, and hopefully, some fresh air will ease the weight of everything you're carrying. Even for a little bit."

Cin turned to look at his hopeful face and shook her head ruefully before giving him a nod. She couldn't say no to his excitement or genuinely concerned attitude.

"Fine. Fine. We can go but only a day trip." She wagged a finger at him as she chuckled to herself. By the time she stopped laughing, they were standing outside her door. He leaned back against the brick wall of her building, studying her as she fidgeted with her keys. The light from the entrance was harsh on his face, casting ghastly shadows across it. It was almost enough to stop her.

She gestured to the building. "Do you wanna?"

He followed her in. The elevator was out. She could feel his presence lingering behind her as they trekked up the stairs to her apartment. She swung the door open and waved Ian over to the small set of chairs she used as her dining room and gathering space. He awkwardly plopped down on the closest one and inspected her small space.

She followed his eyes from the nightstand full of glasses to the pile of unfolded laundry next to the stackables with a frown. She'd forgotten what a mess her apartment was when she agreed to bring him here.

"I'm sorry." She cringed. Why did she apologize? She shouldn't apologize for who she was. Who she'd become under the weight of everything the world had shoved upon her. She didn't ask to be juggling everything, and she certainly didn't plan to be clean about it.

"Don't. I've been there too."

She dropped onto the chair next to his and placed her elbows on the table between them so she could lean toward him. "Really? You've been in such a depressive swing that you can't even wash yourself because some cute guy dropped a lead weight of knowledge on your lap while you're trying to figure out the rest of your mess?"

"You think I'm cute?" Ian winked.

"Ugh. Why did I bring you up here?" She pushed

herself back into her chair and glared at the frustrating man across from her.

"Listen. I understand. I've been in your shoes."

"What do you know? You're not crazy." She huffed. But Ian just bit his lip and watched her. "You're not crazy, right?"

"I'm not your brand of . . ." He waved his hand at her. "We shouldn't call ourselves crazy. We don't need to add to the stereotype. But I've suffered from depression my entire life. I know it's not the same as your swings, but I've been here. I've seen the bottom and am still crawling my way up."

"I didn't know."

"I didn't tell you. I . . ." He bit his lip again, and she forced herself to look away from the temptation. She wasn't here for that. At least, not right now. Not with Mira and all her unresolved feelings swirling in her head. "I should have told you everything to begin with. I'm sorry."

She chewed over his words as she walked away to bring them some water. In the kitchen, she paused, her head in the cabinet, and took a deep breath. She needed to hear him out—no matter what—and yet, all she wanted to do was kiss his infuriating face. She grabbed two glasses, filled them in the sink, and stalked back over to the chairs with the most neutral face she could muster.

"Can you show me how to—" She left it open-ended. She didn't know how to describe it, what he did that first time she saw the magic, but the light in his eyes told her he knew.

Ian took the glass from her, and she watched it shake as he took a sip. "We normally have practice after the meeting, but I think everyone was a little frazzled."

"Do you remember the feeling you got when we first touched? You grabbed my arm to drag me to a table?" She shook her head. "Really? How much did you have to drink? You know what, never mind. It's not important. What's important is that when we touched . . . there was a moment. A spark that tethered us together. You can focus in on that connection to build stronger magic—feed from each other. We can share both magic and as the bond grows, emotions."

"I don't understand." Cin ran a frustrated hand through the end of her braid.

"Why don't we start by calling on the magic?" Ian pulled his hands apart as if pulling apart a ball of yarn. It took a minute, but the image of golden strings started to grow in her mind. Or over the table. She couldn't tell if it was real or not. "You see it. Don't you?"

Cin wanted to say no. But she did. The golden weave in front of her wasn't just a ball of light before. It was a taut string tying them together. It ran from his left arm, where she had first put her hand on him, to the same place on hers. On his arm, where his T-shirt left it exposed, she could see a golden band wrapped around like a tattoo. "Can everyone see this?"

"Only people like us."

"Are we all different?" She chewed her thumbnail. Her words sounded awkward and uncomfortable, but she didn't know how else to say it. She was different; her mom was different. Even Ian had made the comment that he had been to the dark places she had.

"Different is one way to put it. We're untapped. Each of us." He placed a warm hand on hers. She wanted to pull away, but the golden string was still there, tying them together in a way she didn't want to understand. But she couldn't stop digging. "The harder we try to ignore it, the worse it gets. But with proper medication and training, we're capable of amazing things. Each and every one of us is special—with a little help."

"What's wrong with you?" She wanted to curl up into a ball. Why would she say that? What's wrong with you? More like, what is wrong with her? She watched him mull over her words as she waited for the voice to dig into her for her stupidity, but it was absent.

Ian finally laughed, and she let go of the breath she didn't realize she was holding. "According to every psychiatrist I've ever met? Clinically depressed. According to my parents? I'm classified as a weaver. I have the ability to weave magic together like a tapestry."

"Am I a weaver too?"

Ian nodded. "I think so. There are aptitude tests you can take, but . . . well . . ."

"Spit it out."

"A link like this?" He gestured to the golden string running across the table. "They are only possible between people who share the same aptitude. There are rumors about people across skill sets who are bonded, but it's extremely rare."

"So I could be anything?" The prospect of this weird fresh start excited her.

He gave a noncommittal shrug. "Are you ready to learn how to create something?"

He took her hands in his, weaving them into a ball shape. She focused on the golden color in front of them, feeling it burn through her belly, and tried to mask her excitement. With the ball partially formed, she looked up to see Ian grinning at her, the corners of his eyes crinkled.

"You're having too much fun with this."

"No, *you're* having too much fun with this." He chuckled as the ball finally took form. "Now. Make one for yourself."

He bounced the softball-sized globe of light between his open palms. She rubbed her forehead, ironing out the creasing there, before chewing on her nail and narrowing her eyes at the strings. She kept flitting to Ian, his teeth glowing in the light of the ball as he watched her, before she moved her hands in the motion he showed her.

Hers took longer than his did and wasn't nearly as circular. But she lifted the golden egg and presented it to him in her open palm. "Not bad, right?"

"My first globe was square shaped." He drew his mouth into a line. Standing up, he walked over to her kitchen and crouched.

"What are you doing?"

He smirked. "Better watch out!"

His ball smacked her right in the stomach. She let out an *oof*, followed by a trickling laugh. Ian joined in as she lobbed her egg at his head. It cracked apart, spewing golden threads over him like a lopsided crown.

"Every time you practice, your magic will get stronger. More stable." He lifted his ball, rubbing the top a few times, and she watched it unravel like yarn. "This takes years of practice."

"Why was that spell with Link so much easier?"

He clicked his tongue, drawing Link out and giving his golden body a rub. "Link, when I made him, was designed to be part of reality. The more love and affection he got from you, the more real he became. Because he's grounded in reality, spells attach to him easier."

She lifted a glass ball off her bookshelf. "If I used this

to ground my ball of light, it would easier for it to stay together."

He nodded. "Everything we do, when grounded in reality, helps the magic sustain as well as us. We all need to be grounded—hence the medication and lack of self-medication—or we fall apart."

Isn't that the truth?

∽

They worked in silence for a while before Ian turned to her with a frown. "We should talk."

Her stomach dropped. This was it; he was done with her. She hadn't even done anything. "About what?" she hedged.

"Wraiths."

She let out a sigh of relief. That was a subject she was vaguely ready for. Cin gave him a half-hearted smile and nodded. "I guess I should know before we have our surveillance session tomorrow."

"Wraiths are extremely dangerous for a variety of reasons, but the most important one is that they can drain your soul upon possession. The longer you are possessed, the weaker your soul gets until you have nothing left." Ian leveled her with a serious look. "People without souls do really dangerous things."

"Like what?" Cin asked, leaning forward. She didn't expect to be as curious as she was, but after the meeting earlier, she realized she wanted to protect the city she lived in, and it was in danger. A danger she didn't yet understand.

"Do you remember the serial killer a couple of years back?" Cin nodded. "That was a possession that got out of control." Cin gasped. "The situation was so bad, it made it all the way to my coven in Atlanta. This coven has become known for its wraith vigilance ever since that episode."

"Are you saying the wraith made him kill all of those people?" Cin asked, looking down at the golden threads spread between her fingers. She twisted it into a ball, her eyes focused anywhere but on Ian.

"Not quite. Wraiths can only get you to do the things you are already leaning into. You have to have the darkness already in your soul for them to use it. He already had the darkness needed to kill people; the wraith just exasperated it."

"So anything this possessed person does, they could have done anyway under the right circumstances?"

Ian nodded. "This is why we have Sanjit in the coven. He's an expert in his field and helps understand what a person is capable of. He's the most important piece when it comes to possession. As long as we know who is possessed, we can figure out how dangerous that person is capable of being."

Cin took a deep breath and finished building the lopsided ball in her hands. She handed it to Ian, and he inspected it with a smile. "What are we looking for tomorrow?"

"Ah, the signs of possession. I can't believe I forgot to tell you those. They are the most important part of surveillance." Ian handed the ball of gold back to her and grabbed his mug of tea from the table. After a long sip, he looked at her seriously. "The most important thing to look for is consistent vomiting. Being possessed takes a huge toll on your body as you might imagine, and your body will reject the possession."

Cin narrowed her brows. "How do you tell the difference between someone being sick and possession?"

"Good question. There are other signs. Things wraiths like to keep around them to help strengthen the bond with the possessed. There are plants, like witch hazel and lavender, or candles. Specifically red candles."

"Why red candles?" Cin gave Ian a quizzical look. "There doesn't seem to be any significance there."

Ian shrugged. "We've never been able to figure out the connection, but a lot of possessed people have them. I have seen very few cases where there are no red candles scattered about someone's home who is under possession. It's just something we've accepted as a sign despite not truly understanding it."

~

They spent another few hours practicing until her reminder rang, and she had to send him away. He wrapped her in a warm hug, adding to the building warmth in her stomach, before slipping out into the night. It wasn't until she was lying in bed, her body drained of energy, that she realized how easy it was for her to open up to Ian in a way it never was with Mira. Her smile melted as she stared up at the ceiling and tried, unsuccessfully, to justify her feelings.

He'll never treat you like Mira does.

"But is that really a bad thing?" she asked into the darkness. Link snuggled into her belly, where he was curled up, and sighed. His fur was smooth when she ran her fingers through it. "I didn't think so either."

Chapter Fifteen

When she woke up the next morning, she had two messages. One from Mira saying she was going to be late and one from Ian telling her to meet Adam and him at the church after dinner. She reread them both, looking for clues that might unravel her tangled mess of feelings, but they were short and to the point, leaving no room for her to find anything even slightly useful in them.

Cin rolled over, eyeing the bottle on her nightstand, and swallowed her two pills. They went down like weighted anchors, dropping into her stomach with a mouthful of water and a handful of indecision. She rolled the orange bottle between her hands, hoping for some answers, when Dr. Cohen's name flashed in her vision, and Mira's comment about seeing him echoed in her head.

She pulled open the practice's app and sent him a message. He responded almost instantaneously.

Tomorrow at noon.

With a look at the clock, Cin realized she had more

time than she planned that morning, with Mira being behind, so she pulled out her old French press as she heated water up. She didn't really like hot coffee, she would drink it if that was the only option, but when it came to trying to figure out what her next steps were, it always seemed to clear her head. Something about the soothing motions brought her back to her teenage years, watching her mom grind and press her coffee every morning. The smell of fresh-brewed coffee that wafted through the condo as she showered, the smile that her mom couldn't keep off her face in the before—it was a ritual she only pulled out in the gravest of situations, and today seemed to fit the bill.

She pulled out a notebook, getting settled at the bar while the coffee brewed in front of her, and started to write. She wrote a list of all the other places she wanted to look for her mom, starting with talking to Sanjit and Floyd, all the great and wonderful things she couldn't explain about Ian that made her shiver, all the memories with Mira that kept her close to her heart, and lastly—most importantly—she wrote about everything she had accomplished. Because at the heart of everything, Cin wouldn't have been able to cope with any of this if she hadn't put the bottle away and started focusing on the things that made her feel close to her mom.

And that, she wrote, was what she really needed—to be close to her mom. Looking down at the words jumbled across the paper, Cin wasn't sure what to do with any of it. When it came to her mom, Cin was clueless. She pulled out her phone to check the time before pouring her still-warm coffee into a mug and getting pants on. Mira would be there soon, and she hated to wait. She quickly keyed the words into a note on her phone—a reminder of what she wanted.

By the time she made it outside, Mira was leaning against her hood with her arms crossed. What pissed her off?

Cin smiled, giving a little half-wave, but Mira just scowled and got into the car. She felt her heart climb into her throat as she dragged her feet across the small expanse of concrete that separated them.

"Good morning!" she said, adding a little extra pep to her voice.

"Really?" Mira snipped. "I haven't seen you in days! I ran into your brother at the liquor store last night. You didn't even tell me he was in town."

Cin sputtered. "I . . . I don't . . ." She took a deep breath as she got into the car. Mira followed, and she turned to look at her. "I'm sorry. It's been a whirlwind since Mom went missing. I've barely had time to grade papers."

Mira glared at the rearview mirror as she pulled out of her spot and pulled onto the main road. "Is there anything else you're hiding?"

She looked down at her hands and started to pick at her nails, trying to come up with the best half-truth she could manage. After a long enough pause, Mira scoffed.

"You can't even tell me what you're up to? I don't even know who you are anymore."

"That makes two of us," she shot.

"I'm not the one keeping secrets, Cin."

"I meant I don't know who I am anymore either." She tried to push the sadness from her voice, but with a peek at Mira, it was obvious she did a horrible job. That or Mira just knew her too well to hide anything.

Mira placed a hand on her thigh, causing tingles, and exhaled. "It must be hard not knowing anything about your mom."

Cin nodded, refusing to speak in case she let Mira in on her other secrets: the coven, her feelings about this new and unimproved James, and how bad of a job she was doing worrying about her mom when she had found this new connection to her that made it feel like she wasn't truly gone. "I was hoping I could follow you over to your office today. I wanted to ask Dr. Ramesh about any places Mom would be inclined to go to psychologically."

She kept her eyes trained on the parking deck appearing in the distance to avoid the looks Mira was giving her. It was a thinly veiled lie, but if Mira didn't know about his extracurriculars, she might be able to get away with it.

"I think he has meetings all morning," she said slowly.

"I don't mind waiting. The new professor agreed to take my class today to get a feel for the structure anyway." Another lie, burning her mouth as it spilled out. She hated to lie to Mira, but she didn't have a choice. Mira didn't give her any options. A small part of Cin whispered that if Mira truly cared about her, she wouldn't put her in that position, but it was battered by the onslaught of strong, positive moments where Mira was the only one there for her.

She could feel Mira's gaze as she parked the car in the first spot she found. Her voice was slow, careful. "If you want to wait, I guess it's fine."

Cin plastered on a smile as she pulled her bags out of the car and pulled out her phone. She shot Ian a message about class, trying her best to hide the surprise at his rapid response, before suggesting they grab coffees—her treat—on their way to her desk.

You can't afford that.

Cin breathed out a sigh of relief when Mira didn't argue further before linking arms with her and heading onto campus. At least Mira was satisfied. She squeezed their arms together and did her best to ignore the messages from Ian—she would deal with that next.

By the time they made it up the stairs to the psychology department, Mira's face had lost all signs of concern or annoyance from their earlier conversation, and she was happily chattering away about how her week had gone, filling Cin in on details that she couldn't muster more than an "Oh, yeah?" to. It was enough to appease Mira—just another reminder that she never really cared about Cin's opinion anyway—and gave her time to think through her questions for Sanjit.

As if knowing she was coming, he was leaning against the frame of his office doorway when they stepped out of the elevator. "Cinzia, how lovely of you to stop by."

"Dr. Ramesh. I was hoping you would have time to chat this morning?" It came out as a question, but his swift nod and wave toward his office eased her fears that he wouldn't want to speak.

"Don't you have meetings this morning, Dr. Ramesh?" Mira asked, stepping between them.

"Ah, always keeping me in line. Don't fret. My ten a.m. just rescheduled to this afternoon." He pointed to a Post-it Note on her desk. "I was just leaving you a note for when you got in. Come now, Cinzia, let's talk in my office."

She made a meek sound before skirting around Mira and into Sanjit's office. She sat down just in time for Mira to huff. He ignored her, calmly joining Cin and closing the door with a comforting click. She fixated on his calm shuffle to the desk. It was as if she popped by every day.

"Let me guess, you're here to make sure Mira does not find out about your involvement in our extracurricular activities." She coughed, choking on her coffee. "I was close to your mother for a long time and have always known Mira's feelings toward our kind. I expected this day to come eventually. I just wish it was better circumstances."

"I'm glad you've been prepared for this. I certainly am not. I don't even know how to dance around this topic. I've always thought my mom was just crazy." *Different.* She picked her nail angrily. Why couldn't she correct her mindset about this?

"She was something special." A smile flitted across his face. "She was Floyd's right hand until she signed herself into that loony bin." He tsked. "I still don't know the whole story about that. Maybe she'll share when we find her."

His certainty made it easier to breathe. "She didn't sign herself in there," she added. "James helped put her there when there was that police incident."

Sanjay lifted a brow. "Is that what you've been told?"

She nodded.

"Well, that's not right. James was gone for at least a year before she went in."

"James left right after she went in?" It was more a question than a statement.

Sanjay twisted his mouth as he sat down and steepled his fingers together. "James is undercover at a trouble coven. He's been there for almost four years now."

She just stared, her brain trying to piece together the

information being laid out in front of her, but it was useless. Nothing was adding up, and she just didn't know what to ask to clear up the muddled information.

"Wait. No. James. James wasn't like us. He wasn't struggling." She sipped her coffee to avoid biting at her nails again.

"James was and is one of the best of us. He wasn't a weaver like your mom. Or probably you. James's specialty is whispering—like Adam." He tapped a book on the shelves behind his desk. He pulled it out and handed it to her. "Here's the book of specialties and gifts along with what disorders are associated. It's the DSM for magical abilities."

She ran her fingers over the book. The door started to creak open. She shoved the book into her bag as Mira popped her head in, a fake smile plastered on her face. "Dr. Ramesh, your ten thirty is early."

"Well, it's been a very interesting chat, Cinzia. Please keep me up to date on your mother. I do hope you find her soon." Sanjit waved her out. She stood, her legs weak and wobbly, and dragged herself away from Sanjit's calm demeanor and shattering information. Mira's fake pleasantness wasn't helping much either. Without any options, she pulled out her phone to tell Ian she wouldn't be showing up for their session today and she'd see him later that night. Then she headed to crack open the unfinished bottle of gin in her house.

Chapter Sixteen

She managed to avoid actually drinking the gin—pouring herself several shots that she dumped down the drain. The darker voice in her head had booed her, repeatedly reminding her that gin was her only true friend. Gin and Mira. But the voice she'd grown up with, the only one that felt like a part of her, reminded her that she could survive without her crutch. It was those words, coming from the voice she had accepted as part of herself, that pushed her to stay sober.

When the sun went down, she drew another line across her calendar—three days without getting drunk—before getting dressed into all black and putting a leash on Link. He fought her for a few minutes before giving in. He hated being leashed. Preferring to hunt late at night and exercising himself—some nights coming home carrying his leftovers. When they made it outside, walking the mile to the meetup, she couldn't help getting excited as Link smiled up at her. She ruffled the fur on his head before rounding the last corner to find Ian and Adam loitering in the alley behind the building, their familiars next to them.

They crept through the dark, smelly alleyways like shadows—shadows like she imagined when Ian had walked her home not too long ago. It was a smooth, slinking walk until they reached a dirty brick building. Ian pulled the fire escape down.

He gestured for her and Adam to follow him up the metal staircase. She gave him a few steps of space before creeping up and listening to Adam's creaking steps behind her. A small buzz of excitement ran through her. Their familiars slipped away, a line of fur disappearing into the darkness. Despite it being her first mission, she couldn't contain the feeling of pride swelling in her chest battered by the negative, dismal voices circling in her head. She felt like she might throw up or faint or scream with joy.

You shouldn't be here.

You're going to fuck it up.

She ignored the voices easily; they were weaker than usual thanks to the lack of alcohol streaming through her veins. It made it easier to focus, easier to exist in the world. And because she was finally in the right state of mind, she felt confident about her appointment with Dr. Cohen and ready to express everything she was feeling into something constructive. Ian had explained, when he realized she had missed Floyd's speech, that as a new member being out to watch and to learn from missions the team deemed safe enough was critical for understanding their roles in the city. Things like surveillance or magical detainment. Tonight was the former.

Cin looked up the side of the building to the three pairs of eyes watching them from the roof. In the middle,

CHAPTER SIXTEEN

the familiar golden eyes of Link blinked three times in rapid succession as they met hers. She blinked back before bringing her attention to the darkened alcove that Ian had secured for the group. It was big enough for only the three witches, leaving their familiars to keep watch from above.

"Be sure to stay in the shadows here. We just need to know if this student is under the thumb of a wraith. Cin, since this is your first night out, can you give the telltale signs of possession?"

She nodded as if Ian could see her before speaking up. She had listened enough during his mini-lectures while they planned for the next semester to spit out what he was looking for. "Vacant eyes or obvious paranoia. Excessive vomiting. Excessive collection of red candles or red objects. Lavender or witch hazel."

"Good. What does witch hazel look like?"

"Green-yellow spiked balls." Cin peered into the glass windows of the dark apartment. No one was home yet but would be soon. They needed to get their bearings on what was going on before they made it home. The apartment was a one-bedroom flat loft with modern flairs. She scanned the glass table tops for vases filled with spike-topped plants or candles in pentagram formation. It wasn't until she looked at one of the bookshelves on the far wall that she saw a candle placed next to a dark vase filled with witch hazel. She pointed at it. "There."

"I don't see a lot of signs. Are we sure about this?" Adam asked, edging around Cin to point his question at Ian.

"When I cornered Floyd to see the report, it said that the student health center reported that she complained of flu-like symptoms, mostly vomiting. We're just here to check it out. It could be nothing."

The sound of the lock turning and the door creaking shut the group up as they dragged their eyes from one another to the opening door. A tall blonde with a happy expression walked into the apartment, throwing her sparkly flats off and dropping her keys into a glass dish. It took her a minute, but as her blue eyes landed on the window right above where the group was sitting, something clicked within her brain. The face, the flashing blue eyes, the bright white, perfectly straight teeth.

"Elizabeth Marrow," Cin whispered. "She was in my introductory chemistry lab when I first started teaching. She's the happiest person I've ever met at eight in the morning. There's no way."

"We have to investigate every case we receive—big or small," Ian reminded her. "But having her in your class is to our advantage."

Adam shushed them, drawing their attention back to Elizabeth's pacing form. Walking the length of her living room, she clutched her stomach and pinched her eyes shut. "I think she's going to be sick. Someone needs to get a visual on her bathroom."

"I am not watching someone in the bathroom," Cin grumbled. "We're not Peeping Toms."

"You should know better, Adam." Ian shot him a look before turning to scowl at the empty living room. "Where did she go?"

The lights flipped on in the next window down. Cin gestured to it. "Bedroom. Can we get out of here now?"

"Yes. I think we have what we need now. Come on, let's head up to our familiars. We can travel down the indoor stairwell."

Cin gave the lit-up window one more glance before following the guys up the stairwell and over the barrier for the roof. The minute her feet hit the ground, she was pounced on by Link. She lifted him up, carrying him like a baby, and let him lick the sweat off her face with his rough tongue. She rubbed her forehead, wiping away the saliva, as the wind hit her forehead and made her shiver.

"You shouldn't baby him so much," Adam pointed out as he gave his familiar—an extra-large gray cat—a small scratch between the ears.

"At least my familiar isn't a chubby wubby." Cin placed Link on the ground before giving the cat a loving scratch. "You know, if you loved on her more, she probably wouldn't like me better than you."

Adam stuck a tongue out at her but kept his comments to himself as she chuckled.

"You two need to learn balance." Cin and Adam turned to see Ian's husky curled up in a ball at his feet, one eye watching the world around them.

"You know what I don't understand? Why is it I got the illegal fox and you both have animals that you don't need to hide? Even my mom had a cat." The memory of her black cat, glossy and lithe, circling her mom's feet every day while she cooked dinner made her chest hurt, like someone squeezing her just a little too tight. The cat had passed when she went away.

Ian's eyes flashed, a small moment to acknowledge her still missing mom, before responding. "You get what the world thinks you would be compatible with. Apparently, you're a fox kind of person." She rolled her eyes at his shit logic. "Anyway. I'm going to report back to Floyd and Megan about what we've learned, and I'll let you know what our next steps are. Adam, do you want to make sure"—he gestured at her—"she gets home safely?"

She opened her mouth to argue, but when she turned to tell Adam she didn't need him, she caught the look he was making. It was a pleading look. Something Ian must have seen as well. Something had happened with Adam's dad. Hopefully, he would talk to her. He had been slow to open up the first few years—stopping by to visit during her office hours at least once every few weeks—but after this semester, after needing her to support him, he was at almost every office hour, no matter how busy she was. He sat there, eyes peeled, as she ran through equations he had learned years prior.

It wasn't until he leaned over, the room empty, and whispered, "I'm worried I won't have anywhere to live when he dies," that her heart broke for him.

He was like a lost puppy, and she felt an unexplainable pull to save him. To pull him from the frigid, drowning waters he was in and wrap him in a soft, warm towel until his eyes lit up again.

It might have been that she was the only person newer than him or because she was kind to him well before she knew what he was capable of. Whatever it was, she wanted to be there for him. She touched his arm gently, quietly letting him know she was there, as Ian gestured for them to go first as he pulled out his cellphone.

They walked down the stairs without speaking, the sound of her heels clicking on each step echoing in the empty stairwell as the only noise. It vibrated in her chest, calming her nerves. She watched Adam's hunched figure, the gray cat waddling behind him, make its way down the stairs, and tried not to think of worse-case scenarios. She didn't want to believe his dad was sicker than before, let alone if he didn't make it. Adam, holding it all in every day, made her heart drop and her throat tighten.

From the way Adam was collapsing into himself, it was hard to think of anything positive.

When they made it onto the open street, they wrapped around the building to weave through the alleyways. They made it through seamlessly, appearing by the church, and then into Adam's car. Hands on the steering wheel, he finally turned to speak. Cin watched him swallow a few times. "The doctors told us my dad has two, maybe three weeks left."

She sucked in sharply. "Adam. I'm so sorry."

She wanted to hug him, comfort him, but the logical part of her brain reminded her that he was still her student. If they were caught, it would be bad news. She placed her hand on his shoulder and gave it a squeeze. "Is there anything I can do to help?"

He twisted his lips, mulling over her words, as he turned the engine over and pulled onto the road. They drove in silence, heading toward her apartment, and she wanted to speak, to say anything to comfort him. She was at a loss for the boy who was more like a younger brother than her own. She couldn't protect him from life, no matter how much she wanted to.

"Do you think we could stop for a cup of coffee? Just sit next to each other and have something to drink?"

She murmured agreement, fixated on the tenseness in his shoulders. Adam pulled down a side street that held one of those generic, on-every-corner coffeeshops she barely tolerated. When he pulled over in front of it, a small part of her resisted, but when he turned his sad, puppy-dog eyes on her, she got out of the car without complaint. Following his lead, she ordered a hot chocolate, though she added a scone—cinnamon, her favorite—and got situated at one of the benches nearby.

Once settled, Adam stared out the window and watched the people passing by. It was a Friday night, and they were downtown, so there were plenty of different people walking to date nights or parties or barhopping. He didn't say a word, didn't even look in her direction. It was that moment of unadulterated quality time she wanted to keep in her pocket. The belief that she didn't need to make everything better for everyone all the time, but that she could simply exist with someone and that it made them feel better. It wasn't something she was used to feeling from people, especially not her brother or Mira, but something inherent with Ian and Adam.

Her found family. It was the first time she'd thought of it that way, but it made her feel at home. These people—Ian, Adam—were the ones who understood her. Even Floyd, Megan, and Sanjit. The people who accepted her quirks and oddities, even pushed her to pursue them, were her family. These people who included her still-missing mother. Whenever they found her, when they brought her home from whoever stole her, she would apologize. She would explain that she should never have doubted her, that she should have taken her rightful place in the coven instead of insisting she was crazy. They were all "crazy" in society's eyes, but it was that different quality that made them so incredibly special. So incredibly magical.

"Ms. Cin?" Adam's tentative voice pulled her out of her thoughts, and she focused her eyes on him. "Do you ever wish you had stayed ignorant to the world of magic?"

She shook her head. "Why?"

Adam looked down at his empty mug and frowned. "It's hard knowing how capable we are and not being able to help him. You know?"

"We're not miracle workers, Adam. We're protectors. Our job is to protect the world from dark forces."

"And you think cancer isn't a dark force?"

"Cancer isn't magical. It's just a part of our genetic code that falls out of sync. I know you must be struggling, but your dad wouldn't want you to be holding this weight on your shoulders. He'd want you to continue living in the ways he can't."

Adam nodded before grabbing their mugs and dropping them off on the tray next to the sugars. "Are you ready to go home?"

She stood up, following him into the car. He drove her home in silence as she mulled over his words and her own thoughts. When he parked in front of her building, she turned to look at him. "Your dad wouldn't want you to suffer, Adam. Spend your last few weeks with him and make sure you have a chance to let him know how much you love and care about him. You'll regret it if you don't. I know I do."

She didn't stick around for him to respond, her eyes burning as thoughts of her last conversation with her mom reared its ugly head. She didn't need Adam to see her weakness. She didn't need anyone to see her weakness.

Chapter Seventeen

Cin was still reeling from the night before. Her sudden and encompassing need to protect Adam and the high from surveillance pushed against each other, trying to get a hold of her thoughts. But she needed to focus, she needed to learn about herself. She had to know what she was capable of, and this book, the one from Sanjit, held more answers than she was willing to ask of anyone right now. Anyone besides her mom.

Cin was staring at the book when Adam knocked on her door and let himself into the room. She flipped the book closed and turned her attention to him. "What assignments do you want to work on today?" she asked cheerfully, though it sounded fake to her ears.

Adam smiled down at her. "I finished all the work last night while my dad slept. I'm actually good. I thought we could talk about this." He lifted the book and flipped some of the pages. "Sanjit told me he gave you this, and you might need some help going through it."

She smiled back at Adam, swallowing her own trepidation at diving into this wild world of magic she had denied for so long. "That would be really nice."

He took a seat and flipped through to the section on depression. "This is where your powers are from. Or at least some of them."

"What do you mean some of them?" Cin balked. "There's more?"

Adam rocked back and forth. "There could be. Most people manifest the powers of their dominant disorder. Since your dominant disability is bipolar, you have the ability to manifest both sides of the disability." Adam pointed to a paragraph in the book. "We know for a fact that you can create. You are at a minimum a weaver. That is a power that comes with depression, just how it appears for Ian."

"I, on the other hand, have pretty severe ADHD, which manifests itself in whispering." Adam flipped to earlier in the book and pointed to the section on ADHD. "I'm able to whisper into the world what I want from it, and for the most part, it listens. I'm not supposed to use my powers unless they are absolutely needed, but I could show you."

Cin frowned. "Why wouldn't you be allowed to use them?"

"They can be used to control people."

Cin's frown deepened. "How would you show me?"

"I can ask you to do something, something simple like picking up this book, and you would be forced to do it." Adam shrugged. "It comes in handy with possessed people, which is why I think they keep me around."

"Adam!"

"What?" he asked sheepishly.

"People don't 'keep you around.' You're a part of this coven."

"This coven? Does that mean you are officially part of this coven?" Adam winked.

Cin shook her head and laughed. "I guess I am." She turned back to the book. "When we finish looking at this, will you sit with me while I practice? Ian says I should be practicing every day."

"I'll make you a deal," Adam said. "I'll sit with you while you practice if you buy us a round of coffees." Adam yawned. "I'm exhausted."

"Deal," Cin said, smiling broadly at Adam.

∼

Cin was staring at her phone, James's number entered but not dialed. It was this feeling building in her chest that was screaming at her to find out what he knew about Mom before she lost her chance that had her poised to dial. At the end of the day, no matter her feelings about James, he was another lead to her mom.

She took a gulp of her hot coffee, burning the roof of her mouth, and muttered a curse before she dredged up the courage and pressed the send button. She pushed away the nerves as the phone rang, but they made her lightheaded as his voice croaked out, "Cin?"

"Hey, James," she said tentatively. "Are you busy this morning?"

"I was just running out to get coffee. Want me to bring some over?"

Cin breathed out. "That would be great. I only had supplies to make hot, and I'm dying."

She clicked the phone shut. James had cackled, making her skin crawl. Her fingers were tingling, her heart making her head whoosh, her vision shaky. She still remembered his crooked smile, leaning against the silver fridge in her kitchen. The way he promised, "No matter what—it's us against the world." Before he jabbed a knife in their hearts.

Cin had tried to ignore her mom, dismissing her, but after the first month of ignored phone calls, she couldn't deny the truth. Then the letter came. It was short, just a brief note saying he was going to Montana for work. The feeling of the knife in her gut when she visited Mom, and she said, "James won't be coming back."

She did the only thing that felt right; she closed her heart to him. It was easy to pretend he didn't exist, hadn't left her, when Lucy didn't want to talk about him. That made visiting Mom easier than she had expected, which was why she had made it a weekly thing in the first place.

When the knock sounded on her door, Cin realized she had been so lost in thought that she hadn't moved from her spot on the stool. She stepped over Link, who was curled up under her chair. She waited for him to slip under the bed, his golden slits cautiously watching as she opened the door.

James handed her a grease-stained brown bag and a cup of coffee. She breathed in the salty, greasy Taylor ham and gooey cheese greedily before ripping the sandwich wrapper open and taking a bite. "You remembered," she mumbled, mouth still full of food.

"You can't come to New Jersey and not get a proper bagel. The South just isn't the same—started calling them *fagels*." James laughed as he put his empty bag in the trash and met her at the table.

CHAPTER SEVENTEEN

"The South?" Cin narrowed her eyes. "I thought you were in Montana?"

He cleared his throat. "Was. Just got settled in Nashville when I got the news."

"You never did tell me how you heard," she prodded. She couldn't help it. She didn't trust this James as far as she could kick him.

"Really?" He feigned surprised, his eyes arched perfectly and a small frown across his face. "Mira called me when she saw how upset you were."

She mulled over his words, adding this new oddity to her list of things that were uncomfortably different about her brother. She tried to ignore the tension building at the base of her neck. "I thought you didn't like Mira. I'm surprised you answered."

Didn't he just tell you that?

"Oh, you know how Mira is. She didn't stop calling until I answered," he said, brushing her off.

Cin nodded slowly, digesting everything. She kept building his story in her head—a Jenga tower of lies—but missing pieces kept making it crumple. "Yeah. That makes sense. Well, I'm glad you're here. I wanted to run a few things by you."

"Sure, sure. Shoot." He sipped his coffee and watched her through the steam.

"How long did you know Mom was a real witch?"

James sputtered. "Mom's not a real witch."

"Are you sure about that?" Didn't they tell her he had been pulled into a secret mission?

"What gave you the idea that Mom was anything other than mentally disabled?" James touched her hand. Cin fought to keep herself still—she didn't need him knowing how much his touching her made her want to scream. This man who didn't feel like her brother, didn't act like her brother, didn't know what her brother did. She needed him to believe she was fooled. That he was the real James—piece by piece, she was sure he wasn't but not sure who he was.

She shook her head with a practiced rueful smile. "I don't know. I'm grasping at straws now." The lie was easy to tell—much easier than when she had to lie to Mira. She was starting to admit that lying to Mira was getting easier too.

"I hope you aren't falling down the same path she did."

"I have a good handle on my limitations, thank you very much." The voice came out harsh, venomous almost, but James didn't react. Choosing to look around at her apartment, he nodded in absent-minded agreement. It was clear he was thinking about something else, but she didn't know how to prod him. This wasn't the James she grew up with, the one she knew how to push just so to get what she wanted. The man sitting across from her was a forgetful, lying stranger.

You should trust him. He's your brother.

"Do you have any other leads?"

Cin waved a hand in the air. "Not really. I was hoping you'd have something. I'm started to get really worried."

"She'll turn up."

She bit back her retort. James was no help, and she had no interest in spending time with this weird, hollow version of her brother. She held up her end of the conversation, talking about the weather and James's new job—one she wasn't sure existed—until the clock brought her close enough to her appointment, and she could run out of there.

CHAPTER SEVENTEEN

She made it to Dr. Cohen's office exactly five minutes before noon. It had taken longer than expected to get James out of her apartment, so her hair was down in all its knotted glory. She tried to detangle it with her hands as she waited. Her makeup consisted of red cheeks from the brisk winter air and poorly swiped on mascara.

She wanted to feel bad, or out of place, but she was the most put-together person in the waiting room. Besides, it wasn't like Dr. Cohen hadn't seen her curled up in a ball, face red and puffy, with no makeup on before. This sober Cin was a huge step up. She tried to brush away the images from her first breakdown as she was called to wait into the almost-empty office.

Cin took a seat in her usual chair and started to tap on the arm, making herself focus on the noise so she didn't get sucked back into the memory. It was the reason she hadn't been to see Dr. Cohen in a year. It was a wonder that he tolerated her short phone calls and secure messaging to get re-ups on her medication. But she never went without.

When he entered the room, the first thing she noticed was the beard she had never seen before. The next was the frown wedged within the stubble that was directed right at her. She drew a thin line with her mouth but kept her eyes steady as he took his seat and pulled up her file on the computer.

"Cinzia, it's been a while," he started. "I'm glad you've come in. Did something happen?"

"A lot has happened," she replied, the words starting to spill out as they always did with him. "Mom's gone missing. James reappeared. I've stopped drinking. But that's not why I'm here."

"Oh. Well, you don't seem to be spiraling out of control, which I'm happy to hear. I'd like to dive into all of this, but let's start with the standard list, yes?" He slid his glasses up his nose.

He didn't wait for her response, jumping right into her filled-out form of what her moods were in the last two weeks. She nodded along as he checked off each line item while making positive grunts. For the first time in the history of appointments like this, she hadn't even lied when filling out the form. Despite everything going on in her life, she actually felt in control. At least of herself.

"It seems like you've got a good handle on everything going on." He tried his best to hide his surprise. The twitch of his mouth gave him away. "Why did you come in?"

"I'm made a lot of strides, but I've been on the same medicine since I was fifteen, only changing doses, but I can't seem to get rid of the voices."

"Voices? There's more than one now?"

She nodded. "Yes, a few weeks ago another one popped up. Without the alcohol, they have been quieter, but I was hoping they would go away."

"What is this new voice like?"

Cin coughed. "Almost the exact opposite of the usual one."

"Oh. Well"—he tapped his pen on the desk—"that's interesting."

It didn't sound interesting; it sounded like he had never heard this before and thought she was falling down the well she labeled as "definitely crazy," and he labeled as "request in-patient assessment."

"I'm concerned that this is a manifestation of your stress," he added, breaking through her spiraling thoughts.

She didn't want to comment that the voice came before the stress, afraid of where his mind was going. She tried to pivot the conversation back to what she wanted. "So do you think we could adjust the medication?"

Dr. Cohen cleared his throat. "Let's talk about your moods. It seems like you haven't had much in the way of big, spiraling swings, but you've notated irritability and apathy." She nodded. "These are pretty common side effects, so I'm not surprised, but I don't know what else to try." He clicked the keyboard a few times. "Notes from when you were younger say everything else made you cry?"

It was a question for him but a sharp pain for her. The way her chest collapsed into her when Mira waved goodbye, pulling away from the condo and leaving her alone. The throat-crushing croak of tears when she heard her dad's voicemail for the second time that day. It was unbearable. "Y-yes," she stammered.

"Hmm. There are a few new things on the market. Maybe a cocktail." His eyes were focused on the screen as he continued to mumble to himself. "Are you serious about staying on the wagon?"

She nodded.

More desk tapping before he dropped his pen onto the desk and his fingers flew across the keyboard. He didn't speak as he typed away, sheets printing out of the printer under his desk. He pulled them out of the tray, stapled them, and handed them over before dropping the pen in front of her.

She signed the pages, skimming the medicine's name,

as he outlined the new routine, things to look for, and everything else she had heard so many times it was like a mantra she could repeat in her sleep. With a swift nod, she was sent on her way—the stack of paper scrunched in her hands.

A nurse slipped a laminated card, date and time printed in perfect scrawl. "Be back in one month to check on your progress."

When she stepped out into the fresh air, instead of frigid, it was brisk and refreshing. She shot a quick message to Mira telling her she had finally gone and got her meds fixed. When she didn't get a response, she told Ian to meet her at the coffee shop around the corner. With a clear head, she realized they hadn't spent much time planning the next semester and really should get started. His response came swiftly, and she turned down the next corner toward the coffee shop.

∽

She watched carefully as Ian crossed the frosty window of the café, his face bright and cheerful as he bopped to a beat. She couldn't help the smile creeping across her face as he caught her eye and waved. It was easy, the easiest thing in her life right now, and exactly what she needed after breakfast with James and seeing Dr. Cohen.

She lifted his matching black coffee in his direction as he entered. "You are a saint," he murmured, taking a big slurping sip of it.

"You probably should wait to say that after I've destroyed your slides." She grinned. "I hope you brought your laptop!"

Ian spat out the coffee he had started to drink. It dribbled down his chin and dripped onto his burnt-orange felt pea coat. A small brown circle building on one of the lapels. Rubbing viciously at the new stain on his jacket, he said, "No. I thought you had yours."

"We could go over to the library. Everything is saved to the cloud anyway."

"No, no. I live around the corner. We can just go to my place. Do you want to order a pizza when we get hungry?"

Cin just stared. He asked as if it wasn't a big deal. She tried to force her breathing to a steady rhythm instead of the quick one-two that was making her head dizzy. "Uh, sure."

That's all you got?

Before she could second-guess herself, Ian was leading her out. "Awesome. We can just walk to my townhouse; it's just down here."

She stood there, a small uplift on one side of her mouth, watching the gold string that tied them together stretch out before rushing to catch up with him outside the café. They walked silently, Ian weaving between afternoon travelers ahead of her as she plodded along. She studied the couple walking by, two women across the street smiling and holding hands, their heads bent together as they whispered secrets to each other. Her heart twinged. One of them looked up at her, and she averted her eyes to Ian's back.

She jogged, the sound of her heels clicking against the concrete pinging in her head comfortably, and looped her arm with his. The minute his arm slipped by hers, she jumped slightly with shock as comfort spread across her chest, but before she could get far, he pulled her closer with a whispered, "You okay?"

She pulled her arm away, her mind spiraling toward Mira and the looks she would give her. The looks she's given her over the last few dates she had brought home—the girl she met at the student center her senior year that Mira called *immature* because she giggled constantly or the guy she found on Tinder that she thought was only there to sleep with her. It was the same for anyone else she introduced to Mira. Not that she had many dates, but none had survived Mira's tests.

She wasn't willing to admit this out loud, but Mira's constant negativity was one of the reasons she had been avoiding dates for several years. Mira had been such a big part of her life for so long that she had never questioned her behavior. Their sudden lack of quality time made her second-guess every other choice she was making.

She tried to remind herself that she was there to make sure she kept her job, that's all she needed, but as he unlocked the door to his two-level townhome and waved her inside with a smile, doubts started to crawl through her mind.

She stepped through the doorway, closing the door behind her as she looked wide-eyed around the foyer. It branched off to either a set of empty, open dark wood stairs or an open-concept living room area that was separated by a marble island from the kitchen. All the colors were muted neutrals with red and orange pops of color. A small stack of novels sat on the living room coffee table, and she walked over to it as Ian went to find his laptop.

She read through the spines, ticking off the ones she had on her bookshelf with a small smile before picking up one she wanted but hadn't purchased yet. She flipped to the first page, taking long sips of her iced coffee, and read through the opening pages while she waited.

"I have a few more to read before I get to that one," Ian said from the top of the stairs. She glanced up at him, registering how comfortable she had become in his home in record time. It felt so unbelievably close to her own little oasis. "You can borrow it while I get through them?"

It came out like a question, and she studied the spine for a few seconds, running her fingers over it. One chapter in and she was already hooked. "I can return it during our next planning session."

He waved his free hand in the air. "Don't rush. Enjoy it so that when I finish, we can talk about it."

Her heart jumped. Mira only read journals and magazines. The last time Cin had tried to get her to read a book, Mira had laughed in her face. "That won't teach me how to connect with my future clients." She had wanted to disagree, wanted to explain that popular fiction was something to discuss, not cast off, but she had been so adamant about it that eventually Cin just started to keep her reading habits to herself.

"What are you reading now?"

Ian placed his laptop, closed, on the table before pulling out a book near the top of the stack and handing it to her. It was the only one she didn't own or want. "I'm loving it. There's something so satisfying about stepping out of my head, away from the worries and the frustrations, and into the head of someone so badass."

She laughed. "Let me get this straight, you fight literal evil for a living, and you think"—she shook the book in front of her—"jumping into the head of a world-class cop is more badass?"

His eyes flickered. "You haven't done a lot of work

with us. We're pretty awesome, but they"—he jabbed the book—"don't have to deal with the insecurities of being mentality disabled or working with a group of people who don't believe in themselves when they should."

"You're right. I haven't. But what I do know, what you've told me, is that without our disability, without our special brain chemistry, none of this would be possible." She gestured around them. The golden strings hummed with life throughout the living room, always waiting for their command. "Our *limitations* in the eyes of others are our strengths."

Ian nodded. "I'm not disagreeing with you. It's just nice to not deal with them, that's all."

"I get it. It's why I picked up reading in the first place." She lets out a small chuckle. If she was being honest with herself, it was more of a giggle, but she was willing to pretend otherwise. "Before I got diagnosed, when I was starting to swing but no one knew it, I used to buy hundreds of books. Whatever my small weekly allowance would get me. Then I would stay up all night reading until I finished everything in my weekly stack. I read over two hundred books that year."

She could still picture it. The way she made a blanket fort using her dresser and some of her finished books. The lantern she found under the sink that was just bright enough to read by. The way she could catch the sunrise in the morning, book finished, and not feel a wink of exhaustion. It's funny now how she or her mom never noticed how weird it was. Instead, it was her brother—waking up at three a.m. for water—who found her wide-eyed with her nose in a book, and said, "Maybe you should get checked out like Mom."

Maybe Mom was just too used to it, her own tendencies so similar, that she never worried.

Chapter Eighteen

At some point, after the pizza and the hours of chatting, Cin looked outside to see that the street lamps had turned on, and she needed to pop by the pharmacy before getting home to check on Link. Not that he couldn't manage without her—she had caught him on several occasions with a dead mouse or rat caught between his jaws and a twinkle in his eyes—but she had grown attached to him and liked having to take care of him. He was supposed to spend most of his time guarding the neighborhood, her studio, to make sure nothing dangerous would sneak in while she was out or asleep, but she couldn't help herself when it came to spending time with him. He was calming and enjoyable to take for long leisurely walks to clear her head.

Ian promised to go through the slides with her next week before giving her a warming hug, nuzzling his nose into her hair, and letting her slip out into the dark evening.

She was surprised by how quickly she was able to get

in and out of the drugstore that sat between her place and Ian's. She was expecting the usual twenty-minute chat about what these new meds could do to her, watch her new food intake, remember to weigh yourself every day, make sure you have extra water, but instead, the young guy behind the counter told her to sign, handed her a white stapled bag, and sent her on her way.

When she was younger, during her college days, the white bag used to be something she hated. The sound of it crinkling and the bright color were like a mark she couldn't hide. A giant sign that said, "I'm crazy." But she wasn't crazy, she was special, and now she proudly held the white bag in her hands, waving it back and forth like a giant middle finger to the judges of the world.

Bag in tow, she climbed the stairs to her apartment—the elevator was out, again—and threw open the door with a burst of energy and excitement. She looked around for Link but stopped in her tracks as she stared at her bed.

"Mira?" she asked, tilting her head and taking in the sight of her best friend stretched across her bed like the girl from *Titanic*, except dressed. Cin tried not to focus on that part—it was easier than usual, and she was unwilling to admit why. She placed her bags on the counter and closed the door with a solid click. "What are you doing here?"

Mira flipped over so she was leaning on her elbows as she pouted at Cin. "I've been waiting for you. I thought we could have dinner together. Where have you been?"

Cin grasped at straws. She didn't want to explain her budding relationship with Ian. Mira wouldn't approve, especially since she hadn't met him yet. "I had some free time this afternoon, so I asked Ian to meet me at that coffee shop by Dr. Cohen's office. You know the one I'm talking about, right?" Mira nodded enthusiastically. "Ian invited me to dinner after our planning session, so we got pizza." She shrugged in an attempt to give off a nonchalant vibe, but it fell flat as Mira's pout turned into a dramatic frown.

Her eyes glistened under the light of the lamps that Cin flicked on in an effort to fill the silence. Her heart ached to see Mira so upset, but it wasn't like she was seeing Ian. He was just her guide, magically and mentally. That was all she was willing to admit to herself and Mira.

Don't lie to yourself. You're ruining your life with this Ian character.

Before her thoughts could get far, Mira opened her mouth to speak. "I'm worried about you. Ever since your mom went missing, you've been spending a lot of time with this guy." She put air quotes around the word *guy*. "Whoever he is. I haven't even met him."

The way she pouted as she spoke bit into Cin's psyche. It was a tactic she had used in the past. Her poker face. But Cin had spent too much time with her to fall for it. If only she could figure out why she was lying.

Cin twisted her lips to the side in a half frown before walking to sit next to Mira. She ran a gentle hand through the fuzzy blanket that separated them and prepared herself. White lies, or slight side steps of the truth, were easy for Mira to ferret out. She needed to make this convincing, and the only way to do that what to put as much truth in the statement as possible.

You never needed to lie or explain yourself to Ian.

"You're welcome to meet him, but I can't stop spending time with him. I need him to stay in the department. You remember the *incident* this past fall. I need this job."

"That doesn't mean you need to spend weeknights or Saturdays with him."

"I can't lose this job. You know how important this is to me." She was pleading, reaching out to Mira like a lifeline she thought she needed.

"So this guy is more important than me?"

"No one said that."

"But you've made it clear." The words, the look she gave her, stung. It was like Cin had stepped on a hornet's nest, and they all aimed their stingers for her heart. She wanted to speak up and tell Mira everything. But she couldn't. Mira thought everything her mom said was crazy—she made that very clear to not only her but Sanjit as well. Cin couldn't imagine what she would say if she admitted that she was learning about her family heritage and all the things she thought she hated about herself made her amazing.

"Fine. I see how it is." Mira pulled herself up and off the bed before storming off to the door. She paused, staring at the wall, before looking over her shoulder at Cin. "Let me know when you're ready to talk about everything going on in your life. Until then, I'm sure this Ian guy can drive you into work next week. It's clear you don't need or want me."

With that, she walked out, slamming the door in the process. The sound reverberated through Cin, bouncing through her body like a wrecking ball. She wanted to jump up, stop her, beg her to come back, but what would she say?

It wasn't like she could tell her the truth about why Ian was starting to become so important to her. Or what she was really doing all those weeknights. She couldn't just blurt out, "Hey, Mira, sorry I've been weird lately. I'm still in love with you but developing feelings I don't want to admit to myself for Ian. Oh yeah, and I'm a witch. A full-blooded magic weaver who can make amazing things out of nothing and part of a secret group that protects our world from the shadows."

Yeah, no.

Cin blew out a long breath and flopped back onto the bed. It wasn't long before she heard Link's tapping across her hardwoods and felt him pounce onto the bed. He licked her cheek before curling up on her stomach. She rubbed his head. "Where have you been hiding? Somewhere in the bathroom probably, waiting out the argument. Good thing too. I don't know how I'd explain you to Mira." Yet another secret she was keeping.

Link growled as she said Mira's name.

"What? Don't like Mira? It's probably because you've never met her." Cin sighed. "Maybe one day I can tell her the truth. That day is not today."

He huffed, sticking his head under her hand, and she started to scratch between his ears as she contemplated all the tangles that surrounded her: her uncomfortable relationship with James, her new constant of fighting with Mira, and of course, Ian. She didn't even have words for that situation—perhaps she did, but saying it once, even in her head, was more than enough for the week. Maybe the month.

∽

Unwilling to ask Ian for help or apologize to Mira for having a life outside of her, Cin spent most of Sunday on her laptop looking for articles that might include her mom. Obituaries were always last, but like every other Sunday she had done this, she found nothing. She snapped her laptop shut and dialed James's number.

"Yello?"

She laughed despite herself—some things will never change. "Have you ever tried to say hello when you answer the phone?"

"I see you haven't thought about taking your snark down a few levels."

"My *snark* is the best thing about me."

She sighed, preparing herself to fill the silence with why she called when James spoke. "I went by the facility Mom was at. I spoke with some of the orderlies. They said she stopped by to grab her stuff, and then yesterday, I found some of her stuff in the living room when I got home from work."

Cin jumped up, clutching the phone to her ear, and started hurriedly throwing out thoughts. "Do you think she's coming back? She'd probably okay, right? Should I come over? Do you think she'll show back up soon?"

"Whoa, whoa, little sis," James's voice was calm and authoritative. It grated on her. "I was thinking that you could come by Friday night. We can grab dinner and go through everything we know together."

"Why can't we meet up sooner?" It came out whiny, and she cringed. She was almost thirty, not fifteen.

"I have to get ready for a big week of meetings in Chicago. I fly out in an hour or two."

She bit back her frustration. "Who's going to keep watch at the condo?"

"Mira."

The word hung in the air uncomfortably. Cin replied slowly, enunciating every word. "I thought you hated Mira. Why did you call her?"

She wanted to scream, to ask James—this version of James—what the fuck was going on. If he switched his opinion of Mira one more time, she was going to lose it. Scream at the top of her lungs for him to get out, stop trying to help, and leave her the fuck alone.

"We needed someone unbiased watching the place. If Mom comes home and sees either of us, she might bolt. Mom always liked Mira."

Her face pinched. Mom always hated Mira. Had complained about her so frequently it went in one ear and right back out the other. Her face flushed with annoyance. Another lie. "Fine," she spat. "Let me know when you get back into town."

Before he could answer, she ended the call and chucked her phone at the bed. It bounced against the blanket and hit the floor with a thud. She walked over to see the cracked screen and huffed. Just what she needed. One more fucking thing to fix. As if reading her frustrations, Link crawled off the couch and rubbed against her legs until her vision stopped blurring and her heart started to beat normally. She rubbed her hand down his back, and he yipped. "I would be lost without you," she said, leaning down as she placed her phone in her pocket and kissed Link on the head.

Getting out of bed the next morning and running through her usual routine, she didn't even look at her phone, forgetting that Mira wasn't going to be driving her to campus today. It wasn't until she made it downstairs, backpack weighing heavily on her shoulder, and Mira's car wasn't parked out front that it clicked in her head. She sighed, walking back into the building and into the elevator.

Cin didn't want to call Ian for a ride, James wasn't in town, and she felt uncomfortable calling Adam. She didn't even know how he got to the school or his schedule. That left Floyd or Megan, who usually got to the office before she woke up, or the bus. She pulled out her phone, looking through bus schedules while she walked back to her apartment. When she made it inside, she pulled anything unnecessary out of her bag, dropping the magical DSM Sanjit gave her on the counter, and turned around in hopes to make the bus.

It shouldn't have been a big deal, riding the bus—she did it all the time when Mira wasn't around and she didn't want to pay for a cab—but something about today was giving her the feeling of hair on the back of your neck standing straight up. She felt woefully unprepared as if on the bus she'd find the mother that abandoned her or the best friend who suddenly went from uncomfortable to unaccepting and unyielding, but instead, sprawled across two seats at the back of the bus was Adam, his head bent over the second seat with long black strands plastered to his forehead as if it was the middle of August in the South instead of December in New Jersey.

"Is everything okay?" She sat in the row ahead of him and leaned a leather-clad arm over the back of the seat.

Adam looked up briefly from the pages of handwritten notes to give Cin a weak smile. "I had to get Dad set up at the hospice facility this weekend, so I didn't get to study for my final today."

She breathed out. Finals. She had completely forgotten—she hadn't graded the standardized final she gave out last week, and they were due tomorrow. At least she didn't have to teach today like she had planned. She studied Adam's notes. "Organic was my best subject. What time is your final?"

He flicked his eyes to her. "Four, but I haven't even started studying."

"Do you have flash cards?"

He blew out a long, annoyed breath. "No—just these notes."

She reached over and snatched them off the seat. Adam protested weakly, but she gave him a look. "Pull out a clean piece of paper and draw me the caffeine molecule."

"I don't—"

But she cut him off with a hand gesture. "You do. Do you want to pass?" He rolled his shoulders and gave her a curt nod before drawing out the structure. She looked it over. "Perfect. See? Let's get through this study guide—we can work in my office until your exam."

～

When Adam finally packed up to walk through the building toward his final, his shoulders were relaxed, and a determined glint filled his eyes. He gave her a brief hug before skittering out of the door and leaving her with a stack of scribbled-on ungraded tests. She pulled out her department-issued red pen and started comparing the responses to the pre-filled answer sheet.

She marked a few reports mindlessly, wondering how Adam was doing on his exam, before losing complete focus as her thoughts tumbled to Mira. It wasn't that Mira wasn't normally reactive or that she had never expressed jealousy before. Because she had the same reaction anytime Cin had brought anyone new into their lives —whether it was the girl she met in bio lab during her sophomore year that she thought would be a good friend or one of the few other people she met along the way that liked the same books or enjoyed the same TV shows.

It was something she had expected, something she normally ignored until Mira came back with a pout and a cup of coffee to smooth things over with. This time was different—how she felt about Mira, and Ian, were different from every other time. For once, Cin didn't feel the stomach-clenching guilt that made it impossible to eat until Mira was willing to talk to her again, and her decision to keep her growing relationship with Ian wasn't making her question everything—except for maybe not calling him to pick her up this morning. There was no doubt in her mind that he would've been there in a heartbeat if she needed him.

As if hearing her thoughts, his head appeared in the doorway with a large grin and an even larger cup of iced coffee. "I know you're not drinking right now, so I thought you might enjoy some coffee to power through grading."

"How'd you know?"

"I've walked by here a couple of dozen times going from the office to the printer in the department suite. You

CHAPTER EIGHTEEN

haven't looked away from that stack all afternoon. Have you even finished any of them?"

She looked at the small stack of graded tests with utter hopelessness. "Three. That's it."

He laughed before pushing the door all the way in and filling Adam's spot. He grabbed a stack of papers before pulling out a matching answer sheet and pen. She savored a few sips of coffee as he nibbled on the back of his pen and marked his way through the first two on his pile. It wasn't until he winked at her that she dragged her eyes to her own ungraded assignments and started to check answers.

She graded quickly, looking up every few tests to study Ian's profile until there was only one left, and she was stuck watching him finish. His eyes scanned the pages as she took in his sun-kissed skin, unmarred except for the scar that ran on the right side of his face. It was smooth, pinkish-red in color, a few shades lighter than his skin. Her eyes trailed along it until they brought her back to his hazel eyes watching her.

"I'm sorry," she mumbled, turning her face as it heated with embarrassment to the disorganized pile of paper. She carefully alphabetized the pile, noting that Adam had scored very well, before the silence started to ring in her ears.

Ian placed his hand on hers, grabbing it lightly but comfortingly. "Everyone wants to know—I'm not surprised you do too."

"I didn't mean to stare." She tilted her head so she could peer up at his face. He smiled when their eyes met.

"It's okay." He gently followed the line with his index finger and took a deep breath. "When I was younger, around seven or eight, my parents were considered 'unsafe,' and I moved to live with my aunt. My uncle—he wasn't a good man—got really drunk and was playing with a set of knives. It was summer, and he was wearing flip-flops around the house. So he slipped, hit a turned-up corner of the rug or maybe just on the flip-flops—it's hard to remember—and fell. On the way down, he held the knife away from himself, and it sliced through my cheek. My aunt wasn't much of a mother—she could barely handle my uncle, let alone a child—plus we weren't well off, so she got some of those butterfly bandages and did her best to seal it up. I still don't know why anyone thought they would be good for me. My parents were always more loving, if a little eccentric.

"Anyway, it's hard to remember the whole experience, I was so young, but I remember the pain. And then when I finally started back at school, I remember the whispered comments from the other parents and the way the other kids started to avoid me."

Cin snapped her mouth shut in an effort to stop gaping at such a difficult story to process. All her years, when she went to school, she was able to pretend she wasn't different. Her illness was a secret, a mostly whispered, well-guarded secret that she got to tell people. On her own terms. Just like everything else that weighed on her life, it was her choice. But it wasn't Ian's. "I'm sorry I made you feel like you had to tell me. I'm glad you did, but I should have let you decide when you wanted to on your own."

Ian stood up and pulled her into a hug. It was tight, like she was wrapped in a cocoon, and comforting. "I want to share everything with you," he whispered into her hair. "This is just the most obvious story—the first one everyone asks."

She nodded into his shoulder as the weight of his words settled into her belly with a radiating warmth she'd never felt with Mira.

If only she could stop comparing them. See them as their own people. Decide what to do about them.

Chapter Nineteen

Without James to ask about any sightings of Mom, Cin didn't have any other options but to rely on Ian and Adam. She wanted to call Mira, she really did, but she couldn't. Besides, it wasn't like they were talking. She wasn't about to be the first one to break the silence.

The two of them, Ian driving and Adam in the back seat, drove her around the surrounding suburbs to leave posters of her mom on street poles. Adam was most silent but made it clear that he would rather spend time with them than waiting for his dad to die. They made sure to drive when Adam wasn't allowed to visit. She couldn't take away any of their time. With their help, she found it easy to keep her phone in her bag during the drive instead of staring at the empty screen.

She was sitting across the café table from Ian. Adam had been dropped off at the hospice facility. Ian had his nose stuck in a book she'd pick out of her stack. She was reading a book on wetland types when her phone rang. It vibrated, skittering across the table until it hit the pile of environmental chemistry textbooks she was reading through. Mira's image popped up. A photo from when they had visited Baltimore for a girls' weekend. She stood, laughing at something Cin said or pretending to laugh—she was never sure—in front of the harbor with the ocean spread out behind her.

It used to be a happy photo. One that made her smile. Now all she could think about was how Mira had led her on during dinner. The way she laughed, leaning across the table and over the seafood to place her manicured hand on Cin's arm every time she told a joke—most of which weren't funny. The wink she gave her before sashaying past her, her dress too tight and a little too short. The feel of her long fingers against her back as they walked down the street to their hotel. The way her face turned cold, rigid, as she glared at Cin as she said, "What's wrong with you? I'm *not* into you."

"I'm getting my own room." She slammed the door of their room, bag over her shoulder.

She shook off the memory. The words "one new voicemail and missed call" scrolled across the screen. She peeked at Ian, so wrapped up in his book he was oblivious to anything going on around him, and almost chuckled. His ability to lose sight of the world and only focus on what was in front of him made her sink farther into him, into the feelings she didn't name.

She turned back to her phone. The transcript of the voicemail appeared on her screen with a few clicks.

Hey, Cin-Cin. I hope you're doing okay. Was thinking we could do dinner. Meet me at our place tonight around eight. Can't wait to see you.

She read it a few times. Cin-Cin? She hated that nickname. Grumbled every time her mom had said it. She was still staring, her eyes wide, when Ian cleared his throat. "You okay?"

"Yeah, sure." It came out quickly and mumbled. She could feel his eyes on her, but she couldn't face them. At least, not with the message transcribed across her screen.

With a click, it disappeared into cyberspace. She turned to look up at his curious eyes.

"I'll be here when you're ready to talk about it."

She twisted her lips before giving him a slow nod. He turned back to his book, eyes crinkling as he laughed at the pages. She looked down at the wetland book, scribbling notes about the difference between swamps and bogs. It wasn't her favorite subject, but Ian wanted to do one lab with a field trip to a man-made wetland. Anything to show the students there were ways to explore the subject outside of school. It was hard to focus on, her mind repeating the words in her head.

Ian tapped a finger on the table, drawing her attention. "I was wondering if you wanted to get dinner tonight?"

The question tore through her, ripping at the barely tied-together strings holding her anxiety in. She was barely managing Mira and now Ian. How was she supposed to pick one of them? She took a deep breath, her fingers shaking as she placed the book down, before meeting his eyes. "Let me go home and shower, I'll let you know afterward."

His eyes lit up as he nodded wildly while she packed up the books. She slid each one carefully into her bag, trying to look and remain calm. She didn't need Ian to keep worrying about her. This was her thing to figure out. One shaky smile and an "I'll call you."

And then she slipped out the door. Her body flew as

she moved as fast as she could until she was down the street, book bag wrapped up in her arms, running as fast as her legs would take her. It was all she could think to do, the world and her people pressing down on her until it felt like her chest was almost concave with anxiety. All she wanted was to call her mom and talk about everything.

All she got was more stress.

∼

She spent the evening pacing around her studio, Link in tow. She couldn't convince herself to eat, her stomach protesting with the heavy weight of anxiety that was building in her. She had grabbed some bread, picking off small chunks, but only managed to gag it back up. It wasn't one thing, but everything added together that was making her belly gurgle and her throat burn with acid from its emptiness.

She spent several tense minutes crouched over the toilet. Stomach acid burned with each heave, expelling anything she got past the gag reflex.

With wobbly legs, her stomach still cramping, she shoved her sleeping pills down her throat, barely managing a sip of water. It wouldn't last, but she let herself fall into a heavy dreamless sleep. Sleep could only handle so many problems, could only wipe away so much. She felt it first, the world still black. Her stomach clenched, begging for anything. Her chest heaved, filling with dread, as she opened her eyes.

She had woken up like this a lot, before she had taken steps to take care of herself. Every time, the clock glowing with the middle of the night, she threw herself into making a past-midnight snack. Her body did this, pushed

CHAPTER NINETEEN

her to wake up in the quiet of the night. After she'd taken her meds and they were at their strongest. When the voices were just as silent. It was when she had the peace she needed to think through all the words spitting out at her. It was her only time to truly process.

She carefully cut fresh slices from her aged cheddar block and let out a sigh. Middle of the night was easier. She grabbed fresh slices of sourdough.

Link yipped once to let her know he was watching from his spot curled next to the dishwasher.

Most nights, Cin was okay with making late-night ramen, but there was something so satisfying to her about making a grilled cheese sandwich at three in the morning. The process was the best part—like pulling apart the layers in her head.

She was so focused on slathering her bread with mayonnaise—thinking through more places she needed to investigate for signs of her mother—before constructing the sandwich, ensuring the outside was well covered in butter, and placing it on the hot grill. Mira hated this, had gone home the first sleepover she had woken up starving. "I can't spend the night if you won't actually sleep. Some of us need their rest."

It hurt, the memories of the before. She was lost. Barely registered the ping of her phone. She listened to the sizzling of the butter, placing a sprig of rosemary into the pan, and took a giant whiff of the heavenly dish. The voices were silent, but her brain wasn't. What about James? Are you going to finally push Mira away? How do you tell Ian about Mira's behavior?

Her thoughts were interrupted by her phone ringing. She threw in her earbuds—a pair was scattered in each room of her home—and answered it.

"Hello?"

"Oh." He coughed. "I didn't think you would answer." Ian's voice was soft on the phone, giving her a little tingle. She tried to push it away, but her heartbeat wouldn't give up, galloping away in her chest.

"I'm making grilled cheese."

Ian laughed. "It's three a.m. Why would you be making grilled cheese?"

"Have you never made your favorite food in the middle of the night?"

"Well. Uh, no. I guess not."

She could hear his smile and took a moment to savor it before speaking. She wanted to explain how critical this time was for her—to process or cope with the world around her—but decided against it. She didn't want to push him away any more than she already was with her bad behavior. "Did you need something?"

"Oh, yeah no. I called just to leave you a message."

He paused. She flipped her grilled cheese.

"A message about what?"

He chuckled awkwardly. "I just called to tell you that it's okay that you weren't up to tonight. I know you're going through a lot. This is all new to you. I had to make sure you knew that it's okay for you to want to spend the night alone in your pajamas and make grilled cheese when everyone else is sleeping."

She rubbed her lips, which were stretched into an upward curve. "Thank you. Most people don't understand things like that." The messages from Mira with a passive-aggressive "I see how it is" attitude rolled around like lead weights in her gut—a reminder that Mira never understood how hard it was for her to just be. That sometimes she just needed to spend time alone to process or sleep or make her favorite food. That it wasn't always about her.

"I've been there—maybe not with grilled cheese, but we all have our own things. Who knows, might be there again one day. It's okay to have a down night." She let the tension she didn't know was building in her shoulders out. It was silly, her belief that Ian would flee when things got hard. Ian understood—every time without fail. And yet. "I'll let you get back to your grilled cheese. I'll see you in the morning, Cinzia."

He hung up with a click. She couldn't help the silly grin she had on her face. She shook her head ruefully— Ian was a different breed. Her smile vanished momentarily as the acidic smell of burned cheese started to fill her nostrils. She flipped the burner off hurriedly before waving a towel at the smoke alarm. It was like college all over again. She was the middle of the night popcorn burner.

"Shit." She threw the destroyed sandwich onto a plate. "There goes that." Link yipped excitedly at her feet, and she sighed. "Fine, you can have it."

She put the plate on the ground and leaned against the counter as Link ate her sandwich. Even with the burned sandwich, she couldn't hold back the smile Ian had brought to her face. It was impossible, she was quickly learning, to not have all her emotions tinged with the comforting feeling of being appreciated no matter what; that man was the most understanding person she'd ever met.

He would break one day—everyone did.

She couldn't stop the negativity.

Memories of Mira stabbed at the place between her shoulder blades, building tension she didn't want and dragging down the corners of her mouth. She couldn't stop replaying all the moments—the final ones—when people snapped because of her behaviors. The way her high school teachers stopped signing off on extending her deadlines because she was adjusting her medication. The subtle ignoring of texts or phone calls her "friends" started to do until they outright pretended she wasn't there when they passed in the hall or on campus. James had flat-out walked away. Mira regularly left to "come up from air."

Her eyes landed on the photo of her with her mom. She was five, little brown pigtails dangling from her head as she sat on her mom's shoulders, and Lucy was laughing so hard that it looked like they were about to tumble into the pool that was out of frame. She pressed her hand against it lovingly and pulled the frame against her chest. "Mom, I don't know what to do. I can't love them both. You were right. I don't think Mira is good for me. I don't think Mira is good."

The words hung in the air above her like a dark cloud as she lay down, frame still in her hand, and stared at the ceiling. Saying them out loud made it so much harder and real. Real like the feeling of Link's soft fur curled up against her exposed stomach. She rubbed her free hand against him and closed her eyes. She would deal with this tomorrow.

∼

Tomorrow was filled with meetings to discuss final grades with the department and getting grades uploaded. She didn't have time to do anything besides work. Her brain was focused—thoughts of Mira and

James floating out into the distance. She didn't have any option but to finish the semester strong. It was dealing with her problems or keeping her jobs. Problems didn't keep food in the fridge or the lights on.

With Ian's help—driving her to campus, helping her finish the last few ungraded tests, and supplying her with a constant stream of coffee—she managed just that.

Triumphant, she slapped the stack of papers on Dr. Williamson's desk. She slid the roster, final grades calculated and ready to submit online, next to it. Floyd smiled as he flipped through the graded papers. He handed them back with a simple, "You've done well."

The stack of papers he slipped into her hands as he leaned across the desk said, "Two-year contract."

She fixated on the words, Assistant Professor.

When she finally met Ian in their classroom, she couldn't wipe the smile away. His eyes lit up as he read the papers, and he hugged her tenderly. He held her hand driving home, giving her chills and making her lightheaded. She floated up to her apartment.

When the door to her studio slammed shut, it snapped her back into reality. She had five missed texts from Mira that she needed to deal with. Cin scrolled through her phone, looking for missed messages and only finding Mira's, before shooting a message to James. She couldn't remember when he was getting back.

She opened the thread between herself and Mira as if it were a chemical reaction in her organic lab that, with too much oxygen, would blow back into her face. Gingerly, she read each message until hitting the last message.

"After everything I've done for you, the least you could do is respond to me. Stop being a bitch."

The words jabbed at her, ripping holes through her good mood. It deflated her so much that she felt like someone had poured concrete over her feet. She dragged herself across the room, running her fingers absent-mindedly through Link's fur as he greeted her, and started pulling her clothes off.

By the time she turned on the water for her shower, she was naked and shivering. It wasn't cold in her apartment, the heat was on, but the strength of emotions running through her made her jerky and uncoordinated. She lowered herself onto her butt under the stream of hot water.

She didn't know how long she stayed like that, letting the water run over her and wash away her emotions, but eventually, she leaned back against the tub. Hot water had turned warm and ultimately cool as it pelted her chest; it ran off her breasts, down the basin, and swirled into the drain. She watched it through the running water and tried to imagine her feelings running down with it. She hoped one of them would wash away.

She turned her head to look at Link's curled-up form keeping watch as she dealt with her problems. "I can't love two completely different people," she said. He looked up at her and grumbled.

"But I do. I really do." She lifted her hands into a cup and let the water collect there until it went over the brim before dumping it onto her stomach. "I don't know what I'm supposed to do. I'm filled with emotions, with feelings, and I don't even have anyone to talk to. I would talk to my mom, you know, but I don't even know how to find her or where to go from here."

As the words started bubbling out of her, she felt the weight of everything start to lift—making it easier for her to spill her thoughts to the empty bathroom. "James is here. He's trying to help, but something about him . . . I don't know what it is, but he's different—wrong. He's not the James who used to be my ally. He's an impostor. Then there's Mira. I don't even have words for the way she's acting. Maybe she's always been this way." She shook her head. "Mom always said something about Mira wasn't right. That she was linked to death, but I just don't. I want to talk to Ian about it, but I don't know if we're there yet. I trust him, I really do. He's so wonderful but there's this part of me that's convinced he's going to split once things get hard, you know? Just like everyone else has." She blew out her breath as she turned her head to watch the clouds out her bathroom window.

"I don't know what to do anymore." She watched the owl-shaped cloud float by with a bittersweet smile. It felt like a sign—her mom always had something owl-shaped lying around the house, it was her favorite animal. "Mama. I miss you so much."

"Link." He had fallen asleep, lightly snoring, next to the radiator, but he lifted his head and blinked up at her. "Do you think Mom is sending me a sign with that cloud?"

Link yipped. "You're right. I'm just imagining things." She shook her head and stood up to wash her hair real quick before turning the water off, wrapping her hair up, and stepping out of the shower. She stared at herself in the mirror before Link jumped to his feet behind her. "What, boy? What is it?"

He growled at the door.

"Cin? What is growling at me, Cin?" Mira called from the other room. She shushed Link. He growled once more for good measure before sitting next to her with his teeth bared at Mira standing outside the door. "What is that thing?"

"Thing? You mean Link?" She bit back her annoyance. How could she call Link a thing? Link was her only confidant right now and her snuggle partner. She plastered on a fake smile and spit out a lie. "He's my new puppy."

"He does not look like a puppy. He looks like a fox." Cin lifted a brow at Mira. She had used the spell Ian had taught her. Link should look like a puppy—no one had suspected anything when she walked him around the neighborhood.

"Link is a baby pit bull, Mira. Can't you tell?" It came out forceful and slightly hissed, but she didn't know how else to respond. Link was her protector, and Mira had upset him.

Mira wrinkled her nose as Link snarled once more. "He's kind of nasty. I guess that's pit bull-y like."

Cin gasped. "Pit bulls are one of the sweetest, loving, and most caring breeds out there. How could you be so narrow-minded?"

"That 'sweet, loving, and caring' thing"—Mira stuck a finger out at Link—"is snarling at me as if I kicked it. Can you get it to stop baring its teeth at me?"

Cin huffed, looking between Link and Mira. Mira put a hand on her hip and squinted at Link with derision. But Link was ignoring her, choosing to look up at Cin and whine. She twisted her lips before letting out a long breath and glaring at Mira. "No."

"What do you mean, no?"

"I mean, I'm not going to let you treat my puppy like a piece of trash. What has gotten into you? Better yet, why are you here? I didn't answer for a reason."

"Because I don't like that mutt?" She ignored the more important question—making Cin's blood boil.

"Because the Mira that I've been friends with would never say such horrible things about any living creatures. I don't know who you are trying to be right now, but I have no interest in that." Cin took a step toward her and shoved a finger in her chest. "I think you should rethink your attitude. If you decide that you aren't better than a helpless, adorable puppy, you can give me a shout, but if you don't think you can accept my new puppy, then I have no interest in you."

"You can't be serious."

"I'm one hundred percent serious. Get out of my home."

"You're going to regret this," Mira growled ominously, before flipping her hair dramatically and walking to the front door. Cin and Link followed her, watching her stilted, angry walk. Mira rooted around in her pocket, pulling out the key for Cin's place, and slamming it down onto the counter.

She opened the door, looking over her shoulder to glare at Link once more, before slamming the door behind her. The sound of it reverberated in her chest, and she dropped to her knees in the middle of the room, landing with a thud on the shag rug. Link ran over to lick the tears she didn't notice were falling from her face. She gave him a few good boys and a pat.

"I guess that's one decision I don't need to make for myself?"

Chapter Twenty

Cin eyed Ian from across the table, his angular face scanning her proposed lesson plan with no indication of what he was thinking. She'd been working on it all week—right after she signed her contract for the next couple of years. His class had become theirs. A joint venture that made her giddy, made her smile even when she wasn't happy. She started tapping the table in frustration. What was taking him so long? It wasn't until her leg was jingling the leftover silverware from dinner that his mouth quirked into a small smile.

"It's cruel to leave a girl hanging." He didn't look but laughed lightly. She scratched her arm and grumbled. Why wouldn't he just tell her it was horrible and get it over with? It was clear they should never have offered her that position. Why did they offer her that position?

It was a huff, combined with her incessant tapping, that woke up the sleeping fox at her feet. He yawned, making his presence known, before nipping at Ian's socked foot.

"Ow."

"Good boy, Linky." He jumped into her lap and rubbed his soft fur against her arm. She scratched lovingly under his jaw and wrinkled her nose before sticking a tongue out at Ian.

"I still can't believe you named your familiar after a video game."

"Do you have a better name for an illegal fox whose sole responsibility is to protect the 'damsel in distress'?" She gestured to herself.

"You're not a damsel in distress, Cin." He slid the papers over to her.

"I don't know. You're stressing me out right now. All this waiting. I'm pretty sure this is me in distress. Link knows it's not good for me."

"You're so dramatic. If anything, I should be afraid of you." Ian shook his head with a light chuckle. "Besides, this is great. You should be proud of yourself." He tapped the notes with his finger.

"You're right. I'm a badass." She pulled her shoulders back and drew on the golden magic that ran like lightning across the room. She pulled a golden globe, like Ian had taught her, together and lobbed it at Ian. He lifted his hands and caught it midair effortlessly. "Distressed, aren't you?"

He shook his head. "I don't think anyone could ever call you helpless." He studied the ball in his hands. "Look how far you've come in two weeks."

"You're right, but I'm also an unstable recovering alcoholic who can barely hold a job—we're lucky they gave me that contract. We have no idea what this sheik could actually do."

"Did you just make another Zelda reference?"

"Do bears shit in the woods?" Cin cocked an eyebrow at Ian.

"You're in quite the mood today. I guess the magic practice is really helping?"

She nodded as she placed Link safely on the floor where he curled into a ball, and then she began picking up the pile of silverware and plates. She carried them silently to the sink.

"I never realized how much better proper management would make me feel. I've barely heard the voice in the last few days. This morning, I woke up after a full night's sleep. I don't even know the last time I slept so soundly that I woke up refreshed." The corners of her mouth quirked up. "I wish I had listened to my mother a long time ago."

Her heart ached, reminding her that while she was voice-free, her emotions were still more variable than a twenty-sided die. And she hadn't heard from James or found any trace of her mom.

"Imagine what cutting out drinking would do," Ian commented, giving the half-empty bottle of gin a look.

"I haven't touched that in a while. I should really throw it out." She walked over to it and tipped the bottle over the sink. Watching it go down the drain was unsettling but for the best. "You know what would be fun? Reliving our first night together! It's Thursday night." She waggled her eyebrows at him.

"I'm going to regret this . . . aren't I?"

"Who knows? Maybe the night won't end in pizza this time." She winked dramatically, forcing a laugh from Ian, before starting in on the dishes. Over the sound of the water running, she could barely hear Ian's quiet footsteps as he made his way into the kitchen.

"I'm not going to say no to you, but, Cin . . ." Ian placed a warm hand on her shoulder. It made her shiver delightfully. She bit her lip, unwilling to give in to him, and looked over her shoulder. "You should really consider what repercussions this might have."

She leaned her head against his lightly. "We'll be fine." Placing a clean plate in the rack, she turned to look into his eyes. "I'll be fine."

"Be careful."

Ian put away their notes as she finished doing the dishes. It didn't take them long to clean up and walk over to the bar. It was busier than usual, packed in tight, but that didn't bother her. She grabbed Ian's hand and weaved them through the crowd to order a mojito for him and a diet soda for herself. She handed Ian his drink before pulling them onto the dance floor as the DJ changed songs.

"It's our song," she yelled over the starting notes; she downed her soda, Ian following quickly, before adding, "First one to stop singing loses!"

Ian rolled his eyes but started to sing when the first few lines played. She joined in, closing her eyes and letting the music take over. She had always loved this when she was drunk but now, completely sober, she couldn't imagine a better feeling—the bass thumping so violently she could feel it in her bones. The moment felt incredible. Until she tripped over her own feet, falling over and onto the person she didn't realize was next to her.

She opened her eyes and gasped. "Mira? Mira! I'm so sorry." She untangled herself from her best friend and got to her feet before pulling Mira up. She wanted to clamp her mouth shut. She shouldn't be nice to her. But Mira, dazed, just blinked at her with a small smile, and she couldn't be as angry. "Are you okay?"

Mira nodded slowly. "I should probably sit down."

She gestured to an empty table and awkwardly pulled them over to it.

Ian pulled a chair out and helped get Mira situated. "Who is this?"

"Ian, this is Mira. She's my best friend. You remember me telling you about her?"

"Ah, of course. Nice to meet you, Mira." He looked neutral, with an easy smile on his face, but she could see the apprehension in his eyes. She'd done more than just tell him about her—she had blurted out all her jealous behavior and irrational actions over the last few weeks like word vomit. She had felt better at the time, relieved to let go of some of the stress coiled in her stomach, but now it felt like her stomach had dropped out of her body.

Cin watched her friend survey Ian with a critical eye, looking for things she would no doubt comment on later when she cornered her, before reaching out her hand to shake it. "Do you mind giving us a minute to talk Ian?"

Or she would comment on it now.

"I'll get us another round." Ian walked away, beelining it to the bar. She watched him carefully, waiting to make sure he was out of hearing distance to look at Mira.

"I really have no interest in what you have to say about him." It came out as a hiss. She instantly felt bad, but she pushed that away. She didn't plan to take it back either. Mira was clear that her intentions were not pure. Mira didn't want what was best. She only wanted what was best *for her*.

"Nothing. I just . . . I don't like seeing you with some guy." Mira gave a dramatic sigh and a pout.

She's right. You belong with her.

Cin bit her lip as the second voice interrupted her thoughts. It was the first time in a while she had heard either voice. It made so many questions run through her mind.

Where had it come from?

Why was it back?

Was it back for good?

She wanted to rip her hair out. She peeked at Ian by the bar. Maybe it was time to let Ian know what was going on and see if he had some insight. Maybe she should trust. "You don't get to say that. You made your choice a long time ago."

"I can't keep watching you throw yourself at guys," she bemoaned. Cin tried not to roll her eyes. She was used to this, even expected it on some level, but with her new clarity, she realized how annoying it really was. Annoying and cruel.

Unnecessary. "You've said that before, and it's never changed anything. It doesn't need to change anything now."

Don't lie to yourself. You want it to change.

Mira leaned over, her body moving like spaghetti, and breathed out a heavy breath filled with alcohol. The smell made her jerk back—it reminded her of who she'd used to be. "It's always been us, Cin. It should only be us."

Something in her tingled as her heart started doing double time. She tried to take a few deep breaths to slow it down, but she'd been attracted to Mira for so long that she couldn't. Her fingers tingled as her emotions started to tip toward panic. Despite everything that was going on, she still cared about Mira. She was her best friend, her very beautiful, very loyal best friend, whom she had pined over for years.

Take her home with you.

Before she could say anything, Ian was back, handing out drinks. She took hers greedily and gulped the soda as if her life depended on it. She was going to need a lot of courage to get through tonight, and without that, there was nothing saving her. After two rounds—Mira and Ian getting drunker by the minute—Cin had managed to push back enough on her own emotions to ignore the beating of her heart or the tingling sensation of being literally stuck between two roads. Every time she brushed against an arm or a hand—on either side—she was sure that she might faint. But she didn't, and without the alcohol, she felt more and more confident that Ian was the right choice for her.

It was easier than expected as Mira threw on one of her dazzling smiles and chattered away about what classes the psychology department professors were planning for next semester. It was an easy topic, one without the threat to destroy her unstable sobriety, and they fell into easy conversation, littered with additional rounds. She was grateful every time Ian went to get drinks and returned with Diet Coke or club soda instead of something laced with gin.

She couldn't help the grateful smile she sent him each time it was handed to her as if she was celebrating with the group. It wasn't until she stood up to go to the bathroom, Mira clinging to her, that she realized Mira had gone way over her limit. Turning to Ian, she gave him an awkward smile. "Maybe it's time you take us home?"

Ian, who looked far more sober than she expected, looked up from the pile of empty glasses on the table. She could see the disappointment in his eyes, the slight wrinkle on his forehead, but it was easy to ignore once he was speaking. "I'll get you both back to your place. You can make sure she sleeps this off."

She mouthed, "Thank you," as he led them out of the bar and guided them through the dark night. They passed Antonio's, and the two of them shared a longing look over Mira's head. With Ian's help, she managed to get Mira up to her floor and lay across her couch.

"I'll check on you in the morning," Ian whispered into her hair, before giving her a quick hug and heading out of the studio.

It was the silence proceeding Ian's exit, pounding at her sober brain, that started to weave thoughts into Cin's head. The voice was gone, but the urge, the urge to explore what she'd always wanted to, wouldn't be ignored in the silence. She wanted to hit her head until it stopped —until it gave her the peace she wanted. Instead, she clenched her stomach as it started to twist with all the negative thoughts. She rolled to the side. "I'm sorry. I don't feel well."

She slid off the couch and jerkily ran to the bathroom with a hand on her throbbing head and an arm wrapped around her stomach. It was too much—the voices, her feelings she wrote off after Mira stormed out, and Ian standing still in front of her, his hand outstretched to help, the weight of all the secrets she was suddenly carrying alone. She slammed the door shut just before collapsing on the cool tile floor. She laid her heated face on the ground.

Run away. She won't save you.

Kiss her.

"No. Stop." She slammed her eyes shut and moaned.

She had been voice-free for too long; she should have known it would be back. She couldn't get away from it—proper management only held them back for so long.

A knock on the door forced her eyes open. "Cin, are you okay?"

Tell her how you feel. That you want Ian.

"I don't even know if he wants me," she whispered.

Don't be naive.

"I'm not lovable."

Don't lie to yourself.

Kiss her. Mira loves you.

"I'm fine," she called, loud enough so Mira could hear her. "I'll be out in a minute."

To tell you off.

To kiss you.

"You don't get to dictate how I run my life." Cin pulled herself off the floor by the edge of the sink and stared in the mirror. Her blue hair was limp and hanging something akin to the girl from *The Ring*. The huge, black-blue bags under her eyes were almost as horrifying as the hollowness of her skin. She looked like she had drunk three full bottles of gin, but she hadn't touched anything. Everything was spiraling out of control. What was happening?

It was like the voices were draining her energy. Sapping her dry of anything that was holding her together.

It doesn't matter. All that matters is dealing with Mira.

Kiss her.

"Stop it!" she screamed. Her voice cracked in time with the glass of the mirror. She studied the golden threads of humming magic ripping through the glass. The sound of shattered glass falling into the sink pinged like metal chimes. It fell into a pile and glittered in the muted streetlight streaming through the window. Golden lines weaved in front of her—magic she'd grown accustomed to but was still shocked by—and straight through the mirror shards.

"I'm coming in," Mira declared, before the door swung open, slamming against the wall and knocking down a candle nearby. Cin watched it land with a clank before rolling across the floor. She watched as Mira's sock-covered feet walked past it to put her hand on Cin's chin. She lifted her face, forcing her to meet her eyes. She searched the depths she thought she knew but could find no signs of empathy or concern. With narrowed eyes, she noted that she saw the clear signs of sobriety as she murmured, "What happened?"

Push her away.

Kiss her now.

Cin took a deep breath as the voices battered her. She'd grown weak with the ease of voices in her life. She was only so strong. She wasn't invincible. She was only able to take so much. As they studied each other, Mira's eyes began to glisten with love and concern while her mouth quirked just so. Cin knew it was fake, could see the way it played out on her face just so, but her heart wouldn't stop beating like the kick drum in a rock show. Her eyes flitted to Mira's mouth in time to see her biting her lip. It was so well orchestrated that Cin started second-guessing her original assessment.

She tried to rip through the fog in her brain.

A small part of her mind pinged. Mira's sudden lack of drunkenness, her steady frame standing in front of her posed just so, the way the voices spoke out of nowhere. Something wasn't right.

What's not right is you not kissing Mira.

Mira gently rubbed Cin's cheek in circles, her eyes locked on Cin's lips. She breathed weakly, fighting the sudden weakness in her knees and influx of thoughts from the uncomfortable voice in her head. She tried to step backward, but her body couldn't budge. Her mind screamed at her, warned her of trouble, but it was like she was in a trance.

"Are you okay?" Mira's voice was soft, pleading.

Do it.

Cin felt like her mind was a million miles away. The scene was playing out in front of her, she could feel the part of her that wanted Mira, but it was far away. She watched in horror—screaming in her own head—as she pressed her lips to Mira's and held her breath as she waited for some reaction. Mira's hand snaked through her hair and pulled Cin closer as she let out the breath she was holding. It came out as a gasp, and Mira giggled. Watching from away, above, it felt like nothing. All the magic she expected, she'd dreamed of for so long, drained away like dirty dishwater.

"Are you sure?" Mira asked, her voice husky.

Cin screamed no in her head, images of Ian filling her mind, as her head started to nod. Mira spun her around, backing her out of the bathroom with butterfly kisses spread across her face. It felt like a nightmare she couldn't get out of as she guided them onto her bed with a contented sigh.

She wanted to pull away—to run as far from this as possible. Instead, she rolled over, straddling Mira with a cheeky smile, before pressing herself onto her and smashing her lips down greedily. Mira met her with force, pulling roughly on the ends of her hair and eliciting a low growl. Mira flipped them over before pulling back to rip their shirts off—one after the other.

Mira's fingers trailed across Cin exposed midsection, sprouting goose bumps and a tingling sensation she'd never felt before. Something about the way her fingers slid across her skin or the sudden silence in her head, but her voice suddenly worked. She pulled herself out from under Mira with an irritated growl. It was mirrored by Link who had suddenly appeared on the bed. He stepped on Mira's chest and bared his teeth.

Mira rolled from under his claws. Angry red lines spread across her exposed chest. "I think you should leave." Cin pointed a shaky finger to the door. "You were supposed to be my best friend. Not someone else to take advantage of me."

"You came on to me," Mira sniped. She threw her shirt on over her head, wrapping her arms around her cuts.

The last thirty minutes replayed in her head. Had she? She didn't feel like she had been in control. Almost as if someone else was running her body. She put that on the back burner, she'd have to deal with whatever that meant at some point, and narrowed her eyes at Mira's sullen face. "Get. Out."

Link growled, nipping at Mira's heels as she stomped her way to the door. She looked over her shoulder, glaring at Cin. "You're going to regret this."

She slammed the door on her way out. The sound reverberated in her chest, building a void right where her heart was supposed to be.

Mira's words clanked around her head. Would she regret this?

Chapter Twenty-One

When her alarm went off the next day, her eyes were already open. It was like she was in a hypomanic state without the rest of the symptoms. She didn't have the need to drive around the block with all the windows down until her fingers were frozen. She didn't want to paint Link curled up sleeping at her feet bathed in light before giving up halfway out of frustration. There was no voice to tell her to sing at the top of her lungs while she cooked breakfast.

Instead, all she had were bad memories cycling. The moment she got the phone call about her mom. The way James was standing in her apartment waiting for her like a ghost from the past. Every moment of Mira last night before she pushed her away. Every time Mira had done something similar, had played with her head, only to leave her out in the cold—wondering, always wondering. Because that, she realized, was what really messed with her head. She was finally starting to feel something for someone other than Mira, and she knew it.

Mira had always been afraid to lose her but never willing to take the leap of faith Cin was. The whole situation was toxic, and she was getting out. Well, she had been trying to without realizing it. She had actually found someone who accepted her for her. She racked her mind for moments where she felt otherwise, but she couldn't. Ian was everything she needed.

But how would he feel when she blurted out the truth? As if reading her mind, her phone dinged. She rolled over to grab it from the nightstand.

"Do you want iced or hot coffee when I pop by?" Ian's message read.

Shit, she had forgotten he was coming to check on them. She quickly made up an excuse about Mira wanting diner food. He agreed with a stipulation for dinner later. She didn't respond. She knew he would worry, she hated that, but she just couldn't face him. How many times had she fucked up so badly someone stopped talking to her? She wasn't ready for Ian to give up on her like everyone else. She didn't think she could lose another person and make it through. She was only so strong.

She just couldn't lose him. Couldn't lose the way he laughed at her silly traits that most people hated. That Mira had hated.

When her phone rang, she almost didn't answer it. It was probably Mira apologizing or Ian asking if she was okay. But when she looked down, it was neither. Adam's name scrolled across the screen. She picked it up right before it could go to voicemail.

"Adam?" She couldn't contain the worry. Finals were over, she knew he had passed—checked with Floyd herself. "Is everything okay?"

He hiccuped into the phone before blowing his nose. "Can you come to the hospital?"

She wanted to ask if his dad was still with him, but it wasn't the time. Instead, she confirmed which hospital before telling him she'd be there in thirty minutes or fewer. With coffee and breakfast, she added to herself. Her problems didn't matter. Nothing mattered but Adam. Adam who needed her. She didn't know what was wrong, but everything is better with a cup of coffee and food in your belly. And a good laugh—like her mom used to tell her. A good laugh and family.

When she had her first depressive streak. She was barely sixteen and had come down from a particularly bad hypomanic streak. It felt like if she left her bed, she would dissolve in the air—turning into a puddle on the ground of her childhood bedroom. It had been two days, her mom bringing water and grilled cheeses every few hours to make sure she ate, before she finally sat down on the bed next to her.

Her mom's sturdy, steady body made her roll in the bed so she was lying with her face upturned to her mom's smiling face. "Hey, sleepy."

"What do you want?" It was a hiss, eyes narrowed, and she studied how neutral her mom's face had stayed. It was like she was a punching bag waiting to be hit.

"It looks like you haven't eaten. I brought a fresh sandwich."

"I'm not hungry." She felt bad, somewhere under the depression, but it didn't come through. Years later, she still felt bad for how rude she had been. It was uncalled for, especially with how much she was doing for Cin, but teenagers don't understand that until it's too late.

"Would you be hungrier if I fed you some mice?" She

lifted a fake mouse and shoved it into Cin's face. Giggles spilled out as she batted it away.

"Where did you get that?" She was still smiling back at her mom. It was the first real smile in a couple of days.

"It doesn't matter. You've laughed. You know what that means?"

And she did. It was a family tradition. A tradition that would serve Adam well today. No matter what was happening, a good laugh always helped.

By the time she had her hands full of sustenance and made it to the hospital, she heard pages in the hospital requesting doctors to the room number Adam had texted her. She rushed to sign the board, claiming to be a cousin of Adam's—they were only letting family up, but she hoped the frantic look in her eyes was enough for them to believe her—and hopping the fastest elevator.

When it dinged on the floor, Adam was leaning against the wall bent over with his arms wrapped around himself. She dropped her things on the floor quietly and threw her arms around him. He sagged into her arms. Her shoulder was quickly drenched in silent tears. He might not have been silent, she wasn't sure, but the sound of the doctors and nurses behind them covered most of the noise.

She wasn't sure how long they stood there, Adam barely able to stand and her finally being strong for someone else, but when a doctor—a pudgy older man—stood behind them, Adam wasn't crying anymore. "I think they want to speak to you," she whispered, giving him one final squeeze before walking a few paces away to give them space.

She did her best to still her shaking hands as she waited for them to finish talking. She wasn't sure if it was good or bad news, she didn't want to watch, and the doctor was so neutral as he waited for Adam to turn around. Eventually, she could hear the squeaking of Adam's sneakers approaching. His eyes were red-rimmed with heavy bags. She knew she mirrored his expression.

"They said he won't wake up again." And then he was back in her arms, full-out sobbing. She bit her lip to stop her own tears—he didn't need them right now—and guided him into the privacy of his dad's ICU room. With Adam sitting, she quickly gathered her stuff and handed him his lukewarm coffee.

"I didn't even get to tell him I loved him." He sniffled before sipping his coffee. "Thank you for coming. Thanks for bringing this." He waved at the brown bags of food. "How did you know?"

"I've had my days in the ICU. I remember the cafeteria food and how badly James and I would want fresh coffee or a bagel while we waited for my mom to wake up."

Adam nodded, but she knew he didn't understand. He had the look of someone who had never waited for a loved one to pull through an overdose. She was grateful for that. It wasn't something she would wish on anyone. It was painful in the worst way. Cin placed a soft hand on his shoulder. "I'm glad you called. You shouldn't be alone right now."

"She's right." Cin looked up to find Floyd, Megan, Sanjit, and Ian standing in the doorway. She smiled meekly at Adam.

"You called them?"

"We're your family, Adam—whether you want us or not—we're here for you." Cin swiped at her eyes as they started to prick. She wished she had this family when she had spent all those years struggling. She wished she had a lot of things that she tried to give to Adam, but she wasn't bitter. She was grateful she was able to ease the burden of someone she thought of as a brother. More brotherly than James—that was for sure.

Adam blew his nose and tried to smile at the group. "Thank you—you really didn't need to come."

Ian walked across the room and stepped between their chairs. He patted Adam's shoulder. "We didn't need to—we wanted to. Cin was right to let us know."

Ian wrapped an arm around her. She did her best not to jump away—afraid that a single touch would force her to spill secrets she wasn't ready to acknowledge. Especially in front of this group. And Adam. Poor, crushed Adam. Ian's arm, which normally felt just right over her shoulders, made her neck sweat and itch uncomfortably. She did her best to grin and bear it as the group laughed over stories of Adam's dad when he was growing up. By the time the sun set a few hours later, Adam was laughing with everyone.

When a nurse came in to send the others home, Cin leaned over to Adam, and whispered, "Want to get some sleep at my place?"

He gave her a grateful smile from where he was curled in a plastic, uncomfortable hospital chair, small and fragile. Her heart ached as she guided him through the building and into a silent cab. He didn't speak until they were bent over a glass of wine and some Chinese food. "Thank you for being the big sister I never had."

She laughed. "I'm far too nice to you to be a big sister. Maybe your really cool cousin."

"Cool? I don't think anyone would ever call you cool." He jabbed her with an elbow. It was so reminiscent of the nights Mira and James had tried to cheer her up after her mom's first hospital visit that her eyes burned a little.

"Maybe I'm not cool, but at least I bring coffee and poorly timed jokes." She stuck her tongue out at him before taking another sip of her water. She wanted wine, to share with Adam, but he didn't need that. He needed her on her game; he needed someone to steady him as he rocked. She bit her lip, building her confidence, before breaching the subject.

"What did the doctor say were your next steps?"

The words hung in the air between them, punctuated with the scratching of Adam's fork as he emptied his beef and broccoli. It wasn't until the bowl was empty, slid across the table into the pile of dirty dishes, that Adam leaned back, arms over his stomach, and looked at her. His eyes were steady but still red-rimmed from crying silently in the cab over. "They told me he wouldn't wake up and I should pull the plug."

She grabbed one of his hands and squeezed it. "Is that what you want?"

He sniffled. "I don't want him to be a vegetable. He doesn't want that. He made me promise. But I'm not ready to say goodbye."

"I read once that coma patients can hear you. Does he have a favorite book?"

"He always kept a battered copy of Grimm's Fairy Tales in the house. His dad used to read it to him." He hiccuped as his voice wavered and eyes shined. "And he used to read it to me."

She gave his hand another squeeze. "Why don't you read it to him, remind yourself of the good times, and tell him you love him? Then decide your next steps after you've had a chance to bring the best memories you have up."

His shoulders heaved as he breathed out. "I wasn't sure what I was going to do—after he passed, I mean. I didn't think I had any family left; it was just us. I can't afford our place alone."

"Trust me, you don't need to explain. All I had was my mom. If you guys didn't show up . . ." She shivered. "Well, you saw me before." She looked up at him, eyes unfocused and shoulders scrunched into themselves, and frowned. "Why don't you get some sleep. I'm sure last night was a lot."

She stood up, cleaning off the table before making the couch up. With sheets and a blanket on it, she got Adam a glass of water. "I'm going to read in bed if you need me. Get some sleep and we'll deal with tomorrow when it comes."

He didn't respond, just smiled at her from his spot on the couch, and she felt her chest squeeze.

∽

In the morning, Adam got back into his clothing from the night before and slipped out the door before the sun had fully risen. When he woke up—his soft snoring suddenly stopping—she was still awake, her eyes bloodshot from lack of sleep and her mind still racing with thoughts of Mira, Ian, and, of course, Adam and his dad.

She listened to his sniffling and shuffling but didn't speak up. He didn't want to talk to her, not while he was still forgetting the nightmares he probably had. The nightmares she had, waiting for her mom, still plagued her. When the door clicked shut softly, she listened to

Link's soft padding across the floor until he pounced on her leg with a grumble. She sat up and gave him a scratch under his jaw. "What am I supposed to do now?"

He didn't have any answers. What she wouldn't give to have answers. She was left alone with her own wandering thoughts. She still hadn't heard back from James about her mom, hadn't seen any signs that she was trying to get in touch. Then there was Mira. She shivered. What was she going to do about Mira?

With all the self-growth and rebuilding, there were some things that didn't just disappear. The ability to believe your emotions was one of those things. She knew this, she spoke about this with her doctors. Her first therapist, an older woman her mom went to—used to go to—had sat her down at the mature age of seventeen, and said, "Cin, you're going to have to learn that all the emotions you feel, they are extreme versions of what you really think. You can't trust them."

The words had destroyed her self-confidence for years until she started working with Dr. Berstein. He had changed everything for her, had lifted her up. He promised, "One day you're going to see that you know the difference. What's up there isn't always right, but that doesn't mean it's never right. You're allowed feelings, Cin."

His words, and years of therapy, had taught her when to pull out her feelings from the disorders'. She'd gotten so good at it that it didn't require weeks of discussion, she didn't require discussion at all, and he transferred her to Dr. Cohen for medication management only. But it was times like these, when the emotions were so heavily muddled—so tied to all parts of her—that she couldn't see where the disorder stopped and she began. Maybe that's where she always sat, in the middle of two warring sides. The barrier between oil and water, with a little shaking it looks and feels mixed, but something was always off.

Link's weighty paws landed on her chest, pulling her from her spiraling thoughts. She looked up at his big, loving eyes. "Well, Linky, I think it's time for a drink."

She didn't look at the clock, didn't pause to take her pills, before plodding into the kitchen to grab a bottle of gin from her backup stash. It was the second to last bottle in the house, and she would need it to deal with the emotions throwing spears at each other in her head. She knew it was wrong, a mistake, but it burned just right.

Chapter Twenty-Two

Drunk. That's all she could feel, all she could remember. The burn of gin and the swirl of bad memories. It wrecked her psyche, driving her further and further from reality. She tried to pull herself out, Link tried to pull her out, but every time the fog cleared . . .

Mira replayed in her head.

James lied to her. Over and over again.

But that wasn't the worst.

The worst would be Adam's disappointment when she couldn't sober up to be there when he called.

Ian walking away when she told him about Mira—about everything.

Reality. Dreams. Nightmares. They blended in her mind, impossible to distinguish between.

She spent two days racked with guilt waiting for Adam to call, for James to call. Despite her best efforts, for Ian or Mira to call. For anyone to call and pull her out of the spiral she was in. But her phone was silent. It wasn't until she finished most of the gin in her bottle and realized she needed to step out into the world around her that she picked it up from the floor next to the bed. The phone was dead. She plugged it in and in her foggy state surveyed the studio around her. Empty Chinese food containers and greasy bags from the bagel shop next door littered the floor around the couch. The couch, which had gained a divot in the center of the cushion from her constant position there.

When her phone finally turned on, it sounded like a symphony as messages and voicemails pinged. She watched each message come in—mostly from Ian—until Adam's distressed message appeared like a hammer. It slammed through her fog.

"I'm ready. Can you be here?"

She read it a few times, committing to memory that someone needed her. She expected it—wasn't surprised at the request—but she couldn't process it. The empty beer bottle she had found in a cabinet was like a stale, expired stowaway, and the gin bottle mocked her as she tried to stand. She swayed, almost falling back to the bed, before she could finally drag herself to the shower. She turned it on cold, hoping to pull herself out of her stupor, and cleaned her body the best she could without putting in much effort—it was more like jumping into a cold pool. When she stepped out and looked in the mirror, her eyes were clearer than she expected.

She pulled herself together as quickly as possible before letting Adam know she was on her way. When she slipped outside, cold air slipping under her jacket and making her shiver, she squinted at the sun she hadn't seen in days. She covered her eyes before hailing a cab.

She wanted to let the rest of the group know, let everyone support Adam as they had a few days ago, but something about the message made it feel like it was just for her. That he wanted her there and no one else. She didn't even stop at the coffee shop situated inside the entrance of the hospital, didn't wait for the elevator crowded with nurses and visitors, and rushed up the stairs. Her legs burned from sudden use as she sprinted. She wasn't sure if she was rushing to get to Adam or running away from her own problems, but when she finally pushed open the large, mechanical doors to the critical wing, she was out of breath as her eyes scanned for Adam.

She found him crouched, hunched over himself, against the wall outside his dad's room. He was a statue. Cramped in the same spot she found him days before. She slid down the wall and pulled her legs into her arms. "Adam."

He sniffled.

"I want you to do me a favor. Can you do that?" She leaned into him and prodded him with an elbow toward him.

"What?" His voice was throaty, raw, and cracked as he looked up at her with bloodshot eyes.

"Tell me about your favorite happy memory with your dad."

He tapped the hard tiled floor with a shoe before he knocked his knees together. He opened and closed his mouth a few times, clearing his throat before giving her a sideways glance. "When my mom left, I was really lost. She used to do these Oreo nights every time a full moon happened. On the first full moon after, I was a blubbering mess. I had built this fort, had been living in it since I realized she was gone, and I had fallen asleep on my piles of pillows a sniveling, snotty mess.

"My dad woke me up—this big grin on his face. He dragged me out to our little patio and pointed at the moon. But I was so distracted by the giant plate of Oreos with milk." He sniffled out a laugh, wiping his sleeve against his nose. "It was the first time I smiled since she had left. We ended up spending the whole night laughing and eating what seemed like hundreds of Oreos."

Cin placed a soft hand on Adam's and squeezed it. "I want you to remember that every time you miss him."

"I don't want him to be gone." Adam choked up, putting his forehead against hers.

They stayed there, listening to her breathing and his soft sobs, until Adam started to gain control of himself. She pulled back, grabbing his clammy hand, and studied the dark bags under his eyes. "When I was younger, a family friend sat me down after I lost my grandfather. They pointed at the grave where they had just buried him and whispered something I've carried with me since then." She locked eyes with Adam. "She told me that he wasn't there—wasn't in the ground—but watching over me. Whenever I needed him, I could just speak to him—in my head, out loud, whatever made me feel like he could hear me.

"Some days, less often now, I talk to him." She gave him a weak smile. "He's proud of me some of the time, but I'm pretty sure most of the time he's tired of my shit."

He cleared his throat. "I really like that."

"It'll be okay. I know it's not now, and honestly, it'll never not hurt, but you'll learn to manage that pain."

Adam leaned his head over to her shoulder and rubbed his face on her shirt. She tried not to be grossed out, imagining the tears soaking her shirt, but she couldn't help the frown on her face as she rubbed his arm. "I thought I was ready, but I haven't even made it in there yet."

"Why don't we do it together?"

He nodded before clamoring up the wall. She followed him up, linking her arm in his, and guided him into the room. A plain curtain covered most of the bed, leaving just two pale feet sticking up through the blanket. She edged them around the other side of the bed, ignoring the machines he was plugged into, and brought him to his dad.

She put his hand on his dad's frail, papery one before slipping a step away. "Say goodbye to him. Say everything you need to—everything you want to make sure he knows. Then we can talk to the doctors together."

He looked at her, mouthing a thank you, before kissing his dad's hand.

"I'll go grab us coffees so you can have some space." She watched his shoulders drop gratefully before slipping out the door. She took the stairs slowly, meandering in an effort to give Adam the time he needed, and ordered two coffees when she made it to the coffee stand on the main floor. She leaned against the wall, waiting for her coffee and watching hospital staff march by, when someone called her name.

She looked up, blinking a few times, before it registered that it was Ian, not the barista. She looked over his frazzled appearance, his chest heaving as he gasped for air, and smiled weakly. "What are you doing here, Ian?"

"Besides getting irritated that you didn't tell me today was *the* day?" He narrowed his eyes at her. She stood there, mouth slightly agape, studying this version of Ian she'd never seen before. This hurt, angry man she barely recognized. His annoyance rolled into her like a tractor-trailer.

"How did you know there was one?" She pinched her lips as his shoulders tensed.

He shot her a pointed look. "I'm not stupid, Cin. I heard them whispering last time."

Before she could respond, her order was called. She scurried to grab the coffees, hoping to give her face a few seconds to cool down, to give her mind a few seconds to cool down, before squaring her shoulders and facing Ian. "Adam asked me to come alone. I wasn't going to overstep."

The lie slipped out before she could stop it. His anger was blurring with Mira's. She fell into the trap of how she responded to her, but he wasn't her.

"That doesn't mean the rest of us don't want to support him. We could have sent flowers, food, something—anything." Ian took a deep breath, his frustration ebbing away, and took the coffees from her hands. Shaking his head, he guided them to the elevators.

"If you really want to help, he's worried about not having a place to live."

Ian clicked his tongue. "I'll keep that in mind."

As she pressed the button, he added, "I had texted him, just to check in, and I knew. He didn't sound right. I couldn't let him do this alone." He shot her a sideways look before stepping onto the elevator. "I should have known he would call you. I would have done the same thing."

"I think he—" She stopped herself, slowly working her way back through his words. "What do you mean you would have done the same thing?"

"I don't know. It's just that you're so easy to talk to."

He shook his head ruefully. The tension, tight and harsh between them, cracked apart and slid away. "Despite your behavior that first week, you're like an open book. You have no secrets to hide, and you spill your heart and soul out to people. It's hard not to open up back."

Except you still haven't told him about Mira. Or James.

She bit her lip, chewing over his words and the voice's very accurate interjection. She was speechless and grateful when the bell for the elevator dinged to let them off. She beelined for Adam who was talking to a nurse outside his dad's room. She linked their arms and gave him a squeeze.

"I'll go collect the doctors, and we'll meet you in the room," the nurse said, before leaving her alone with a disgruntled Adam and Ian, who handed over Adam's coffee.

"Did you call him?" Adam whispered in her ear. She shook her head.

"I ran into Ian in the lobby. He's worried about you. He said he wanted to come check up on you."

Adam drew his mouth into a straight line. "I didn't want to make this a whole big thing." He ran a hand through his matted hair, getting caught at the ends. "But I'm glad you're here. I should have called you too."

Like the sound of silence from inside a lab first thing in the morning—the loud whooshing of the instruments, the eerie ringing that came with the emptiness of the fume hoods—was palpable in the air. The critical unit had this bated-breath feel that couldn't be broken by anything but the incessant ringing of a coded patient.

Ian wrapped an arm around Adam's shoulders. He slumped, releasing his worries into the two of them. They were weighed down with the joined burden as they shuffled into the cold, barren ICU room.

～

When Adam stopped crying, instead sniffling into his sleeve as he cleared the mucus from his nose, he asked Cin to take him home. He didn't want to go home to an empty house. He probably didn't want to float through all the memories. She couldn't blame him; she had stopped visiting her mom's place as soon as James moved in to avoid all the heartache that lived there.

Ian offered his house, large enough for all three of them to stay, and she gave in when Adam looked at her with pleading eyes. She couldn't deny him any comforts, no matter how uncomfortable something might be for her. They stopped for pizza, her running in to say hi to Antonio and grabbing two large pies, before spreading themselves across Ian's living room.

"Personally," Ian said, walking in from the kitchen with waters, "if we're going to watch a movie, I think a romantic comedy will be less depressing."

She chuckled. "You, my friend, have never cried at the point where they break up before the end of the movie. I vote we watch something sci-fi." She pointed at the series of space movies she had pulled up on the TV. "Blood, guts, gore. Nothing better. Nothing to pull at your heart."

"What about a thriller? I just picked up a copy of the newest Jorden Peele." He walked to the media stand and pulled out a DVD.

Adam cleared his throat. "I'm just wondering—if someone could tell me—do I get a say in this choice?"

Ian had the decency to look ashamed, but she just smirked as Adam chuckled. It was weak, barely audible, but undeniable. "That really depends on your taste in movies. If its anything like your taste in chemistry teachers, you might have a point."

Adam snorted. "You are *so* full of yourself."

"I made you laugh. If there is one rule in my house, it's that once you laugh, you're not allowed to be sad anymore."

"We're in my house," Ian commented, waving his arm around.

She shot him a look. "My rules still apply." She waved her arm at the TV. "Well, Adam. What'll it be?"

He studied them, flipping his eyes between the two of them, and smiled. "Thank you, guys. Really. I'm not sure I would have been okay without you." He hugged each of them, stealing the remote out of her hand as he did, and got situated back on the couch. "You both are wrong, by the way. I pick . . ."

She watched him flip through movies until he landed on something with zombies. She shrugged, grabbed another slice of pizza, and settled in for Adam's pick. Zombies beat a broken heart. Maybe even a broken home.

∼

During her movie pick, the third one of the night, Adam and Ian fell asleep. Adam was curled up on the couch with his cat perched on the armrest next to him. Ian was sprawled across the floor. Milo—Ian's husky—had his head propped up on Ian's stomach and was bobbing in time with his breath. She smiled at the boys before clicking the TV off, covering each of them with a throw blanket, and slipped out the front door with Link.

By the time she opened her the door to her apartment, the weight of the day, of the week, of the month, had mounted onto her shoulders. She had been carrying the world on her back for too long. Her mother was still missing. She couldn't get a hold of James. There was no way she could confide in Mira. No way to deal with Mira. She didn't know how to explain herself—her new voice and her constant state of emotional disarray that Mira had spiraled her into—to Ian in a way that didn't make her sound like a total disaster. And she needed to be strong for Adam so he didn't fall down the rabbit hole she fell down every time her mom lost control. It was far worse for him, and she wasn't willing to give up on him.

She screamed, letting her voice get raw and ragged, before dropping to her bed. Link's claws clicked on the floor as he made his way across the apartment to curl up by her side. She listened to his silent breathing, tried to let it calm her, before ripping herself from her bed and crawling to the kitchen. She grabbed the bottle off her dining room table. There was still some left, swishing around the bottle. She ripped the lid off and leaned against the cupboards as she gulped down a few shots of gin.

It landed in her stomach like fire. Instead of the warm burn she got from magic, the fire burned so hot she clutched her stomach. She whined, a low-pitch noise escaping from her slightly parted lips, and Link ran to her side. She slid a rough hand through his silky fur, trying to pull herself back together, but it was useless. She could feel herself spiraling as if she wasn't attached to her body anymore.

CHAPTER TWENTY-TWO

Below her lay the pale, matted version of herself. She tried to swallow down the little bit left of the bottle but only got a small dribble of gin, then roughly wiped her mouth with the back of her hand. The burn was easier this time—the alcohol started to fog her mind, loosening her burden. It was all she could think about. The more she drank, the easier the world seemed.

It was a vicious cycle, but it was hers. It was all she thought she had.

Chapter Twenty-Three

When Adam had called to tell her that he needed help with the wake, she was so fuzzy she thought he asked if she was awake. It took three more tries until the words clicked, and she offered to get a cab to his house, to roam the empty hallways with him. But when the cab pulled up, she was shaking. Whether it was from the alcohol withdrawal or her nerves of trying to hide her buzzed state, she wasn't sure.

Cin took a deep breath, letting the cold December air burn her lungs and clear her head, before she knocked. And knocked. And knocked. After ten minutes, she tried the knob. It was unlocked. Easing the door open, she was temporarily disoriented by the brightness of the lighting in their living room and the white accents. When she gained her bearings, she found Adam curled up on the floor next to a brown couch.

Trying not to startle him, she slipped her shoes off and sat next to him.

Adam cleared his throat, rubbed at his red-rimmed eyes, and handed her a glossy photo. It was a younger Adam riding his dad's shoulders through a pumpkin patch. Both of them wore matching flannel and grins. The rosy-colored man in the photo looked almost nothing like the man they had said goodbye to in the hospital. "I don't know how to be without him."

"He's still here with you. His soul watching over you."

Adam eyed her. "You sound like a Hallmark movie."

She rolled her eyes. "There's a reason people like those so much." She surveyed the empty living room. "You didn't invite anyone else?"

"I don't have any other family."

"I texted the coven to bring over comfort foods and to shuffle in and out for the next week." She gave him a weak smile. Whatever her own struggles were, she wouldn't leave Adam to do this alone. She wouldn't abandon him in the multitude of ways that others had abandoned her.

He leaned his head on her shoulder. "It's funny. You struggle so much to manage your life, but you always know what I need. You're the best surrogate big sister anyone could ask for."

She didn't say anything, just turned to stare at the candles burning on the table. After a few minutes, she got up and closed all the curtains, padding around silently as Adam mourned. It was a small place but filled with light and love. Pictures of Adam and his dad adorned every surface, all of them smiling back at her with a joy she wanted in her own home. But now, with the strong whiff of despair and mourning, the house had darkened shadows.

She stopped when she found the kitchen. Adam didn't

have much food, she was glad she asked the coven to bring more, but she found enough to make him chicken noodle soup. She was stirring the warm broth when he joined her.

"You really do know just enough to be dangerous."

She searched the cabinet for a bowl and poured him some. "Here. Eat something."

Adam took a seat at the table and slurped the soup. "This is fantastic. Why don't you cook more often?"

"Because I'm an unbalanced mess. One day I'll cook for a living—when I've paid off my loans and can get the echoing memory of being told that being a chef wasn't a career out of my head." She sighed. "I'm sorry, I shouldn't be complaining."

Adam opened his mouth to speak as a knock sounded on the door. He moved to get up, but she waved at him. "I'll get it. Just keep eating."

He sighed dramatically but didn't stop her as she wound through the house to open the door. Standing on the front steps, her arms holding a brown paper bag of supplies, was Georgia. Of all the people to show up, Cin did not expect Georgia. Georgia who didn't like anyone in the coven, who only showed up for meetings when she had to, who ignored everyone who she wasn't being shitty to. She didn't smile when Cin met her eyes, just gestured to the house.

"Can I come in?" she asked, her voice wavering slightly. Cin nodded before taking an awkward step backward to keep the door open for her. "Where's the kitchen? I brought stuff to make cookies."

"This way." She latched the dead bolt before leading her into the kitchen where Adam had finished his soup.

"Georgia," he said cautiously as he leaned against the sink. "I didn't expect you to come."

She bowed her head. "I should have come to the hospital. I'm sorry." She placed the bag on the counter and started unpacking ingredients. Adam shot Cin a look, but she just shrugged. She didn't know what to think about her being there either. Georgia never asked for help, stiffly mixing the batter and placing the filled sheet into the oven. Once the timer was set, she sat down at the table and clasped her hands together.

When the house filled with the heavenly scent of chocolate chip cookies, she spoke again. "I know I've been really difficult lately." She looked up at Cin. "I've never even properly welcomed you to the coven."

"It's fine," she said. It spit out of her on instinct. It wasn't fine, but it wasn't the time for that discussion.

"It's not, but I appreciate the sentiment." She looked between the two of them and dropped her shoulders. "I'm going to do better."

"Well, cookies are definitely a good place to start," Adam said, chuckling. "Where'd you learn the recipe?"

Georgia gave him a grateful grin before launching into a story about her mom showing her how to bake as a kid. Cin nodded along but tuned out as they discussed the different childhood things they carried with them into adulthood.

When the rest of the coven started to show up, Adam and Georgia were bent over a plate of cookies giggling about something she hadn't been paying attention to. No one commented on the sudden niceness of Georgia until Ian slid next to where she leaned against the fridge.

His nose brushed her ear as he whispered, "What's up with Georgia? Did she hit her head?"

She shrugged, eyeing the pair who still seemed to be in their own world. "I don't know, but whatever changed has been for the best. This is the happiest I've seen him all semester."

Cin turned her head as something flashed past the window. She caught a glimpse of what looked like Mira staring her down. But when she blinked, whatever she thought she saw wasn't out there anymore.

∼

It didn't take long for them to plan a dinner in place of a wake. One that the coven chipped in to cover for Adam. It had been bittersweet but filled with good memories of the man that Adam had lost. Georgia had offered Adam a ride home against Cin's wishes. It left her alone in the car with Ian, and she was not ready for that.

But there she sat, arms crossed, in Ian's car. He flipped his blinker and shot her a look before turning onto the highway. "Are you sure you're okay?"

She bit her lip. "I'm fine. Just a lot to process." It wasn't an outright lie. "I just need some time to process."

Just tell him.

Ian patted her hand. "I'll be here when you're ready."

He didn't bring it up again, flipping on the local classic rock station and letting it fill the silence. Her heart beat in time with the music, reminding her of how little she deserved someone as good as him. She opened her mouth a few times to talk, but as Ian pulled in front of her building, she didn't have the courage. She gave him a hug goodbye and promised to call him soon.

"Stay safe, Cin," he said, waiting for her to get into the building before pulling back onto the road and slipping away. She bit her lip, making her way upstairs, and poured herself a drink before she breathed out.

"I'm the fucking worst." She took another swig of gin before collapsing into a heap on her bed with Link.

Chapter Twenty-Four

Cin turned on the shower and stepped under the scalding water. Her skin reddened, the old scars starting to etch like red pen lines on a notepad across her arms. They were reminders of how far she had come from her childhood, leftover mistakes from a difficult time, but tonight they were laughing at her. She hadn't gotten anywhere. She was just as unstable as she was when she was sixteen. She wanted to be stable so badly. If only it was that easy.

You'll always be crazy.

The voice was right. How could she have ever believed she had gotten anywhere? She finally thought she had her life together. Proper medication, no more self-harm, the belief that she had a place in the world—she even gave up alcohol—but it was all disappearing. It was slipping through her fingers as smoothly as downing a well-made gin and tonic was to drink. Cin crouched, letting the water run down her back, and reveled in the burning sensation as she worked to shut off the voices in her head. She thought she was done with them, but as she lifted her head and let the water wash over her face, they started battering her.

You can't wash it away, Cin.

"Stop it!" Cin screamed into the muffling water. She dropped herself against the cold porcelain and let her face press into it so her back was pelted with water. She focused on the cool surface, hoping to numb the thoughts inside. The longer she sat, the cooler the water got. Until it was freezing, sapping all the warmth from her bones, and she had to force herself off the bottom of the tub and out of the bath. With a soft towel wrapped around her and the water turned off, Cin lay down on the tile floor.

That's right, give up. Give in.

How did she let it get like this? She was better than this. This person lying on the cold, hard bathroom floor bemoaning her life and the demons inside of her. She had climbed the mountain—she had won the battles. She was Cinzia freaking Clark, a slightly unstable but completely badass chemist and *witch*. She was capable of more than just giving in to the monsters she was living with. She had conquered her limitations and graduated with her masters in one of the hardest sciences all while juggling her mother and her own illness. She was more than this— she had proven that, right?

You'll never be more than this.

"Shut up! You don't own me." She pulled herself off the floor and dragged her body to the sink to stare at her reflection. With her blue stringy hair hanging off her head like a dirty mop, her usual blueish black bags, and the dead look in her eyes, she scared even herself. She couldn't keep doing this, falling apart every time some-

CHAPTER TWENTY-FOUR

thing crazy in her life happened. She couldn't let someone else's bad behavior drag her down. She couldn't let Mira control her anymore. She was stronger than that. She needed to believe in herself the way Ian believed in her. She was capable of that. Right?

Cin lifted her hands in front of her, watching carefully for the golden strings to weave together. She repeated the same pulling and threading she had done to make the ball of light with Ian the first time. He had gotten her to weave light out of nothing. When nothing happened, Cin smashed her palm onto the counter. This was what she got for drinking so much. She knew she shouldn't have picked up that bottle.

You're not special.

"You don't know that." Maybe she just needed to sober up. Didn't he say something about that? About magic needed proper medication and a clear head to work, to funnel through her. When had she last taken her pills? Maybe she hadn't taken her medication this morning. Cin blew out a long breath and walked to her nightstand to pick up the orange bottle. It was new, recently refilled, and looked untouched. When did she get this?

Everything felt like it was blending together. She hadn't been this out of sorts since her first episode when she was fifteen. Her mother had forced medication on her as soon as she realized Cin was "blessed" with the family condition. She didn't feel blessed today, especially not when she couldn't manage to function on her own. She should have listened to her mother. She should have listened to Link. They hadn't liked Mira from the beginning. That should have been her first sign.

You aren't special like your family.

"SHUT UP!" Cin ripped the lid off, cracked the plastic, and took two small tablets out. She couldn't listen to this voice anymore. She swallowed them with the last bit of gin on her counter and dropped onto her bed, soaking the sheets. She grabbed the sheets and used them to pull herself into a sitting position before rubbing her temples. She needed to get a grip or at least something real inside her belly to help clear her head. What was the point of all the work she'd done to get in control if she was just going to give it all up?

She rolled off the bed, stumbled to the kitchen, and looked around her fridge for a water bottle. Or food. Anything. All the shelves were empty except a few rotten, open takeout containers she forgot about.

When did she get groceries last?

How long had she been like this?

When was the last time she had water?

Was Adam okay? Had she checked on him?

How did she let herself slip like this?

She needed something stable to hold on to—needed someone stable to hold on to. She reached for her phone before walking over to the kitchen to pour herself a glass of water. She flipped through her contacts as she drank.

Mira? No, Mira had ruined more than enough in her life. There was no going back from that. Her last words still slithered in her belly like a vicious snake.

Her mom? If only. What she wouldn't give to have her mom home and safe again. She still couldn't believe that the trail had gone cold.

Her brother? No. He had told her he would reach out when he had another lead. That was their only connection now, and she wasn't going to change that. It wasn't like he had responded to any of her messages since he left for Chicago.

Cin shook her head as she landed on the last contact. His name scrolled across the screen as the phone rang. It rang and rang. She wanted to scream. But when she was ready to hang up, his voice came through loud and clear.

"Cin? Are you okay?"

"Not really." There was a rustle.

"How can I help?" His voice was earnest, warm. The way it had been when he explained to her who she really was, when he confirmed everything her mother had told her for years. The way it had been when he supported her through all her struggles—teaching her magic, believing in her to pull together class plans, helping her stay sober. It warmed her chest as butterflies fluttered in her stomach. How had she ever thought Mira was good for her when Ian was so right?

"Cin?"

"Come to my place." She looked down at her towel-clad body and sighed. "One hour and bring food, please." She didn't give him a chance to respond. She didn't need his answer to know he would show up, and if he didn't . . . if he didn't, then she would need to rethink her plans. She would need to figure it out alone.

She grabbed jeans and a sweater, but when she went to get dressed, she realized that she had never really showered—she had just stood in the hot water and soaked herself. In fact, she couldn't remember the last time she actually cleaned herself. She sniffed herself and tried not to gag before turning on the shower and taking the coldest shower of her life.

Clean and dressed, she tied her hair into two pigtail braids, running her hand over them affectionately, and swiped on some mascara. Peeking at herself in the mirror, she felt like she was staring at a shell of herself. A shell she wasn't willing to accept any more. A shell that was the direct result of Mira's incredulous behavior.

"I am no longer willing to let you have the power here," she said. Mira wasn't there to respond. The voice didn't respond either, finally subdued by the medication starting to kick in. At least it hadn't been long enough for a full withdrawal. She smiled triumphantly at herself. "You are not in charge. Not now, not ever again."

Cin spun on her heel. Walking into the living space, she surveyed the damage. Trash and empty glasses littered the whole place. She picked everything up, wiping at day-old stains from the gin. New rings etched into the table. She grumbled before setting out to dust. She was done letting the demons win. She wasn't weak anymore.

By the time Ian showed up, cooking supplies in a reusable tote, Cin had lost the momentum and power she willed upon herself before cleaning the apartment. Ian pushed past her, eyes scanning the studio, crinkling as he noted the sudden cleanliness, before dropping the bag on her counter.

He opened a few cabinets, before calling over his shoulder, "Where are the pans? I need something deep."

He clicked at the oven, it pinging as he hit start. She hadn't moved, hand still holding the door and eyes wide. Ian pivoted, focusing his warm, smiling face on her, and tilted his head. "Is everything okay?" His forehead puckered. "I know you're upset, but I thought we'd eat first, get some food in your belly."

Her mouth agape, she shrugged. "Yeah, let's get to it."

He waved her over. "Come, cook with me. We have time to talk about whatever you're struggling with. Right now, give your mind some time to think about a recipe. Something routine and simple."

"What are you making?" She pulled a dish out from below the oven. "Is this good?"

"It's my lita's arroz con gradules and pork chops." He looked at a bone-in pork chops he pulled out of the bag. "Do you eat pork?"

She nodded. "How can I help?"

"Here." He handed her some tomatoes and onions. "Cut these up."

She pulled out a cutting board and a knife. She chopped rhythmically, Ian frying the pork chops next to her. They cooked in silence except for the few commands Ian issued. By the time the food was ready, smelling like heaven and making her mouth water, they had gone a full forty-five minutes working together in silence. Her heart wasn't racing; her mind wasn't trying to feed her lies. They were silent, enjoying the moment with her.

She helped him plate the food, picking at pieces of rice and sneaking them into her mouth, before bringing them to the table with glasses of water.

"Eat a little first, please. We can talk as soon as I know you've eaten something." He pleaded with his eyes.

"It smells delicious." She forked a spoonful of rice and pigeon peas, as Ian had explained when he pulled the can out, and moaned. "And it tastes delicious. Jeez, I owe your lita flowers or something. I didn't know you could cook like this."

"My lita used to teach me every weekend." He smiled, giving her hand a squeeze, before starting in on his own food.

She took a few more bites, cut off a piece of the salty

pork chop, and slowly chewed it, before clearing her throat. "Something happened."

Ian put his fork down, focusing on her. She fidgeted under his gaze. "Did something happen to your mom? Brother? Is Mira okay? Is Adam okay?"

She sucked her teeth and shook her head. "After you left us last week, something weird happened." And then she spilled her guts. She told him everything that happened, including the ominous way Mira left her and the second voice that popped up. She admitted to relapsing, her utter collapse under the weight of Mira's behavior, and how she hadn't checked on Adam. That she was completely useless, a waste of space. When she finished, out of breath and fingers twitching, Ian was watching her calmly. "What?"

He sucked on his lip for a second, his eyes giving nothing away, before taking a sip of water. He calmly placed the water on the table as her heart raced. She tapped her fingers on the table nervously. Then their eyes locked, and she felt like she could breathe. "Do you remember your lessons on wraiths?"

"Sure. What does that have to do with this?"

"I think—and I could be wrong—but it's very likely that you are being tracked by a wraith. Especially with the behavior from Mira and Link." He ran a hand through his hair. "It's likely that the wraith is possessing Mira and the blonde student. I'm not surprised—I looked into her record, this Elizabeth Marrow—she switched to psychology this semester. I bet she spent a lot of time in the office with Mira."

"Do you remember the first night we met?" She gave him a second to respond—of course he did—before continuing. "I think I saw them both in the bar that night.

Elizabeth Marrow took your spot at the bar when you bought my drink. I should have recognized her then, but I already had a few." She quirked her lips, a smile and frown fighting each other. "Do you think this is linked with my mom?"

"Has anything else weird happened?"

"No." The word came out slowly and unsure. Was there anything else she was missing? She didn't think so. She felt like she had covered it all despite the unease in her brain.

"Something weird is going on, but I'm not sure. I can't place my finger on it yet. Maybe you shouldn't be alone right now."

She poked at her food a few times. "I wish I could go stay at my mom's. Make popcorn and watch a rom-com."

"Why don't I stick around? I can sleep on the couch—I won't impose on your space—but that way you aren't alone." He used his fork to move a few errant peas around his mostly empty plate.

When he looked up, she rubbed a hand over her mouth. "Would it be easier to go to your place? You have a guest room. I don't want to make you sleep on the couch."

"Why don't we invite Adam? He's just been moping at home since it's winter break. I'm sure he could use some company."

Guilt washed over her. She should have checked on Adam before unburdening herself. "I'll call him. Can you put the dishes in the sink?"

Ian stood up, grabbing the plates, and walking into the kitchen. She listened to the banging, the sound of water running, as he started dishes. How did she explain to Adam she needed him after she had failed him so much?

He was smiling when he answered, she could tell. She spilled out everything, talking to him was just as easy as it was for Ian, before inviting him to meet them at Ian's.

"You'll be glad you invited me," he whispered, hanging up on her.

She grinned at Ian before throwing some clothing into her backpack. Ian drove them across town in record time, pulling up at the same time as Adam's cab. Before Adam could get out, Ian opened the passenger door. They stayed there, locked in discussion, before he handed the driver a bill, and they both jogged up to the front door where she was waiting with her bag.

Inside, Adam pulled out a bag of gummy worms and handed it to her. "Eat until you puke or feel better. Preferably feel better."

"No. If anyone is puking, it'll be me." He took the bag out of her hands. Ripping it open, he shoved a few worms in mouth. Grime covered the remote as he clicked on a comedy.

She grinned at them. What a family she had.

Chapter Twenty-Five

She spent three days wrapped up in a blanket on Ian's couch. It was comforting, being surrounded by this family of people she welcomed, instead of exhausting. Exhausting like the way spending time with the James who came back or the Mira who showed her true colors was. It was like being with her mom, back before the facility. Before she disappeared.

Mira had called every few hours. Cin asked the boys to read through voicemail transcripts so she didn't have to. Her heart was shredded, pieced together with duct tape and the kindness of Adam and Ian. Mira—her loving, sweet best friend—held a special spot in her heart. It was a place she had made especially for her, filled with late-night ice cream and the way she wrinkled her nose when she didn't want to tell Cin she was being ridiculous.

Just thinking about her wild red hair and deep, caring eyes made Cin's heartbeat speed up and a tingle run through her. She had been building the Mira shrine for a better part of ten years, and Mira knew it. She had never been interested, had blown her off when she explained her feelings. She had always told her it wasn't the right time, wasn't the right place.

She could shake off the devastation—heavy bags under her eyes as she lay awake replaying every moment. Reliving every single touch, every breath they shared together. She had been so wrong. How had she fallen for it?

"Here," Ian said, handing her a plastic cup filled with coffee. She smiled up at him. "Don't beat yourself up too much. A lot of people love people who aren't good for them."

Ian had never made her feel that way. Ian always put her first, always encouraged her to believe in herself, and never wanted more than what she could offer. He showed her what she was truly capable of without discounting her. With him, she could do anything that she put her mind to. But it wasn't only his belief in her that kept her up at night. It was the way he looked at her, like everything about her was just right.

He fought, unconsciously, to make sure she knew so that one day she wouldn't suddenly decide he wasn't good enough.

Truth was she probably shouldn't be thinking about dating. Even now without the pressure of battling alcoholism or the voices in her head. She was standing, again, but on wobbly legs that swayed too much. Ian never made her feel bad about what made her who she was. Not the way Mira did, who pulled her up from her darkest days, always reminding her of how much she had to give to save her. For Cin to function. How she had been blind. How she had ignored her mother's words of caution when, without her burdens weighing them both down, Mira only cared about herself.

She wanted Cin to need her. Mira wanted to be needed.

The realization, strong and truthful, hit her like an arrow to the heart.

She'd been free-falling. Falling through the empty space Mira called love without a parachute. Ian had been the parachute. A support system, the real, honest one she never knew was missing. He was damaged but recovering like her. He was true to who he was and loving of who she was. He was the one she didn't need but wanted.

And she wanted him. From the deep pits where her heart was rebuilding to the voices that circled in her head, she wanted Ian. She had to tell him.

As if reading her mind, Link yawned and nipped at her fingers.

"I know," she muttered, getting off the couch and starting her search through the house. Link padded behind her, watching her carefully, as she inspected the bottom-floor bedroom. Adam's bag was missing. She plodded upstairs, turning to Ian's office, and smiled.

"What are you reading?" she asked, stepping into the room.

He showed her the cover. "Some chick told me to give this a chance."

She sat down next to him on the couch. Plucking the book out of his hand, she placed his bookmark into it and snapped it shut. She slid it on the cherrywood side table before surveying the room. She'd passed it at some point while roaming the house late at night. The lighting was yellower, muted in a warming way, compared to the rest of the house.

"You feeling okay?"

She tapped her finger against the couch, eyeing him sideways. "This is me trying."

"I don't understand."

She turned her head, leaning it on the back of the couch and watching him. "No. Ian. This is me. This is who you are willing to jump headfirst into the deep end with. I'm damaged. I'm the girl who runs through the rain in heels. I'm the person who hears voices every day of her life. I'm an emotional wreck. This is me. I'm trying. I'm not perfect, but I'm sure as shit trying."

"Cin." He pulled her into a tight hug, and she let go of the tension in her shoulders. "I know who you are. I've always known. Did you think I've never cared?"

"Well."

"You adorable, crazy, lovable pain in my ass. Come here." He grabbed her hair, pulling it gently to lift her lips to his and kissed her. She shivered as her body tingled. God, how had she ever thought Ian was anything other than her person?

Cin pulled away, grabbing Ian's hand to pull him off the couch. He moved easily behind her. They made it a few steps, the feeling of his lips on hers lingering, before he stopped them.

"Are you sure?"

"Yes, I'm sure."

"Did you take your meds this morning?"

Cin's heart beat double time. How had she managed to snag someone so utterly caring and selfless? She knew if she told him no, he would have dragged them back to talk on the couch. He wouldn't let it go any further. She turned on her heel to look him in the eyes. She didn't want him to have any doubts that everything tonight was pure, unadulterated Cin. "Yes. I swear."

"Well . . .if you swear."

He laughed before scooping her up and carrying her giggling body to his bedroom. He laid her out on the bed and slid her shirt off slowly, running his fingers up her stomach and over her breasts. The sudden cool air gave her goose bumps. Ian, leaning over her, started to pepper lingering kisses down from her shoulder to her navel, pausing just above her lacy underwear. Cin shivered, her body reacting to the sensitive spots. She tried to push herself up to her elbows, but he placed a gentle hand on her chest.

"Let me treat you." She took a shaky breath. She couldn't remember the last time she was treated, that sex wasn't just an outlet for her own demons, but she lay back down. Ian grabbed her wrists and lifted them above her head, holding them as he ran his tongue up the base of her throat. He blew on the wet, sensitive spot, and she lifted her hips in anticipation. Her heart ached for the man nibbling on her ear, and her fingers ached to touch him back.

She pulled her hands free, Ian letting go easily, and she reached for the hem of his shirt. Ian let her pull it over his head. She ran her hands down the soft planes of his chest and stomach. Ian smiled down at her before placing a soft kiss on his lips. As the kiss intensified, Cin closed her eyes, letting her mind focus on the feeling of his lips pressing into hers. She felt his hands unbutton her jeans before pulling them off her.

Ian stood up to take his own pants off, and she quickly unclasped her bra. She dropped it off the side of the bed as Ian crouched on top of her. She watched as he leaned back and down to nip at her lacy thong. Using his teeth, he slid it down her thighs. Completely exposed, she shivered as he chuckled against her thigh. He dropped the useless underwear to the ground.

Ian leaned forward, hovering above her, to kiss her again before slowly lowering himself on top of her. He pressed his hard length against her, and Cin arched her back. Feeling the pressure of him against her, she let out a soft moan before dragging her fingers down his back. He growled before sliding himself inside her. Cin cried out in pleasure. She slipped one hand into his hair and the other on the lip of his headboard. Ian rocked against her, and she studied the pleasure mirrored in his face.

After a few minutes, Ian pulled her off the edge and spun her around. She pushed herself against the bed and lifted her ass in the air as he pushed himself back inside of her. He pushed deeper and harder until Cin cried out in climax. It wasn't long until Ian was crying out, finishing shortly after her. They stayed there, panting for a moment, before collapsing on the bed.

She couldn't feel anything besides the unending pleasure rolling through her. She wanted to roll over to kiss him but only managed to loll her head to the side. Ian placed his hand on her cheek. "This was worth the wait."

"Yeah, sure. You say that now. You won't when you realize you're stuck with me."

He shook his head. "You're amazing, Cin. Everything about you. From the adorable dancing routine you do when you cook to the way you look at me when I hand you three hundred slides to review because I got excited."

She snuggled into his arms. "I still can't believe you thought that was an acceptable way to introduce your teaching assistant to your teaching style."

"I was excited," he protested, pulling her in close and nuzzling his nose into her hair. She sighed, placing a kiss on his chest. She quickly jumped out of bed to run downstairs and down her sleeping meds, before sliding back into Ian's embrace.

When her eyes started to droop, their breathing in sync, he whispered, "We still have a lot to figure out. We've been avoiding."

"Tomorrow. We'll figure it out when the sun is shining and coffee is brewing."

∽

Adam had returned as dawn was starting to stream into Ian's window. She could hear him pacing, his sneakers squeaking on the hardwood floor before the stairs creaked under his weight. He called up, "I have fresh coffee for the first person who comes down decent."

She smiled, peeking at Ian who was still sleeping, before slipping out of bed and back into her clothing. She sneaked out of the room and stood at the top of the stairs. Adam was shaking her black iced coffee. Even if she wasn't first, it would be hers. Ian usually drank his hot filled with cream.

"How did you know I'd be up first?"

He handed her the coffee. "He sleeps like the living dead." Adam looked at his watch—it was old, but something she'd never seen before. "We have two hours for you to tell me why you have sex hair."

She snorted, coffee burning the back of her throat. She widened her eyes innocently. "What are you talking about?" She tapped his watch with her free hand. "Where did you get this?"

Adam rubbed it. "It was my dad's. He left it for me."

"It's lovely." She guided them to the kitchen island. "How are you holding up?"

"I'm functioning. There's a lot to go through at the apartment."

She bit her lip. "How much longer do you have?"

"They're kicking me out on New Year's." He looked at the calendar hanging on Ian's fridge, squinting as he read the dates. "Another week or so."

"Where are you going to go?"

He ran a hand through his hair, suddenly aging in front of her eyes. He was barely twenty-two, but she could have sworn he was turning fifty. Gray hair had started to pop up at his temples in the weeks since he had first told her. "I don't know. I've been looking, but everything is so expensive."

"I wish you could stay with me. You know I would offer if I could."

He bumped her with his shoulder. "I know. How about instead you tell me about what happened when I went home last night?"

Her face burned. "I should never have trusted Mira. I was stupid for thinking she wanted anything good from our friendship." She pointed at the ceiling and lowered her voice. "He's been nothing but sweet to me. I almost missed something wonderful."

"At least you finally got your head on straight. I've been waiting since you met for this."

She jabbed him with an elbow. "You're a pain in my ass, you know?"

"Isn't that what brothers do?"

Her stomach dropped. James. She had forgotten about him. Him and her missing mother. How could she forget something so important? She twirled her straw around as she thought. Giving Adam a look, she pulled out her phone. "Hold on."

"Is everything okay?"

She shrugged. When was the last time she had heard from him? It couldn't have been that long ago, right? One week maximum. But the date on her phone didn't lie. It had been over two weeks. Nothing from James. Was he back in town? Who was watching for their mother? "I lost track. I dropped the ball."

"It's been a hectic couple of weeks."

"That's not an excuse to stop looking for your mother. It's not an excuse." Her voice was rising in pitch, making them cringe. "I should have kept looking. I haven't even heard from James."

"Who's James?" Adam stood up and started making more coffee. She looked down at her glass; it was mostly empty. Noises had started to emanate down from Ian's room.

"James is my brother. He just came back a few weeks ago. Right after . . ." She trailed off.

"Right after your mom went missing?" Ian asked, walking down the stairs. She watched him ruffle his hair, before stretching out and walking into the kitchen. He gave her a light kiss on the top of her head before sitting. "Are you making coffee?"

"Brewing now."

Ian yawned. "I might just keep you around if you keep this up." He placed an elbow on the counter and looked at her. "So your brother. How long has he been back exactly?"

"I didn't think anything of it. I always expected him to come back—no matter what he said." Ian shot her a pointed look. "He came back a week after Mom went missing."

"And you didn't think this was relevant? How would he have even known?" Ian arched an eyebrow.

She stood up, walking across the white kitchen. "It's not like I knew he had magic or anything when he showed up. He wasn't diagnosed with anything. I just thought he was worried about Mom. I guess it's a little weird. I should have realized something was wrong. Mom didn't have him on any of the paperwork. I don't remember why he knew."

Ian scratched his neck as Adam placed a milky-looking coffee in front of him. She poured herself her own mug, Adam waiting to fill his new cup as well, before handing it back to Adam. She eyed it warily before putting it on the counter. "Your brother isn't in town. Floyd would have told us."

"Why? It wouldn't have been relevant."

"Your brother, he was one of the most talented witches our coven had seen. I had heard rumors about him while I was down South. Someone like that comes back to town, and it's a big deal."

Adam leaned against the fridge and pulled her to a stop. "Your pacing is making me nauseous. Just breathe. We'll figure out what this means."

"Easy for you to say. You don't have a toxic best friend and potentially fake brother living in your mom's abandoned condo," she snapped. She drew her mouth into a tight line before taking a deep breath. "I'm sorry. Everything is starting to really get to me."

"I think we should call an emergency meeting. Let me make some calls." Ian stood up, grabbing his coffee, and walked out onto the back patio. She watched him, her hands getting clammy. She rubbed them on her pants a few times.

"It'll be okay." Adam gave her shoulders a squeeze.

She smiled at him. "Either way, I need to shower, or no one will want to sit in a room with me." She walked upstairs, grabbing her bag of things, and turned the water on freezing. Maybe it would be enough to shock her out of this nightmare.

Chapter Twenty-Six

When Floyd showed up, the doorbell dragged her back to reality. She sprung out of her chair and opened it to find Megan and Sanjit standing behind Floyd like a grim shadow. The midday sun, high behind them, made their expressions dark and shaded. It hurt seeing the frustration and disappointment she felt displayed on their faces. Ian coughed behind her.

"Sorry, please." She let them in with a wave of her hand. She surveyed the crowd around her. Adam and Ian sat on the two brown, cracked leather chairs positioned across from the empty couch. Their faces were neutral masks—masks that covered the nerves she could see rattling them. Ian couldn't stop flicking his fingers, his eyes locked on the guests. Adam tapped on the wooden arms, running his fingers through his hair every few seconds. It was starting to grow in size. She grimaced before waving at the couch. "Feel free to sit anywhere."

She leaned against the side of Ian's chair, grabbing hold of the wooden armrest, and watched as the group took their seats. Sanjit was the calmest—leaned back in his seat, hands folded in his lap. The only sign he was as worked up as the group was the sudden pallor to his dark tan skin. Megan's relaxed mask was cracking—her eyes darted around the group, never landing anywhere for too long. Her hair, normally blow-dried into a clean style, was wet and hanging limply around her face. Floyd was the most concerning—she'd known him for too long, had seen his concern too many times, to fall for the elbow rested on his leg, wrist holding up his chin. Not only were his dark tufts of facial hair, normally shaved, peeking out, but also his dark skin was barely hiding the red undertones. Something that was normally impossible to see. It was Floyd's face that told her more than she needed to know—seeing her brother was a really bad sign.

He spoke first, eyes glued on the stack of books Ian had on the living room table. "Megan and I spoke on the way over. I know this may be tough, but we need you to tell us everything that's happened since your brother has entered the picture." He glanced up, pinning her with his stare. His angry eyes bored into her. She had messed up, worse than when she had upset the board. "Anything you've kept to yourself."

Ian looked between the group. "What are you talking about?"

"She's been hiding things. Keeping important details to herself," Megan added.

"Are you accusing her of lying to all of us?" Ian frowned at the group. He clenched his fist. "You can't just heft the blame of this situation on her. She's new."

"No one is blaming her. But it's time she fills in the group." Floyd gave her a pointed look.

She turned her head upward, watching the fan spin a

few times, before taking a shaky breath. "I haven't been completely honest, and that's my fault. It's been hard to trust anyone—especially with . . . It doesn't matter. I told you a lot of it." She patted Ian's thigh. "It's time I tell the group everything."

She closed her eyes in an effort to clear her mind and then spilled. It tumbled out, faster and easier than when she told Ian. Adam pulled at her hand, grabbing it firmly in his. Ian grabbed the other, both warming her. She gave them a silent squeeze, a thank you for the support. She explained the second voice, the one that she could still hear when she was close to Mira or James, and everything it had been saying to her. Keeping her away from Ian and pushing her closer and closer to Mira and James. When she finished spilling her secrets, it felt like a burden had been lifted—the last burden truly weighing her down.

She tried to not feel guilty about burdening her friends. Of pushing her own worries and fears onto others. But when she peeked an eye open, no one looked distressed. Instead, the group looked less concerned than before. A myriad of resigned yet determined expressions scattered through the leaders.

"We found our wraith," Sanjit said. His eyes had turned fierce, protective like a father.

"Mira's not a wraith," Cin said reflexively.

"Don't be silly, Cin. Of course, Mira's not a wraith. She and this Elizabeth Marrow girl are being possessed by one. They are under the influence of a malicious spirit, and one of them is posing as your brother." Megan huffed, standing up and striding across the room to jab a finger in her face. "This is very serious. Wraiths are dangerous. Especially ones that can get into your head. Your mother raised you better than this."

She bucked. "Do not bring my mother into this. She's still missing. Not that you people have done anything about that."

"Your mother would never have let it get this far."

"What do you know? When was the last time you visited her?" Her blood was boiling. Ian tried to rub her arm, to soothe her frayed nerves, but it was useless.

"I'm just as worried about her as you are."

Cin scoffed.

She opened her mouth but snapped it shut when Floyd stood up. "That's enough. Fighting isn't going to help this situation. It won't deal with our wraith problem, and it certainly won't bring your mother home. We need to strategize."

She rubbed her neck, giving herself a second, before nodding. Megan took her seat again. Silence pinged through the air, everyone frozen in their own frustrations.

Ian pinched the bridge of his nose. "What are we supposed to do about this?"

"We're going to have to kill it in human form—exorcise it from Mira. If it shifts back into its spirit form, we'll need to call in reinforcements. Trapping a wraith is nearly impossible." Floyd tapped his chin. "Do you think she's holding her somewhere?"

"James was staying in my mom's apartment. He wouldn't let me over last time I tried. He said Mira was watching for her to come back. This was right after he told me he called the facility. Claimed that she picked up some of her things and he found them in the condo. I don't know how I missed it." She rubbed her forehead. "James and Mira could be—most likely have been—working right under my nose."

"When was the last time you spoke to the facility?"

CHAPTER TWENTY-SIX

She bit her lip. "James had been doing that."

"Add that to the list of things to tackle. Tonight please." Floyd scratched his head. "Do you have a key?" She nodded. "Good. Once we have all the information from the facility, we'll send you in to get her. You'll pose the smallest threat since the wraith thinks that he has you deceived—even with your rift from Mira. It doesn't know you know about James. Use that to your advantage. You'll need to grovel, most likely, but I think you can manage that."

He scanned the two boys with a critical eye. "Ian and Adam, you'll accompany her but head up the fire escape. I want you both waiting in the wings in case the wraith catches her."

"We need to account for Lucy," Sanjit interjected. "She very well might be held hostage in the apartment."

"Who knows what kind of state she's in. If you"—Floyd gestured to Cin—"can distract it while we get her out, it will make this much easier. Once she's out, there are fewer variables to worry about, and the boys can give us the signal. Megan and I can head up to rid ourselves of the wraith."

"Absolutely not. We're not sending her into that alone," Ian growled. She snorted. "Don't. I'm allowed to be protective of you. I don't plan on teaching next semester on my own at the very least."

"I'm capable of taking care of myself." She pushed off his chair and paced in front of the blank TV screen. "Don't underestimate me."

"I'm not underestimating you. If anything, I'm overestimating the wraith. But I'd rather overestimate than bury you."

That shut her up.

Floyd cleared his throat, dragging everyone's attention to where he sat. "We're not sending her alone; you both will be there. We can't send you in with her. It'll be far more suspicious if three adults are trying to sneak into an apartment. We'll tip off the neighbors. It'll be bad enough to send us in after Lucy's out. Who knows how many people this wraith has control over."

Ian blew out a long breath but agreed. Floyd directed them all to the dining room table as he outlined the timeline, Friday night around dinner, before diving into all things wraith. Her basic lessons with Ian and their surveillance were nothing compared to his anthology of knowledge. He covered how to see beyond the mask, to see the darkness within. How to signal to the rest of the coven if we were in danger, how to keep them out of our heads, and most importantly, what could and couldn't kill them.

With everyone on the same page, Floyd pulled her aside. "Cin, your mother used to have a necklace. It was a rare amber that was charmed to see through the glamour of the wraiths. She told me she gave it to you. Do you still have it?"

Cin frowned. "No, I don't have that necklace."

Floyd placed a soft hand on her shoulder. "Look through your things and see what you can find. If you have it, it is essential for you to wear it during this."

Cin nodded, adding that to her mental list of things to do when everyone left.

"All right, everyone," Floyd said, pulling them back to the group. "I think everyone knows what they need to do. Let's get this done with."

With that, the group said their goodbyes, and she hugged each of them a little tighter, holding on a few extra seconds, before watching their car's headlights disappear down the street. They left her alone with a pacing, sweaty, frustrated Ian and still slightly stunned Adam to ponder how she was going to get the courage to sneak into an apartment potentially holding a wraith hellbent on ruining her life.

Adam was the first to speak. "Do you think you should call the facility?"

She sucked her lip. "Probably. Ian, can you take me home? I think I need to do this alone."

He agreed, grabbing his keys as she packed her things, and drove her home silently. Adam stayed, unwilling to go back to his own place, so the only noise in the car was Link's heavy panting in the back seat and the low whine of the car's engine. When her building came into view, the sound of her pulse whooshing in her ears drowned out whatever Ian had said.

"What?"

"Nothing. I just . . . Can you let me know you get up there safely?"

She gave him a kiss—the casualness of it almost tripping her up. "I'll be fine. I'll call you after I get in touch with the facility."

He nodded his head begrudgingly. She slipped out of the car, letting Link out the back, before giving him another kiss. It burned through her, warming her chest. "Don't worry so much."

"Someone needs to worry."

She stuck her tongue out. "Trust me, I do enough of that for the both of us."

He chuckled, waving goodbye before leaving her standing outside her building. Every moment she had come home, finding Mira or James waiting for, replayed in her head angrily. She clenched her fist, trying to stop it from shaking, before letting herself into the building and into the elevator.

"You'll bite anyone in the apartment, right?" She scratched Link's head. She could have sworn he winked as the elevator dinged, letting her out. Her hands shook as she jimmied the lock and cautiously opened the door. It creaked, revealing nothing but darkness. Link sniffed before padding into the studio. She watched him pacing the large room before jumping onto her bed. He curled into a ball and shut his eyes.

"Good enough for me." She started to flip on lights, putting her stuff away, and finally got a glass of water before pulling her phone out. "I should have done this to start with."

Link lifted his head, watching her as she paced the living room area of her studio.

She dialed the number, the familiar digits being hit like muscle memory. She stared at the numbers, her eyes blurring them briefly, before hitting send. It rang twice before a woman's voice spoke. "Riverhead Facility. Agnes speaking. How can I help you?"

She quickly ran through her own information, what they needed to confirm her identity to be able to share medical information about her mother. Once they verified her, she broke down what she had been told, what she knew, and what she wanted to know about her mother. She let everything spill out so quickly the woman was stunned silent. She couldn't imagine the reaction if she told her about the wraith.

"I just want to know about the night she signed out," she added.

"Hold on." She heard the phone hit the desk, the

sound of drawers opening up. Somewhere farther away she could hear different adults screaming and the sound of nurses' sneakers squeaking through the halls. "Okay. I've reviewed the notes from her case file. It looks like your brother came to visit, helping her sign out and move out all of her belongings." She could hear her ruffling the sheets of paper. "It looks like someone notated he wouldn't speak to anyone but your mom. Interesting." More ruffling. "It says there's something still here . . . I think she actually left something behind."

"Excuse me?"

"Records say it's in an envelope, let me find it." She was barely holding her phone up, her vision blurring. She clutched her neck. It couldn't be—she couldn't still have it. She couldn't still be watching out for her even now.

"Here it is. It looks like a small charm on a block string. It looks like a piece of amber filled with brown flecks. Does that sound familiar?"

"Yes," she squeaked out.

"You can swing by to pick it up at any time. It looks like there's a note in here, too, but I'll leave that sealed to you." The phone beeped to signal the other party had hung up, but Cin barely heard it. Over ten years and her mom still had it.

∽

They were sitting, cross-legged across from each other, on top of her childhood twin. The flannel sheets warm and scratchy underneath her. She couldn't stop fingering the fraying end of her jeans. They were too long, hand-me-downs from her brother, and she kept stepping on them with her Converse. She rolled them up nervously.

"Cin-Cin. Can you look at me?" Her mom's face was warm, loving. Her hair was amber colored—soft, cascading down her back in waves—and her smile was patient.

She nodded, biting her lip.

"You're getting older now. Developing into your magic, into the family tradition." She reached behind her, grabbing at something. "It's time I pass down what my mother gave me at your age."

Her mother handed over the stone with little ceremony; it landed softly in her outstretched palm. She turned it in the sunlight, watching the amber reflect. "What is it?"

"It's a charm—amber filled with sage and cinnamon." She closed Cin's hand around it and held it between her own. "When all else fails, this will protect your mind from outside evils. Keep you safe."

Chapter Twenty-Seven

No matter what anyone said the day before, what they claimed, James was still her first family. She wanted to give him a chance—wanted him to be the brother that left her behind. Wanted to give Mira a chance—wanted her to be the friend she thought she was. There was something about James's sudden aversion to spending time with Mira, the way the voice was stronger with them. Supporting them while tearing down the others that made it hard.

She needed to at least see what they would say when pressed.

She sent them a message inviting them over for dinner. When her phone pinged with new messages, one right after the other, she expected a no from at least one of them. But when she saw the yeses, the hair on the nape of her neck stood on end.

Surveying her apartment, she dashed around to clean up empty glasses and straighten her books. She grabbed anything magic-related and slid them into her backpack before slipping it under the bed. With one last glance, she leashed up Link and headed out the door. If they were really possessed, if what Floyd said about amber the day before was true, she would need to stop by the facility before they made it over.

The walk was empty, the streets cleared of students and the masses at work. She turned on something alternative, slightly edgy, and focused on the sound of the music to keep her feet steady and her heart even paced. It worked, for the most part, until the ominous door of the facility appeared in her vision.

She tripped, almost falling over Link, before grabbing at the railing and forcing her way up the stairs. At the top, she tied Link up. "Stay here."

He whined.

"I'll be back soon. I promise." She edged away, slinking into the building. The whiteness of it, blindingly bright and sterile, made her cringe. The place reeked of fresh antiseptic.

"Can I help you?" She turned to look at the younger nurse. He wore the standard white scrubs but had a smile she'd never seen in this place.

"I'm looking for something my mother left behind. Lucy Clark?"

His eyebrows shot up. "They left me a note to expect you. Wait here." He walked, a slight skip in his step, to the attending booth. He dipped down below the counter. She looked around, searching for signs of her mother. Signs she had been there. Had an impact. Only the squeaking of the attendant's shoes echoed in the halls. Even the normal sound of screaming was subdued.

"Here it is!" He popped up, reaching out over the counter and waving an envelope.

She plucked it from his hand, gripping it close to her chest, and mumbled a thank you. She gave him a quick wave before jogging out the door and falling to her knees next to Link. She could feel it, the weight of the amber and the sharp stab of the pointed end. She gave Link a kiss before standing up and untying him.

They ran the whole way home. Her heart beat double time, racing inside her chest from more than just the exercise. Her lungs burned as she tried to suck in air through her panic attack. Her legs and fingers, arms even, tingled under the sudden burden—exercise and panic battering her body. When she let them into her home, her shoulders released their tension. She poured herself a glass of water and sipped it slowly, rubbing the necklace through the envelope lovingly.

~

"I'm not going to fall for your shit," she had hissed. Her hand snaked up and ripped the necklace off. She held it out, a sneer spreading across her face. "This hunk of sentimental garbage isn't worth anything."

Her mom's face had dropped. Dark bags hung under her eyes. Her hair was frayed and limp, brushed back roughly into a pathetic ponytail. She reached for the stone. "I swear, Cin-Cin, I'm not lying. I can really do magic. You can too."

"Really?" she snipped, dropping the stone onto the tile. It clanked against the ground before sliding under the nearby fridge. "You can barely stand straight. You're drunk again."

Her mom dropped to her knees, reaching weakly

under the fridge. "You don't understand. You've barely experienced this. You've barely scratched the surface."

"Trust me, being bipolar is enough." She stormed out of the kitchen, grabbing her bag and eventually leaving the apartment and her mother behind.

∼

When Mira and James showed up, one right after the other, she had tied the amber around her neck. Link scurried away, hiding under the bed as she had asked. He winked before disappearing from sight.

She saw it immediately. The darkness, the deep shadows following them, was so prevalent it was choking her. Mira walked in first, a trail of dark mist following her, but James had followed. His mist was different, shimmery purple. It didn't trail but shimmered in the air between them. Underneath it, she could just barely make out the blond ponytail and blue eyes of Elizabeth.

The hairs on her arm raised. If she could see Link, she was sure he would have his hackles up. She was stupid—to fall for Mira's barely disguised manipulation, to fall for the James who came home, for any of it. But she didn't have time to focus on that. She plastered on a fake smile. "I thought we could order pizza and clear the air."

Mira flicked her eyes around the apartment. "Wouldn't it be better to sit somewhere public? In case we disagree?"

She ran her tongue along her teeth. "If you don't feel like you can have a civil conversation, you're welcome to leave." She waved at the door.

"Whatever." She plopped onto the couch, kicking up her feet and putting her dirty booties on the coffee table.

James sat down next to her. They exchanged a look as she got settled on the chair across from them.

"I'm surprised you sat next to each other." She waved to the empty barstools. "There are more than enough chairs."

James narrowed his eyes at her. "What did you want to talk about anyway?"

She nipped at her nail beds. The words tumbled out, burning like too many tequila shots. "I think since you both have been helping me look for our mom, we should be putting our heads together."

"I have nothing new to add," James shot, flipping his eyes up to the ceiling. Another lie.

Mira flicked her eyes between them. "I didn't think you wanted me involved anymore."

"I was upset the other day," she replied, digging her nails into her palm. They bit into her, releasing some of the tension in her body. "We've gotten through worse."

Mira sniffed. "You really hurt me."

She choked on the water she was drinking. Hurt her? Was she kidding? She cleared her throat, taking a slow sip of her water, before nodding slowly. "You're right." Ouch. "I should have considered your feelings before reacting so harshly."

"You've never considered me. Especially with this stupid *witch* business."

You've always been crazy—nothing more.

She rubbed her neck, trying to push out the voice. She could see it now, something she missed before. The darkness was snaking out, thin tendrils pushing into her. It slithered around the amber. She was positive it slid into her consciousness through her ear, but the reflection from the fridge was barely visible. "You're right." It ripped through her, but she didn't have a choice. She invited them in. She had to prove that something everyone, including herself, knew was true the night before.

Why did she always need to prove things?

"I know I'm right," Mira said, flicking her hair. She jabbed James.

"You know how I feel about this."

She flipped her head between the two of them. "I see you've become buddies."

"Mira did me a huge favor when I went out of town," he said.

"That's because I'm a good person." The darkness around her pulsed. Cin bit her lip, nibbling at the ripped skin as she processed. The Mira she grew up with, the one who actually supported her, was gone. She had watched it happen despite never believing it. Mira had spoiled, had been left out in the sun too long. It gave an opportunity for her to be influenced by even worse forces. The revelation, the belief that her best friend was no longer who she thought she was, had been sitting on the tip of her tongue for way longer than it should have.

But eventually is better than never, right?

"I know you are. I'm glad you both are here to help me. That you are willing to work together with me. Can you tell me everything you've found out since the last time we spoke?"

James spoke first. Nothing to report; everything was quiet in the condo. No signs of Mom. Mira echoed him. That she believed their mom didn't want to come back. She watched them feed off each other, both in words and in darkness. It ebbed between them. She fought her instinct to ground herself on the amber, to give away what she really knew.

CHAPTER TWENTY-SEVEN

With no leads, as expected, James ordered pizza for the group while Mira picked out a movie. Something cruel—where the mom dies. She wore a vicious smile the whole time, the pair cracking jokes back and forth. Cin didn't move, rooted in her seat by their savage behavior. Only her head swizzled, cautiously watching the two of them grow in their malcontent.

As soon as the title credits started, she jumped out of her seat and closed the pizza box. "Thank you for coming. I have an early doctor's appointment tomorrow."

Mira narrowed her eyes but offered to drive James home and guided them out the door. "Talk to you soon," she added, poking her head into the almost-closed door with a ruthless smile.

After James and Mira left, the two of them still cackling together until she heard the elevator snap shut. When their voices had died out, she scratched at her goose bumps before shivering. It wasn't until Link crawled out from his hiding space under her bed, running up to rub his head on her exposed ankles, that the weight on her chest lifted, and she could breathe. She opened a window, letting the cool air wash away her unease, and pulled out her phone to fill Ian in.

"Tomorrow at six."

∼

Getting the group organized was easier than planned. Ian gave the group meeting information. They met at a nearby coffee shop where Megan and Floyd would wait for the signal and clarified roles and responsibilities. Ian and Adam left first, headed up the fire escape as the sun set. Their eyes were cast at their feet as they shuffled down the street. She frowned at their retreating figures. "Do you think they're okay?"

"Dealing with wraiths is serious business, Cin. Be glad they are taking it with respect," Megan said, placing a kind hand on her shoulder. She shook it off and took a step back.

Floyd stepped between them, fitting into the new space she had created, and handed her two coffees. "Take this on your way up. Tell James you just stopped by for an evening coffee."

She eyed the hot coffee. "Can I throw this at him?"

Floyd gave her a look. "You're there to look for Lucy and get out. Don't antagonize them."

"They might, probably do, have my mother. Why can't I give them a taste of their own bullshit?"

"If you do the wrong thing, you might cause her harm. Do you want to be the reason your mom doesn't make it?"

The words he didn't say hit her chest. *Do you want to be the reason she dies? Do you want her blood on your hands?* She took a shaky breath. The sip of bitter coffee cleared her head. "No one is getting hurt today." She looked between the two of them. "I'll see you on the other side."

Then she walked out into the dark night, her shoulders pulled back and her head held high.

Chapter Twenty-Eight

By the time she made it up the stairs to her mom's condo, she was shaking. The coffee was raining down on her hands, dripping softly onto the tile of the hallways. She could hear her pulse whooshing in her head, could feel the tingling in her fingers. The telltale signs of panic building. It wasn't a usual one, one where nothing brought it on but her own disorder. It was direct, the image of her mother behind the door held hostage, her throat being sliced open, ripped at her consciousness.

Leaning across from the door, she placed her head between her knees as she tried to build the confidence she needed. Her eyes were closed when the elevator doors dinged. Mira's boots were the first thing she saw when she lifted her head.

"What are you doing out here?" Her face was twisted into a sneer. Cin just stared.

Standing up, she lifted the coffee weakly. "I thought I would bring James some coffee."

"Great. I'll bring it to him." She reached for the coffee.

She pulled it back. "I'd like to bring my own brother coffee."

"I don't think having a panic attack in the hallway counts. Just give it to me."

She shook her head. The darkness trailed behind her best friend like a savage shadow. It followed as she shrugged. "I'll go see if James wants you to come inside."

Her face burned—this thing telling her she couldn't come into her own mother's condo. How dare she? If she missed all the rest of the red flags, this one smacked her so hard she reeled for a second. The door shut behind Mira before she had moved.

"Fuck." She balanced the still-dripping coffees in one hand and rooted in her bag for the key. She pulled it out and jammed it into the door. She took one final sip of the coffee, knowing it wouldn't survive this and unwilling to waste a full cup, and then slammed her shoulder into the door as she turned the knob. She thought they would have barricaded it, kept her out, but it gave away easily—forcing her to tumble. She caught herself, halfway into the living room, but the coffees went flying. They sprayed the couch and James who was sitting in the armchair. His head swiveled to her, looking away from Mira who was trying to haul her mother out of the room.

"Put her down." She kicked the door shut as she studied her mom. She looked thin, wasting away in her soiled pajamas from the facility, but her eyes were awake. Wide orbs unclouded in a way she hadn't seen in years—her mother had returned. They blinked at her, taking in her slightly disheveled appearance and crinkled just slightly. Her shoulders relaxed. She was okay—she was more than okay. She was there—mentally. Mira snarled, the darkness growing like a cloud behind her, and threw her mom to the ground.

Cin startled. "Don't you dare hurt her."

"Do you think you can stop us?" James asked, standing up and prowling toward her. She took a few steps back until the knob of the door stabbed her back. Her eyes flitted to her mom. Mira was tying her back up, shoving her onto a chair, but she nodded just slightly. She was up to something.

She just needed to give her a chance. She needed to distract, not attack.

In the brief second she looked away, James took advantage. He swung his meaty fist into her head. She staggered, blackness pulling at the sides of her vision. James grabbed her wrist, tying them together with a zip-tie she hadn't seen him grab. He shoved her into a chair across from her mom and jerked his head toward the bedrooms.

Mira followed him out silently.

"Cin-Cin, I knew you'd get my note." Her mom's voice was hoarse but solid—a lighthouse in the dark.

She gave her a wan smile. "I should have found it sooner. I'm so sorry, Mom."

"Shush. We have bigger worries than that. Do you have reinforcements?"

The door to the bedroom creaked open. Mira sauntered out, Elizabeth behind her. The James persona wiped away like notes on a chalkboard. Elizabeth crossed her arms and leaned against the wall as Mira placed her palms on the dining room table between them.

"What happened to you?" she whispered. "I thought we were stronger than this."

Mira laughed. "Me? All these years and you've always underestimated me. Overshadowed my problems for your own. How could I possibly be tired of you and your whining? How could I possibly want to be the important one?"

"She's right, Cin. You've been a burden to everyone you know," Elizabeth added. Mira shot her a look, and she shrugged. "I've seen enough over the years."

Mira focused on her, eyes burning into her. The darkness swirled angrily. It snapped at her body and tried to wiggle into Cin. She wanted to touch the pendant, to thank it, but she couldn't. "What, Cin? Are you really that surprised that your inability to deal with your own demons has dragged those around you down the same dark paths? This is your fault. It's always been your fault."

It's not your fault.

This is your fault.

"It's my fault you kidnapped my mother? How the fuck did you get there?" Cin spit at Mira as she pushed her shoulders back. Her wrist burned against the plastic. Everything hurt from Elizabeth knocking her in the head and throwing her down, but she refused to look weak. She was better than the voice, better than the wraiths strangling her life. She could fix this. Had to fix this.

"I wouldn't have had to if she would have just listened to me. You're dangerous—just like she was. People like you are an abomination. Can't you tell? Mental illness is the reason for most of societies' problems." Mira snarled at Lucy.

"Mira," Cin pleaded weakly. It was hard when all she wanted to do was punch her stupid face. Her fist itched. She put on her best pout and eyed Mira. "I never meant to hurt you. I'm so sorry that I hurt you. Please. You don't want to do this. You don't want to hurt anyone."

Mira's face hardened into a mask of disinterest and anger as she pivoted back to Cin. "You could not imagine what I want to do. What you have driven me to. You're a plague on the world. If you had just given me a chance to be in the spotlight. If you had just cared. If you weren't such a burden."

"Please." Cin lolled her head to the side with a long sigh. She wasn't getting anywhere. She couldn't make eye contact with the boys; her mom couldn't be sneaked out the window. She couldn't figure out if her mom had a plan to get out. They were stuck.

"Don't waste your breath, Cin. This will be over soon enough," Elizabeth said. She stepped up to the table and leaned against Mira. Their darknesses mingled violently. It wriggled behind them like an angry hurricane waiting to blow her into oblivion. She peeked at her mom, catching her shoulders twitch, before narrowing her focus on the two women holding them hostage. Distract. She needed to distract.

Whatever her mom was doing, they needed to be looking at herself to succeed. "You know what I never understood?" Mira tilted her head, Elizabeth parroting. "How is it that, after over a decade of friendship, you never said anything? Why didn't you just tell me how you felt? I would have listened."

Mira sucked her teeth. "Would you have? After all this time, I've learned you don't know how to."

"We've been friends since we were teenagers. Don't you think you should have trusted me? Don't you think I've earned that?"

"Trust you?" She snorted. "There would have to be something redeemable in your batshit crazy ass."

Cin frowned, twisting her head to look at her mom.

She winked. "My dear, miserable Mira. You've forgotten something very important." They turned their attention to Lucy. Cin took advantage of the moment to search the windows for the boys. She couldn't find them but knew they could see her slight nod. They would know to call in reinforcements. She pivoted back to her mom who wasn't tied down anymore. Instead, she sat cross-legged on her chair with a wide grin spread across her pale face, her hands folded in her lap. Red rings wrapped her wrists.

She didn't know how, but her mom had managed to cut the ties. They lay on the floor below the chair. Her eyes were sparkling—like she had waited for just the right moment. That all this time had given her the opportunity to gain control over her magic in a way the facility hadn't. Cin tried not to gasp.

"Lucy." Mira's voice warbled. The darkness started to recede back. It slithered back from her mom, from her, and into the bubble of deep gray that looked like a shadow on the girls. It knew. It was about to be bested. She didn't know why she thought that. Maybe it was the confidence her mom was pushing out, or maybe it was the way the wraith energy seemed to die as her mom pulled back her shoulders.

"Do not 'Lucy' me, you little shit. How dare you. Cinzia and I—we aren't abominations. You don't know what you are talking about. You don't know anything about who we are and what we are capable of. I should never have let you spend so much time with Cin. I knew you were bad; I knew something was off about you. But she loved you so much. You didn't love her, did you?" Lucy unfolded herself to stand tall in front of the chair. The darkness pulled farther away, threatened by the sudden confidence from Lucy. "All you've done is twist her love for your own benefit."

Her mom weaved her hands together, golden strings being drawn in the air. Before her eyes, she laughed as a sword materialized in front of her. The laugh was dark, haunting. The darkness deepened, readying itself as if it had a chance. Cin knew it didn't. Her mom had been leader for a reason—she was stronger, better than the rest. She was more capable than the wraiths. She breathed out as her mom's sword solidified. It glimmered in the light, giving off an ethereal glow against her mom's face. "Did you think I wouldn't be capable of magic because you changed my medication? Silly, pathetic, wraith-controlled girl. You should have thought this through before messing with my family."

Her mom growled. "I was on the wrong medication at the facility. Had facilitated it to protect myself and now you know why. Without the misdirection, you would have put me on something less conducive. Thank you for falling into my trap. No matter how strong you are, you'll never be clever. At the end of the day, I'll always best you." She waved the sword in front of her in a low sweep. "No one hurts my Cin-Cin."

Elizabeth took a step backward, pulling Mira with her. They put their hands up as Lucy edged them into the corner of the kitchen. The darkness tried to slither away, knowing it had little chance in this battle with Lucy fully coherent. "They think we're crazy, they think magic is dangerous, and then they are corrupted even further by spirits that feed on the darkness. But they haven't seen anything yet. Please close your eyes."

Cin squinted.

"Suit yourself. But I warned you." Lucy grabbed the

handle of the sword. It changed from an image in the sky to a solid, steel weight. She murmured a chant, something in Latin—of that she was sure—and heaved the sword into Mira's chest. She screeched as the darkness leaked out, pooling on the ground.

"Cinzia. Get one of the mason jars in that cabinet that I can put the darkness into. It can't get into you." Her mother ripped the sword out, and Mira collapsed, her face pale. She lifted the chair and waddled into the kitchen. "Did they teach you nothing? Child, you have so much to learn."

Lucy tsked before pulling out a knife from the block on the counter and slicing open the tie. She twisted her wrist before pushing the chair away and getting on her knees. She pulled out a glass container, focusing her eyes on the pooling darkness as Elizabeth screeched. She cupped her hands and poured the darkness into the container. The darkness was like a black sludge—it burned, stinging her and covering her hands in welts. She wanted to scream, to cry out in pain, but she pressed her mouth together.

This hurt less than the pain of missing her mom.

Elizabeth's body collapsed on top of Mira's as she hiccuped. Cin sniffled as her eyes watered from the pain and thoughts of a crushed Mira before closing the lid with a satisfying click. Rising up from her crouch, she placed it on the counter and turned to her mother. She stood a few feet away with dark bags. Her body wavered, but she pulled her shoulders back when they met eyes.

"Shush, child. It'll be okay—they'll live." But it wasn't. Her heart was crumbling to pieces. It was too much for her to process. She just wanted to turn back the clock, to go back to the time when she believed the best of Mira. "I'll be okay now. We're safe."

"Are we? Look at what we're capable of, Mom. Look at the string dangling from me." She gestured to her arm. "Look at what that brought on. Can we ever be safe?"

Her mom looked out the window. "Perhaps, but that string will also keep you safe." She touched her arm right over the string. "Whoever you're tied to—the both of you will survive the threats on your life. It will be a lot to protect yourselves constantly, but that's why we have the coven. Our kind, we'll always live in the gray area of life. Where death and destruction go hand in hand with beauty and rebirth." Lucy pulled a hand away to weave a golden rose into the air. "Do you see the beauty we can create? I know that you've never believed me before. Believed that we were more than the demons inside."

"I believe you now. I'm sorry I was so stubborn." Cin smushed herself into her mom's shoulder. She smelled as if they hadn't even let her shower. She had to hold her breath, but it was worth it. "I shouldn't have ever doubted you."

A knock sounded on the door.

"That's probably the coven now. They're not going to like that I didn't follow instructions," Cin said.

"Don't worry, they're used to my antics by now." Her mom gave her another squeeze before answering the door. Floyd pushed his way in first, scowling until he saw Cin zip-tying the women up. Megan pulled her mom into a tight hug, holding her so fiercely she thought her mom might pop. When she stood up, Ian and Adam smashed her into a hug.

She laughed when they let her go. "I'm fine guys."

"I know but did you see that waste of coffee?" Ian said. She rolled her eyes.

"Thank you for worrying about me."

Adam stuck his tongue out. "I wasn't worried at all."

"He almost peed himself out of terror when you tripped." Ian jabbed an elbow at Adam who dodged it easily.

"At least I didn't screech like a little girl every time Mira glared at her."

"That's enough guys. I get it—I'm the only badass here."

They snorted. She gave them a big grin before guiding them into the living room for the debrief.

Chapter Twenty-Nine

The debrief was uneventful—beyond the excitement of having her mom back, of making it out alive. The team deliberated who would be in charge of ensuring the women were cleared of malicious spirit and returned safely to their lives. Cin and Lucy were ruled out immediately, given explicit instructions to spend time bonding and reuniting, and Floyd agreed that he and Sanjit could perform the task. They pulled the two disoriented women into her old bedroom, whispering the next steps and gaining the necessary consent for the coven to cleanse their bodies of the remaining darkness before taking them back to the church.

She watched it all happen as if she were floating above the group. Mira looked so delicate, crumpled on the floor; Cin could almost convince herself she wasn't filled with hate. It wasn't a hard sell, she'd done it for years, but something clicked for her, crushed her belief of goodness in Mira, leaving darkness and toxicity. When everyone left, she curled up on the couch and studied her mom. "Can I stay here with you tonight?"

"I'm surprised you asked, my little Cin-Cin. I wasn't planning to let you go just yet." She wrapped an arm around her. "I'll make some popcorn, and we can watch reality TV until our eyes melt."

She choked out a laugh, leaning her head behind her, and let out the tears she'd been holding in. Tears for her loss, tears for who she thought Mira was, tears of joy that her mom was safe. No matter what the cleansing did, the wraith wouldn't have been able to attach itself so thoroughly if she didn't harbor some of those feelings. If she didn't feel that Cin was a burden on her life, among other horrid things. The tears were wordless streams of salty emotions dripping onto the couch. Her mom didn't comment, giving her another squeeze, and turned on the TV.

She cried for hours until her mom pulled out the mattress, laying it across the living room next to the couch, and she finally fell asleep curled up next to her mom.

The next morning her mom rubbed some balm she whipped up with their delivered groceries into her hands. It stung, but as her mom chanted in Latin, the red welts started to thin out until her hands were left red, raw, but healing quickly. After that, they didn't leave the living room for the rest of the weekend, ordering food in and watching movies until Sunday evening.

All day Saturday, she had spilled her guts, told her mother everything until her throat was raw, and then finally, with tears in her eyes, she hugged her mom so tight it hurt. "I'm so sorry I never trusted you, Mom.

You've been right this whole time—about our skills, about Mira, about everything."

She laughed into her hair, her warm breath giving her goose bumps. "Your old mom here is most definitely not always right. I chose to run, hide from everything going wrong, instead of talking to you. I chose to keep James's abilities from you when I thought you weren't ready. If you had known, things would have probably turned out differently."

She wanted to smooth over everything, but it wasn't that simple. Her mom and her had a long road ahead to learn to trust each other again. They had a long road ahead to welcome back the real James. She grabbed her mom's hand and squeezed it three times. As long as they had love, they could do anything.

They didn't talk much Sunday. Silently circling the apartment in preparation for Cin's departure back into the real world. She didn't know how to explain that even with Mira's dark influence gone, she still saw things in the shadows. Still felt underprepared for the world around them she didn't know. They hadn't spent much time practicing over the week, but she had made the promise to learn from her mom or Ian or Adam. She wouldn't be caught underprepared again.

Cin stared out at the amber sunset. There were no tears left for now, and she needed to start getting herself back into a rhythm, or she would never pull herself out of this. She pulled herself up and hugged her mom. "I'll see you Thursday. Dinner afterward?"

She smiled. "I love you, my darling. See you soon."

The week was quiet. She still had planning sessions with Ian. He didn't ask, didn't demand she blurt out everything she was processing, but offered silent companionship. With all the craziness that crashed through the end of the semester, there was no time to break from the world and experience peaceful, nature-filled alone time like Ian had suggested before everything spiraled. He leaned over, a soft smile on his face, and asked, "Do you want to get away from the madness this week?"

"Yes, please."

He booked a two-bedroom cabin near Bear Mountain. She had started to pack the next morning, the day before they were leaving, when there was a knock on the door. She stopped shoving her shortest-heeled boots and heavy winter sweaters into a tattered backpack and walked to the door.

Cin peered through the peephole and frowned. She opened the door a crack and looked out at Mira's slumped body. They had cleansed Mira of any remnants of dark energies and released her back to her own life. But the stress of being possessed by a malicious force had sapped the life out of her, making her look small and fragile in the empty hallway. She was sure a single gust of wind would knock her over.

"What do you want?"

Mira toed a cardboard box out from behind the wall. It was filled with mementos from their life. Picture frames Cin had made when she was hypomanic, books she had left at Mira's apartment, and several candles she had gifted her for Christmas the year before. A few pieces of clothing were shoved into the bottom, peeking up in bright swatches of days past. "I just . . . I wanted to return these."

Cin pushed the door open a little farther and slid the box inside with a crooked finger before leaning against the doorframe, one foot kicked out to keep the door from slipping open and her arms crossed. "Thank you, but you could have skipped a trip. I'm just going to trash this."

"Cin," she pleaded, "I'm sorry. You know that wasn't me. Think of all the good times."

She pulled her shoulders back, squaring them before locking their eyes. "I don't blame you for the behavior this vengeful spirit enacted through you. You can't control that. But here's the thing, we've been us"—she waved a hand between them—"for longer than you've been possessed, and honestly, one thing I've learned this past month—which I was so *blind* to before—was that you, and you alone, were holding me hostage in our relationship. Your behavior is how the wraith got control of you in the first place."

Mira opened her mouth, but Cin cut her off. "Whether you meant to or not. Until you are willing to deal with your unresolved feelings, my developing relationship with Ian, and my incurable disability that you think makes me unstable, I have no interest in rebuilding this. No good memories, which are now marred with your vicious behavior, can change that. Because the most important lesson this has taught me is that there are people in this world, a lot of them actually, who believe what you think makes me crazy actually makes me special and amazing."

She stepped back from the door, reaching to close it, and said, "I'm choosing to believe those people."

"I'm sorry," Mira whispered as the door shut. Cin leaned against the closed door, avoiding the box of belongings, and let herself have a few minutes of crying before sealing the box and, with the help of Link, thrusting it into the trash room at the other end of the hall. She stared at it, her life with Mira that was never really a life, sitting crookedly on top of a few black bags of trash, and smacked her hands together before spinning on her heel and walking back to her apartment with her head held high.

Never again would she let a toxic friend turn her life inside out.

Chapter Thirty

With her bags in the back of Ian's car, a nondescript silver hybrid sedan, they swung by and picked up her mom on the way to the coven meeting. Her mom slid out of her building like a whirlwind—her brown hair freshly curled and blowing behind her, a light layer of makeup, and bright-red nails. Cin beamed at her as her mom plopped into the back seat and leaned over to hug her around the seat. It warmed her heart to see her doing so well.

"Hello, my beautiful loves." Her mom's voice rang out loud and clear in the car.

"Mama. You sound…"

"I sound like I finally got back on the correct medication?" She laughed. "It feels good to be back to proper management."

She shook her head—that wasn't it. "You sound like Mama."

She rolled her eyes jokingly before leaning back in her

seat as Ian pulled out. She watched him peek at her in the rearview mirror. "I'm glad you're back on your feet, Ms. Clark. The coven is going to be ecstatic to have you back."

"Ms. Clark? You do not need to call me that. Lucy will do." She eyed their linked hands before giving Cin a look. "I have a feeling we'll be spending a lot of time together."

Ian grinned. "I hope so."

~

When the three of them walked in, Lucy's arm linked in hers, the coven stared wide-eyed for a second, no one moving a muscle, until Sanjit bounded across the room. He pulled Cin's mom into his arms, spinning her around in a circle—the two laughing—before handing her off to the crowd of people starting to encircle her.

Standing with Adam and Ian, leaning her head on Ian's shoulder, her heart ached lovingly as she watched the larger group welcome her mom back.

"I'm glad she was all right," Adam whispered, before giving her hand a squeeze. She nodded, wishing she had been able to save his dad like he'd helped to save her mom, but their magic wasn't meant to change the balance of the world. They couldn't save the sick or bring people back. Adam knew that, accepted it, but that didn't make her feel any less horrible about the turn of events.

She pivoted her attention to his neutral expression and dark bags. "What are you going to do now?"

"Without my dad? I don't know—I still need a place

to live. His life insurance policy will only cover the rest of the bills. I used my savings to cover the last mortgage payment. I only have a few days left."

"Well, that's good," Ian cut in.

"Why is that good?" Adam asked. It was obvious he was trying to hide his skepticism, but it was thinly veiled. His forehead puckered as he studied Ian.

"I could really use someone to help out around my place—keep it clean, make delicious coffee—you know?"

"Really? That would be great. That means a lot, man."

"I meant to ask sooner, but this week has been hectic. I'm sorry it took so long."

"We'll be gone this weekend, so that will give you enough time to get your things moved in, right? Maybe someone could help you?"

"And that would be us," Floyd butted in. He stood next to her mom and smiled. "Ian already asked us to help since I have a car."

Adam rubbed his eyes. "You guys don't know how much this means to me."

Ian chuckled. "Trust me, you're saving me from a lifetime of bad coffee." He clapped Adam on the back and slipped away as they started talking logistics. She tuned them out and scanned the room. Everyone was in small groups laughing, even Georgia. Her chest warmed—she was so lucky.

Her eyes landed on Ian. He had made his way to the table for the kosher meal the three physics students had brought in. He was pouring two bowls of matzah ball soup, and her heart leaped. He balanced them, one in each hand, and jerked his head to the table. She bit her lip. How had she managed to meet someone who was always thinking about her?

She joined him at the table and watched her mom joke with Adam and Floyd. She couldn't help the upturn of her mouth as she took in her new world, her found family.

∽

Cin didn't know what to expect when she agreed to go to the cabin, but the first night was quiet and unassuming. She felt at home in the woods with the sounds of birds chirping happily. When Ian asked her to cook that night, she didn't know what to expect. But finding her dancing across the kitchen and singing at the top of her lungs was not it. To be fair, she probably shouldn't have turned her earbuds up to top volume, but he swore he'd be gone for the hour hiking. It didn't help that with all the magic practice and mediation adjustment, along with the return of her mother, she was finally feeling lighter than she had in months, maybe years. She was so happy that she had flipped on her favorite '80s playlist and was rocking out to Bon Jovi.

There she was, screeching out an '80s power ballad, bent at the knees and singing into her wooden spoon, when she caught Ian doubled over in laughter near the slightly ajar front door. She stood up, pulled her earbuds out, and narrowed her eyes at him. "How long have you been standing there?"

"Long enough," he said through fits of laughter.

"You tell anyone, especially anyone in the coven, and . . ." She waved the spoon menacingly in his direction, which earned her more laughter. "Well, I guess I'll have to eat this homemade gravy and spaghetti on my own."

Ian threw up his hands in mock surrender. "Okay, okay. I won't tell anyone. I swear." If he wasn't grinning at her like a fool, she probably would have believed him. She heaved a sigh. "Are you going to at least play that on the speaker I brought so I can join in?"

She smiled before pressing a few buttons. The room filled with music, and Ian made his way into the small kitchen area. "No, no. Go over to the table. There's barely enough room in this kitchen for me. I don't need to be hip-checking you with my dance moves."

"There's more than enough room in this kitchen— you're being dramatic." He backed out. "Next time, you can cook in my kitchen. I know it's big enough."

Cin pulled her spoon from the sauce pot and pointed it at him, flinging sauce across the kitchen and dotting the white rug. "Your house is cold and poorly decorated." She stuck out her tongue.

Ian grabbed his chest and widened his eyes. "Ouch. That's a lie. Besides, you're welcome to decorate it. You could *take me on*."

Cin laughed. "You want me to make it into a *love shack*?"

"Don't *girls just want to have fun*?" He blotted at the flecks of sauce on his ratty workout shirt with a napkin.

"Okay, that was just bad. Almost as bad as the *video killing the radio star*."

"Just had to throw that in there, didn't you?" Ian threw a crumpled napkin at her. "I'm pretty sure the eighties would have eaten us up. They'd be *all out of love* for us."

"That's okay. I would rather *dance with myself*." Cin

shook her hips and turned to stir her sauce, taking a big whiff of the roasting garlic bread. She listened to Ian's quiet footfalls as he reentered the kitchen and leaned over the sauce next to her.

"This smells amazing. Who taught you to cook like this?"

Cin smiled at the memories of her mom helping her stir pots of sauce when she was barely tall enough to see the top of the stove. It was one of her favorite memories. "Mom was a great cook. Taught me everything I know."

"I guess we'll have to ask her to help you cook for Adam's moving-in party."

She grinned. "I'm so glad you're taking him in."

"I'm glad I'm taking him in. I can't make coffee worth a shit."

∼

Armed with the coffee Ian had run out to get and the newest novel from her stack, Cin curled up next to the fireplace. Link was snoring at her feet, his head propped up on Milo's back as he spread his stomach out against the warmth. Ian had his nose firmly inside his environmental chemistry textbook for the next semester, hand scribbling notes on Post-its and slapping them into the book.

She poked him with a finger. He looked up at her. "What's up?"

She leaned over and kissed him. "Thank you for letting me be me."

He didn't respond, just squeezed her hand three times. Warmth bloomed in her chest. She was a long way from healed, a long way from understanding her family heritage—she still needed to call the real James to reconnect—but she was on a better road. One filled with acceptance and support from Adam, Ian, and her mother.

As she leaned her head in her hand, smiling at Ian, she couldn't help but break out into a grin.

She could get used to this.

Acknowledgments

This story started because I needed to find the words to how devastating bipolar can be. I poured all my own pain and suffering into Cin and then I twisted it until there was some light at the end of the tunnel. Because I needed that light as much as Cin did. I hope this story showed you that there is a light at the end of the tunnel, no matter how dark it feels.

To my husband for always encouraging me. For being the first to read any story I write. For rereading every story I write until I feel like I've gotten it right. For your steadfast encouragement and excitement for my career. And most importantly, for loving me unconditionally, even when I'm hard to love.

To my best friend, Caitlyn, for encouraging every story to be its absolute best. For reading every first, second, and third draft. For being honest with me every step of the way.

To editor, Chrissy, for pushing this story into something I am proud to share with the world.

To Quinn, Juan, Cynthia, and Kevin for encouraging me to keep going.

To my dad for helping me find the light when I didn't think there was any.

This story would be no where without the people I

have surrounded myself with. Thank you for every word of encouragement, for listening to me every time I needed to talk, and most importantly, for being there for me when the light didn't exist.

About the Author

J.C. Warren is originally from New Jersey and is currently located in Raleigh, North Carolina. She studied biochemistry at George Mason University and loves to use her science background to help develop her novels. When not writing, J.C. spends her free time with her two loving dogs and husband.

instagram.com/jcwarren_author

Also by J.C. Warren

Life After

More MTP Books

"What is more fearsome? The monster that stands before you? Or the one that lives within you."

Elora Leigh is in hiding.

As an Enchantress, she has spent the last several years running not only from a king that hunts magick, but from the guilt and grief of losing her mother.

Content in her solitude, Elora's life among the trees is disrupted when she crosses paths with the most unlikely of allies.

A thief determined to keep his village afloat, Sorin will do whatever it takes to provide for his people, especially now that the lands have been hit by Mother Gaia's fury. Fishing has ceased, crops won't grow, and the animals they've relied on for food have mostly disappeared leaving him desperate for a change.

When Elora and Sorin discover a common thirst for justice in the Kingdom of Valebridge, they set out on a journey to fend for those who cannot fend for themselves and take back power from the corrupt king.

But the deeper they go through the Wicked Woods, the more Elora realizes those she thought she could trust may not be who she thinks they are.

Family secrets, ancient magick, a kindling romance, and tangles of lies begin to reveal themselves. Elora must make a decision; trust this stranger to help defeat those harnessing magick in the Kingdom, or let the demons of her past push her back into hiding and away from who she was born to be.